NIGHT OF THE WOLF
A WEREWOLF ANTHOLOGY

EDITED BY
ANTHONY GIANGREGORIO

OTHER LIVING DEAD PRESS BOOKS

THE DEADWATER SERIES

COMING SOON

NIGHT OF THE WOLF

Copyright © 2010 by Living Dead Press
ISBN   Softcover ISBN 13: 978-1-935458-57-9   ISBN 10: 1-935458-57-4

www.livingdeadpress.com

Table of Contents

CUTE AND FURRY FULL MOON KILLERS

DAVID BERNSTEIN

Droplets of crimson stained the pine laden forest floor of the Adirondack Mountains. The trail of blood glistened in the full moon's intense glow; the werewolf bleeding profusely from its wounds. It was dying fast, injured by the hunters, its ability to heal damaged by the silver bullets. The beast crawled along the pine needle covered ground, fur caked with twigs and woodland debris. With a final gasp, it fell to the hard earth, shuddering before falling dead. Its Lycan blood seeped from the bullet holes in its body, creating a small river that ran along the ground and into a nearby rabbit hole.

Inside the burrow lay eight baby rabbits all snuggled up against each other. The mother was out scavenging for food. The hungry babies smelled the sweet werewolf blood and began lapping it up. The thick liquid warmed their bodies and made them wiggle with energy.

The mother rabbit approached, the beast's scent striking her nose. She moved carefully toward the burrow, hoping her children were okay. She saw the downed creature lying still, smelling death in the air. Feeling more at ease, realizing the beast was dead, the mother rabbit hopped toward the burrow. Upon reaching her children, a silver bullet pierced her hide, blowing her to pieces. Rabbit intestines, muscle, and bone splattered the surrounding tree trunks and ground.

"Shit," one of the hunters said. "Just a damn rabbit."

His buddy came up alongside him, laughing.

"Fred, you dumb-ass," Jim said. "Ya blew the poor thing to smithereens."

"Hey, I saw movement, Jim," Fred replied. "I'm not taking any chances."

"Hey, look over there," Jim said, pointing to a bushy mound. They crept over to it to find the werewolf's body lying in front of them; its blood soaking the ground around it.

Jim prodded the body with his rifle. "I think its dead, but I'm gonna make damn sure." He placed the rifle against the beast's head and pulled the trigger, sending brain matter and skull fragments flying into the air.

"That ought to do it," Fred said as the two men high-fived each other. With the beast dead, they no longer needed to rely on night vision and used their flashlights to help brighten the area. They each took turns taking pictures with the dead werewolf, still in its beast form until the full moon ended.

"Finally got the son-of-a-bitch," Jim said, relieved. His mind could rest now, knowing the beast was dead. Upon searching the area, his light found the rabbit hole. "Oh, shit."

"What?" Fred asked.

"The rabbit had a litter."

"Bunnies?"

"Yup."

"They won't survive without the mother."

"Shame," Jim said. "Sorry about your momma, little guys."

"Let's take them," Fred said. "We'll sell them to the pet store and I'll give one to my boy. Kyle's always wanted a pet rabbit."

Jim thought it was a good idea. He could save the critters and give one to his daughter, too. The men gathered up the small bunnies, placing them in a rucksack.

They cleared the area of twigs and brush before setting the werewolf aflame. Once the carcass was nothing but charred bone, they gathered the remains and took them with them. They'd grind the bones down later and bury the dust in the woods behind Fred's house.

Jim brought the bunnies home, placing them in a small, open pen that had at one time been used for baby chicks. The next morning, he came out to check on them. To his relief, they weren't only still alive, but hopping around and nibbling on the grass. He must have misjudged their age for they should barely have had their eyes open. They looked bigger, too. He figured the night had played tricks on his eyes.

He let his daughter, Mary, have the pick of the litter before traveling to the pet store in town. Fred had already taken one home for his boy. Mary had named them all, and the one she kept was called, Sherman.

"They look to be about two months old," Bob, the owner of the pet store said as he looked into the cardboard box of bunnies. He bought them all, paying five dollars each. The thirty bucks would buy groceries for his family and that was better than nothing.

Jim lived in upstate New York, in a small town called Crown Point, near Ticonderoga, in the Catskill Mountain region. He worked as a handyman repairing people's houses, barns, or whatever needed fixing.

He and Fred—his life-long friend—were hunters. The area was plentiful with game, supplying them and many other families with fresh meat.

Jim and Fred had been out hunting, staying out past sundown when they came upon the werewolf. They'd seen it off in the distance, at first thinking it was a bear. It moved with incredible speed and agility, something no bear could've done. Its form was humanoid, making each believe they'd stumbled upon an eastern Sasquatch. They tracked the creature to the Willibee's farm, a local cow and chicken breeder.

The two friends, like black-op soldiers, snuck up to one of the barns housing the cows. They heard them mooing in distress and upon entering, saw the creature. It was hunched over, eating a cow, its face buried in the animal's stomach. It repeatedly tore into the meat with its claws and teeth, ravenously gobbling the bloody flesh.

Both men began firing their rifles, hitting the beast square in the back. It spun around, revealing its blood-stained teeth and growling like a rabid dog. Rising on its hind legs, it stood seven feet tall. It had the face of a wolf, but the arms and hands of a man and it peered at them with glowing yellow eyes. The men fired again and the creature took off out the back door. Old man Willibee came out with his double-barrel shotgun, asking what the hell was going on. Both men agreed not to say a word for fear they'd be ridiculed and mocked around town. They said it was a couple of wild dogs and that they'd scared them off.

3

After that night, they researched the legend of werewolf's, coming up with different ways to kill one. Neither knew which myths were true but through trial and error, they believed that silver bullets and fire could harm one, figuring enough shots could kill. Luckily for them, they had been correct.

A few weeks later, Jim stopped in the pet store to buy rabbit food and scoffed at the twenty dollar price tag on the rabbit cage.

"Howdy, Jim," Bob said, exposing his eggshell white teeth. "These buggers grew fast. Unlike any animal I've ever seen." He'd only had them a few weeks and they were twice their size.

"I know," Jim said. "Mary's is huge already."

"I almost want to ask where you found these guys, but the New York State Regulatory Board for Domestic Animals only cares about dogs and cats. Rabbits are never on the news for attacking people." He laughed, nudging Jim's arm. "It's always the dogs."

There were only two rabbits left from the litter. With the cost of a cage, food, and other accessories a customer would spend, Bob was making a bundle off the not-so-little critters.

Jim arrived home, carrying the bag of rabbit food into his daughter's bedroom. Sherman had grown to the size of a small dog and would need a bigger cage soon. He grinned, delighted that his daughter had a pet, and one that didn't require constant attention or money. A little food here and there was fine, and if things got too crazy, he'd just tie the critter outside and let it eat the grass.

He thought back to Bob and his shit-eating grin. The man was making out on his catch. He shook his head. "And that's why you're a repairman and Bob's a business owner," he told himself, muttering under his breath, as he left his daughter's bedroom.

Another week sailed by, the full moon awaiting the night. Jim was relieved he and Fred had finally killed the werewolf. It was going to be the first full moon he didn't have to lie about where he was going, staying out all night hunting the beast. After work, he'd pick up a bottle of bubbly and celebrate with his wife. She wouldn't understand, but he'd just tell her he was a happily married man and wanted to show his adoring wife how much he loved her. *Better add a dozen roses then, too,* he thought.

On his way out of the house that morning, his wife reminded him to pick up some rabbit food at Bob's. He rolled his eyes.

Damn, that rabbit ate a lot but at least it didn't need school supplies and a college fund, he thought.

The same day, after a long day at work, Jim was on his way home when he remembered he needed to stop and buy rabbit food also. He turned his pickup around and headed for town. As he passed the Reckford's house, he saw an ambulance and police car were parked in the driveway. He kept on going, hoping everything was all right and praying everything was okay. The Reckford's were good people.

Upon reaching town, he parked in front of the pet store, his truck's headlights reflecting brightly off the plate glass. The window was obscured by a red splatter of some kind. Paint maybe? Jim looked out the pickup's windows, to his left and right. All the stores were closed, Bob's and the mini-mart the only ones still open. He got out of his pickup and approached the window. Looking through, he saw the inside was trashed.

Birds were flying about, fish tanks were smashed and water and dead fish were all over the floor. A cat was up on a shelf, looking petrified. Cages had their doors torn off, the insides covered in blood and animal parts. He looked down and saw three hamsters scurry past the window.

He approached the front door, the glass now shattered. Shards of glass lay strewn about like uncut diamonds. His feet crunched on the broken pieces as he entered the store.

He heard a moan.

"Hello?" he called out.

"H...help," a voice whispered.

Jim turned the corner to where the manager's office was located. He went inside the little cubby and saw Bob lying in a pool of blood. His chest had four, deep, claw-like gashes running across it and he had bite marks on his neck and arms.

"Bob," Jim said, kneeling by the man. "What the hell happened?"

"It was..." he coughed up blood, dotting Jim's shirt with speckles of red. "It was...the rabbits."

"What?" he said. "The rabbits?"

"Not...rabbits," Bob managed. "Monsters." He began coughing, his body shivering.

5

"Hold on, buddy," he said. "I'll call for help."

But it was too late. Bob gasped one last time and stopped breathing, his eyes going vacant. Jim had seen that look before in the eyes of the animals he hunted and killed. In a slight case of shock, he took out his cell phone and dialed the sheriff.

"Sheriff's office," a woman said. "Can you please hold?"

"No I can't!" he shouted. "I'm down at Bob's Pet Store and something happened here. I think he was robbed. Bob's been killed."

"Sir, the sheriff and his deputies are currently occupied in the field. I'll send someone over as soon I can."

"Are you hearing me? I said he's dead!"

"I heard you, sir. We have emergencies all over town. Get to a safe place and stay there until the police arrive." Before he could reply, the line went dead, the woman hanging up.

"Damn it!" he yelled. It didn't make sense. Crown Point was a small town. The worst thing that happened was a bar brawl. Jim left the store after seeing a snake slither by. Wondering if it was poisonous, he knew he didn't want to wind up needing an ambulance when they were most likely out on calls with the police.

Upon exiting the pet store, he looked up, the moon's glow catching his gaze.

No, he thought. *It couldn't be. Another werewolf?*

He and Fred would've known. He thought back to the night they killed it, then about the rabbits and all the werewolf blood that had been everywhere around the body. He remembered the bunnies had gotten some on their fur. It must have gotten into their system somehow. Maybe they drank it. During all his research, he'd never read anything that stated a werewolf's blood was contagious.

Like a bolt of lightening, he thought of his daughter.

He ran to his truck and sped home. He passed a number of houses with ambulances in front of them, their lights flashing wildly. It was the damn rabbits, it had to be. Bob had sold them to people around town and now they were becoming deadly monsters with the full moon— they were turning into wererabbits.

He almost laughed at the thought, but his daughter and wife were in danger. He called his house, but no one picked up. He tried his wife's cell phone but received no answer, the line going right to voice mail. He floored the gas pedal, shooting forward.

He pulled into his driveway, the truck screeching to a halt as he almost hit the house in his haste. He took his .30-30 from the rifle-rack on the rear window. Inside the glove box was a box of the remaining, home-made silver bullets. He didn't think he would have needed them again but he was glad he had them now.

He loaded the gun with all five bullets, all that was left.

He approached the front door, and seeing it was ajar, he kicked it open. "Deborah?" he called out to his wife. "Mary?" He heard the cat-like hiss from the living room. Stepping inside, he saw droplets of blood on the floor, leading toward the living room. He stepped quietly to the living room's entrance way, his back to the wall. Peering around the corner, he saw the wererabbit scratching at a closet door, his daughter's muffled screams coming from within.

The creature was four feet tall and stood on hind legs. Blood was trickling from holes in its back, telling him that Deborah must have shot at it with the .22 he had given her for her birthday a few years back.

The fur on the wererabbit was shaggy and it had long dagger-like claws. Jim raised the rifle, banging the stock against the wall to get its attention. The wererabbit turned; its furry face scrunched into a menacing snarl, saliva dripping from its mouth. Its two buck teeth were now large pointed fangs, and its eyes were narrow slits, gleaming yellow, like the werewolf he and Fred had killed. The creature hissed at him as Jim fired. He missed, the wererabbit launching itself sideways with its powerful hind legs. He tried getting a bead on it, but the creature kept bouncing off the walls, zigzagging its way toward him. He backed out of the room, know-ing he'd only have one chance to nail it. He aimed at the doorway, waiting for it to appear. Inside the living room, he heard the crea-ture crashing into lamps and furniture, destroying the place. Finally, it appeared in the doorway, hissing, its paws spread wide. It crouched to spring, but Jim fired, sending a silver bullet into its head. Brain matter and skull fragments splattered the wall like a smashed cherry pie, the creature falling dead to the floor.

Jim ran, jumping over the dead wererabbit, into the living room and to the closet door. "Deborah?" he yelled. "Mary?"

"Oh my God, Jim?" his wife called from behind the door.

"Open up, it's safe now. I killed it."

The door creaked opened slowly. His wife and daughter were all right. Tears slid down their cheeks and they were shaking. His daughter was covered in sweat, her curly blonde hair sticking to her face, her eyes red from crying. They stood, embracing each other, letting the love that is family sink in.

"What the hell was that thing?" his wife asked.

"It was Sherman, Mommy," Mary said.

"Honey, stop it."

"She's right, Deb," he said. "That was her pet rabbit."

"What? Have you two gone mad?" his wife asked.

"Look," he said, grabbing her shoulders. "I'll tell you the whole story, but first I have to check on Fred. Okay?" His wife nodded. Jim pulled out his cell phone and dialed Fred's number. It rang and went to voice mail. "Shit," he said. "Honey, I've got to go to Fred's and check on him."

"Why?" she asked.

"He might be in danger."

"From one of those things?"

"Yes, he brought one home too when I gave Mary one."

"No, Jim, let the police handle it," she begged.

"They're busy. I already tried. I was at the pet store," he said, looking down at the floor. "Bob's dead and his store is trashed."

"Where the hell did you get those rabbits, Jim?"

"I'll tell you everything later, Deb, I promise. But in the meantime, I need you to stay inside and lock the doors until I get back."

She was still hesitant but with a little more discussion, he got his wife to understand. He left the house, leaving her with one of his other rifles just in case. Being a country girl, she knew how to shoot a gun.

Jim drove like a madman over to Fred's house. Upon arriving, he saw Fred's car was still parked in his driveway. He knocked on the front door, and when no one answered, he tried the doorknob. The door was unlocked and it opened easily.

The house was shrouded in gloom. He found the wall switch, flicked it on, and almost vomited at the sight that greeted him.

Fred and his wife and son lay in a heap of mangled flesh. Their stomachs were empty cavities while their chests were missing their hearts. The wererabbit had killed them, piled them in the room, and feasted.

Jim searched the house, but the creature was nowhere to be found, and he figured it must have run off into the night. He knew no one in the town would know how to kill the things and they wouldn't believe him if he told them the truth.

Jim got back in his truck and went home where he waited with his family until the full moon phase was over.

News vans from all the major networks came out to Crown Point. They were reporting a wide range of stories, from traveling serial killers, demonic cults, to killers dressed as monsters. None were of course true and Jim knew he needed to tell the sheriff.

He waited until the press left town for good before approaching the sheriff in his office.

"Sheriff," he said, sitting in a chair in front of the man's desk. "What I'm about to tell you...well, you're simply not going to believe it."

"Jim, with everything that's happened in our little town, I'm damn well ready to believe anything."

Jim told him the story about the werewolf, ending with his theory about how the rabbits became infected by the werewolf's blood. After he was finished, the sheriff eased back in his chair, fingers in a steepled position before him.

"So what you're telling me is that I've got supernatural were...rabbits going around killing people when the moon is full?"

"That's correct," Jim said. "And if I'm right, if the affliction or whatever you want to call it is transferable to their offspring, you're going to have a bunch more on your hands. These things grow at an alarming rate and who knows how long they take to reproduce?"

The sheriff held up a finger. "Hold on one second, Jim." He picked up the phone and got his secretary, who also answered the radio for dispatch. "Yes, Margie. Could you send Officers Renfield and McCormick in here, please?" He sat back with a grin. "Just wait a minute."

Jim's stomach began to feel queasy. The sheriff didn't believe him and he looked up as the two deputies entered the room.

"Please escort Jim off the premises." The two officers walked up and stopped in back of Jim.

"Let's go, mister," one said.

Jim stared with disbelief at the sheriff who stared back with hardened eyes. "You're lucky I don't lock you up for public drunkenness," the sheriff said.

"I'm not drunk, Sheriff. I'm telling the truth."

"Let's go, sir," the other officer said. They each placed a hand on Jim's shoulders. It was no use. The sheriff wouldn't believe him and neither would anyone else. He stood up and walked out, the officers seeing him off as he left the police station.

Not knowing what to do, he went home.

"We're moving," he said to his wife when he walked in the door. He told her his conversation with the sheriff and his theories on the rabbit population. "They'll be hundreds of those things soon. But if I'm wrong, and I hope I am, I'll come back and hunt the remaining few and wipe them out."

They left town later that week, after tying up some business and putting their house on the market with the local realtor. They then traveled to Albany where Deborah had relatives. As the weeks past, a few more incidents of bizarre and gruesome killings were reported in the Crown Point area. The F.B.I. was brought in to investigate, saying the killers would be brought to justice soon.

A few months later, during the full moon cycle, the town had its annual Halloween festival. People set up craft and food stands on Main Street, picked pumpkins from the local farmers' fields, and enjoyed hay rides through the woods. A local news crew was there as they were every year. Extra security was brought in to help the F.B.I. keep the town safe from the Full Moon Killers as they came to be known.

That night while Jim was watching television in Albany, a startling, yet not surprising, news report came on. Images of the wererabbits tearing through the streets and attacking people were caught on camera. The scene was right out of a horror movie. Jim sat back in his recliner, as he shook his head sadly. It was his fault that the town was dying. There was no use trying to hunt the wererabbits down, there were too many as they had been breeding like...well, rabbits. He knew this for he had tried and found out the futility of it. The last image on the screen before the cameraman was attacked, the picture going black, was the sheriff getting eaten by one of the creatures, his chest ripped open as the wererabbit tore his still beating heart from his ribcage.

Jim turned off the television; his wife and daughter were sound asleep upstairs in their new apartment. There was one thing he could do to help, and then it would be out of his hands.

Jim walked into the kitchen and began writing the story of the werewolf and the wererabbits, along with the different ways that could be used to kill them. He would mail the letter to the F.B.I. the first thing in the morning, leaving it up to the authorities to decide what to do with the information.

THE STRENGTH OF THE PACK

REBECCA BESSER

I pressed the brake pedal, bringing my car to a halt in the gravel parking lot. The bar looked seedy and disreputable; a good place to find someone that no one would miss.

I got out, careful to balance on the unstable stones as I stood in my four inch heels.

A couple of bikers who were drinking beer and looking at their motorcycles turned their heads in my direction as I walked by on my way to the door. One whistled and the other tried to entice me to join them; with a saucy smile I continued inside.

It was early so I didn't expect many people to be around. I just needed to find one person, one good sized man. I stood just inside the door and surveyed the early drinkers stationed throughout the bar and grill.

There was a man and a woman at a table in the back eating burgers and talking quietly. A couple of guys were sitting hunched over the bar drinking beer and recounting stories of days past. Then I spotted him beyond an archway, playing pool in the back room.

I headed that way, hoping he was alone. I watched him as he moved. From his carriage and posture I could tell that he was strong and agile—he would be fun.

Leaning against the arch, I surveyed the room. I continued to watch him and waited for him to notice me. It didn't take long.

He was bent over the table, lining up a shot, when he glanced my way. His head turned back, then he did a double take. Once he was focused, his eyes traveled from my high heeled shoes up my bare legs and over my tight blue dress to my face.

He stood and leaned on his pool cue. "Howdy. You wanna play, beautiful?"

I grinned and nodded. We had time for a round or two of his game before it would be time to play mine.

"Sure," I said. "Rack 'em up."

He grinned, collected the balls, and arranged them in the plastic triangle.

"You wanna break?"

"Sure," I said, leaning over the table to line up my shot, knowing that I was giving him a good view of cleavage.

I pulled back and then slid the cue swiftly forward, breaking the formation and sending the back two balls into the far corner pockets. The game ensued. He was a good player and gave me a challenge.

I flirted with him mercilessly while we played game after game, brushing up against him whenever I could. He didn't seem to mind. I knew when he grabbed my hips and brought them roughly back against his that it was time to leave and get on with my real purpose for him.

It didn't take much convincing for him to leave with me, and it took even less to get him to go out in the woods with a blanket for what he thought would be some hot sex.

The sun had almost set when we came to a small clearing. He spread the blanket and lay down on his side.

"Come 'ere, babe," he said and patted the blanket beside him.

"Natalie," I told him as I grinned. This was almost too easy.

"Robert," he replied.

I slipped off my shoes and knelt beside him, bending forward to kiss him. He was eager and pulled me down beside him, before crawling on top of me.

I sighed as the final rays of the sun began to fade. Soon I would get to have my fun.

I let him strip me naked. That way I wouldn't lose my clothes by them getting shredded when I changed. No sooner did he remove the last scrap of fabric from my body then the darkness swallowed the world and the moon shed its light upon us.

I growled as I felt the beginning of the transformation.

He growled back as he kissed and nipped at my neck, mistaking the sound for passion.

My dark blue eyes reflected the dim light around us as I scraped my nails up the back of his shirt. My tongue darted back and forth in my mouth, rubbing against my teeth as they grew longer and

13

sharper. My jaw popped as it dislocated and elongated. That's when he pulled back.

"Holy shit," he said. "What the hell are you?"

I could hear the fear and disgust in his voice.

He jumped up and stared for a moment in morbid fascination as black fur sprung out of my flesh, covering my entire body. I felt my bones and muscles shift as he swore again and fled.

He did what they always do, he headed for the car. I'd locked it, so I knew he couldn't get too far. Besides, the pack was out there; they would catch him if I didn't.

I stood on the blanket, stretching my front two paws out in front of me, with my butt in the air. Yawning, I shook myself, my black fur shimmering in the moonlight. Putting my weight on my front paws, I stretched my back two legs, holding one at a time in the air.

I heard the man in the woods, breaking twigs, swearing, running in fear. His heart would be beating frantically by the time we ate him, his blood laced with adrenaline.

Just the thought of sinking my teeth into and tasting him got me excited. Throwing back my head, I let out a wild howl. It wasn't long before I heard my howl echoed by others further off in the forest, each one getting closer and heading my way.

I took off at a loping run, tracking the man in the night. I knew that he wouldn't be able to see well, but I could see just fine. As a matter of fact, I could see much better now than when it was daytime and I was in human form.

It didn't take me long to find him. He hadn't gotten as far as I thought he would. He must have fallen and hurt himself because he was limping and wasn't before. I caught the scent of his blood as I got closer, confirming that he had indeed caused himself harm.

He heard me behind him and tried to speed up, which didn't do him any good. In a couple of bounds I was almost right on top of him. I veered to the right and ran beside him for a moment, my tongue hanging out in a wolfish grin.

I barked playfully and leapt sideways into the air, knocking him down and landing on top of him. He screamed as I sunk my teeth into his soft neck. Hot blood spurted onto my fur and down my throat. I growled and shook him violently, ripping and tearing until

I had the meat free. I chewed it slowly before swallowing, savoring the fresh blood.

I heard the pack close by and howled to let them know where I was before I indulged in another mouthful. Sinking my front claws into his chest, I ripped and tore more flesh free.

A low growl emanated from behind me and I turned my head to see Isis. She bared her teeth in a snarl and snapped at me. Licking my chops, I slowly climbed off the man and backed away. She may be the head female, but it was my kill and I wasn't going to cower in front of her.

Kirk was the next to enter the clearing, just as Isis snapped at me again when she moved forward to eat. He growled at her in warning and yipped at me. This was supposed to be my official initiation into the pack, the proof that I could contribute and provide food when needed.

I watched as Kirk and Isis took what they wanted, then I was allowed to choose my portion, before the other three got what was left. I chewed on a leg bone and watched Isis eat, her white coat shining brightly even in the darkness.

She glanced up and saw me looking at her. Growling, she picked up her meal and walked off into the darkness. When we were finished, we dug a deep hole and buried everything that was left: scraps of clothing, identification, and anything that we hadn't eaten.

Once the body was buried, we yipped at each other and went our own ways into the night. Kirk and Isis headed off together. He glanced back at me before disappearing but Isis pretended not to notice.

I wandered back to the clearing and collected my clothes and shoes, wrapping them in the blanket to make it easier to carry them back to the car. Not having the use of my hands was one of the major drawbacks of being a werewolf, it made objects more difficult to handle.

When I reached the car, I set my bundle beside the rear tire and lay down to sleep.

* * *

I woke up freezing. Holding up my arm to keep the sunlight out of my eyes, I looked around. For a moment I was disoriented and couldn't figure out where I was. Then I remembered. I licked my lips and was pleased to find they still tasted of blood.

Shivering, I quickly stood up and put my clothes on, thankful that today was Saturday and I didn't have to work. From the position of the sun, it looked like the morning was already half over.

I quickly got into the car, started it, and turned the heat on full blast. I had the blanket wrapped around me, but it wasn't doing much good. I hated wearing such skimpy clothes, but it helped me get food in my stomach.

Humans were easier to manipulate when you were offering something they wanted. When I could feel my fingers again, I drove home. No one seemed to be around as I snuck into my apartment. It's a good thing, too. I wasn't dressed as the people in my building usually saw me. Normally, I was fairly modest.

My muscles ached from the change and from the exertion. A long hot shower made me feel better. Pulling on an oversized t-shirt, I curled up in bed to get a couple more hours of sleep. With a full stomach it didn't take long for me to drift off.

I was startled awake by the phone ringing. Grumbling, I reached for the handset on my night stand. "Hello," I murmured.

"Natalie, it's Kirk, wake up sleepy head," he teased.

"No," I muttered. "I don't want to."

"We're having a meeting at two o'clock," he said, all business now. "There are some things to be discussed."

I looked at my alarm clock and moaned. It was one o'clock. "Where?"

He chuckled. "At my house. Try to be on time."

The line went dead. I stabbed the end button and placed the phone back in its cradle.

I got up and dressed in a pair of jeans and a sleeveless blue button down shirt. Grabbing my purse, I headed out the door. It would take all of the remaining time to get there.

Driving to Kirk's house was always a chore for me as I usually got lost. He lived in a huge house out in the middle of nowhere. I was almost late because I passed the entrance to his driveway and had to turn around and go back.

I was the last to arrive, so I had everyone's eyes on me as I entered the living room, where they were lounging.

"Ah, you made it," Kirk said, coming forward to greet me. "On time even, I think you had two minutes to spare."

I blushed. "Yes. You said to be on time."

I looked around the room. You would never have guessed that we were all werewolves. Clothed and in human form, we looked perfectly normal. Only another of our kind could spot us during the day. Our scent distinguished us from humanity. It was faint, but very distinct.

"Have a seat," Kirk said.

I nodded and sat between Frank and Angela. They smiled politely and turned their attention back to Kirk. It was a new experience for me to be part of a pack. I'd never been around others like myself before.

"I would like to welcome Natalie into the pack," Kirk said. "She has proven herself more than once, and last night she provided us with a meal. She has done all that we've required of her so join me in making her feel welcome."

Everyone murmured warm words of welcome, everyone except Isis. She sat in her chair and acted like she didn't care what was going on around her, like she wished she was somewhere else.

Kirk glared at her.

Sighing and rolling her eyes she said, "Welcome, Natalie."

Kirk's jaw clenched at her sarcastic tone. But, since she was his sister, there wasn't much he could do about her insolence. Or rather, not much he *would* do.

"Furthermore," Kirk continued. "Natalie, I would like to invite you to come and live here. It would be safer for you than the apartment where you now live."

Isis' head whipped around and she growled. Kirk ignored her as my jaw dropped. I didn't know what to say. I couldn't believe they were offering me a place to live. The rest of the pack didn't live here so why had he asked me?

"I don't know what to say," I stammered.

"You don't have to decide right now," Kirk said with a grin. "Just think about it and let me know."

I bit my lip and glanced at Isis. She looked really mad. I nodded and looked down at my lap. I didn't know if I could live in the same house as her.

The room had gone silent. Everyone's eyes were on me and I don't think I was the only one shocked by his offer.

"Does anyone else have anything they would like to discuss?" Kirk asked.

No one answered.

"I guess this meeting is over then," he said. "You're free to stay if you like, but if you have somewhere you would rather be, you're free to go."

Frank and Simon got up, said their goodbyes, and left.

I glanced over at Angela to see she had a smug smile plastered on her face as she watched me.

"What?" I asked.

"Oh, nothing," she said, grinning. "Either he really likes you, which wouldn't surprise me, or he's using you as a pawn to piss off Isis. I haven't decided yet, but I'm thinking it might be a bit of both."

I blushed and looked down again, thinking I should probably leave. I started to rise, but as I did so, I saw Isis walk over to Kirk.

"I would like to talk to you, brother," she snapped.

"What about?" he asked, turning to face her.

She crossed her arms over her chest and raised an eyebrow. "You know what about."

He smiled sadistically and nodded. "I'll be right back. Natalie, I would like to talk to you before you leave, so please wait."

They turned and walked out of the room together. I watched Isis' platinum blonde hair swing back and forth as she walked out with sharp, jerky movements.

Angela laughed. "I know he's succeeded in making her mad. This is fun to watch. There hasn't been this much excitement since Kirk had to fight for leadership."

I shrugged and stood and wandered about the room with nervous tension. How was I going to turn him down without offending him? If I did say yes, how was I going to live here with Isis? I didn't know what to do. He'd put me in a difficult position.

Kirk returned a short while later. His face was flushed but I couldn't tell if it was from anger or another emotion.

Angela winked at me and grinned. "I think I'll take off as well. I have a couple of things to do before tonight."

"Bye," I said softly and looked out the window.

"You know where we're meeting?" Kirk asked Angela.

"Yes," she said. "Bye for now." The door thudded shut behind her, causing me to jump and turn. Kirk was standing in the middle of the room with his arms behind his back, watching me.

"Have you considered my offer?"

I nodded and tucked my long black hair behind my ear. "Yes, and I still don't know what to say."

"Is it Isis? Is that why this is a hard decision for you?" he asked, slowly walking toward me. "Or is it me you don't think you could live with?"

I laughed nervously. "I guess I just don't understand why you offered in the first place."

He paused and nodded. "I can see that. You're young and you haven't been a werewolf long. I would like you to come here for security and training. I want you to be comfortable with fighting before we have to deal with another pack trying to move in on our territory."

"Another pack?" I asked with a gasp.

"Yes," Kirk said, coming to stand in front of me. "Another pack. I have to defend our territory and I can't do it all on my own. Everyone has to be able to fight. I can't be worrying about all of you when I'm fighting myself."

I nodded and shuffled my feet. "I suppose I should learn how to defend myself. But couldn't I come here in the evenings or something? Do I have to live here?"

He laughed. "You make living here sound like torture. Would it really be so bad?"

"No," I whispered. "I suppose not."

He walked across the room and sat in an overstuffed chair. "Look," he said. "I know that you and Isis don't get along. She's made her objections clear. I'll deal with her. It's your best interest

I'm thinking about. In that tiny apartment, with humans so close by, how many nights do you think it'll take before you're discovered? Think of that before you say no."

I turned back to the window and crossed my arms, gripping my shoulders with my hands. Closing my eyes, I let my head fall forward, hiding my face behind my hair as it cascaded forward. I stood that way for a while, just thinking about what he'd said.

Kirk was right. I risked discovery staying where I was. Apparently, I also needed to learn to defend myself. I could no longer be selfish. I had to think about what was best for the pack. With a heavy sigh, I admitted to myself he was right.

"All right," I said, lifting my head and brushing my hair back. "I'll move here. But what should I do about my job? It'll be a long drive everyday."

"Quit."

I turned and looked at him to see he was gazing at me intensely. I tried to read his expression, but I couldn't.

"Quit?" I asked.

"Yes, quit," he said, standing. "You won't need a job after you move here. I'm not charging you rent and it's not like we have to buy groceries."

I laughed. "No. No groceries."

"So it's settled?" he asked. "You're going to come live here?"

I nodded and bit my bottom lip. "Yes."

"Great," he said and clapped his hands once. "I'll have a room prepared for you, and I'll send someone to help you move tomorrow."

"Tomorrow?"

He grinned and nodded. "You better go home and start packing."

"I guess so," I said as I walked to the front door and opened it.

"See you tonight," Kirk said.

"Tonight," I said as I left.

I was busy packing for the rest of the afternoon. I didn't have much, I'd just moved here after all. The apartment had come furnished, so I didn't have to worry about anything big.

As the daylight waned, I prepared to leave. We were meeting in the same forest we'd been in last night and I didn't know what we would be hunting tonight, human or animal.

When I arrived, I was informed that Simon had tracked some deer, and that we'd be hunting them, though we preferred human. For some reason, human meat was much more satisfying than any other living beast, but with modern society and the rate at which people were reported missing, it was risky to eat them too often.

It was fun romping through the woods, the wind blowing through my fur, seeing the others around me. I felt like I was part of a family. It didn't take us long to find and kill all the deer. The herd had been small; two does and three of their little ones.

We'd just separated out our portions when I heard Kirk growling deep in his throat. I looked up at him and followed his line of vision and that's when I heard it.

Something was slinking through the woods beyond the break of trees. I sniffed the air and the hair on the back of my neck stood on end.

There was another werewolf out there—an unfamiliar one. The words Kirk had spoken that afternoon chased themselves through my head. Fighting. Defending our territory. In a way I was excited, in another way I was scared. I'd never had to fight before. Would I be able to hold my own if I had to do so now?

Kirk took a couple of steps forward and growled louder, followed by a menacing snarl. Isis joined him, doing the same. I glanced at the rest to see how they were reacting. Simon was lying down with his venison angled between his front paws. Frank was standing, focused on the leaders. Angela lay calmly chewing on a leg bone, watching as if she was amused with the whole thing. All of their ears were up and they were alert. I did as they did and kept my peace and watched, ready to spring into action if it was needed.

As we watched, a nose peeked out from the shadows, followed by a gray head with reflective yellow eyes. The wolf sniffed before extending its long pink tongue to test the air. Kirk took a couple more steps forward, crouched lower on his front paws, and snarled.

The newcomer licked its nose and slid back into the forest. Isis and Kirk stopped snarling, but they stayed alert and watched for a few minutes until they were sure the stranger was gone. I glanced back at the pack. They were all eating again, so I did the same. It wasn't long before Kirk and Isis ate, too.

After the normal yips goodnight, we went our separate ways. I turned to go back the way we came, when Kirk barked. I glanced over my shoulder and he tossed his head in a *come with us* gesture. It hadn't occurred to me that I should go with them, but it made sense. I would be doing so all the time once I was moved in.

I followed them back to their house. I didn't know the way and would have gotten lost on my own. It helped that Isis was so bright, with her white fur, because at times Kirk's reddish coat blended in with the blurred landscape as we ran.

For the first couple of nights after I moved in I sparred with Kirk. After he thought my skill had increased I sparred with Isis. She didn't hold back as much and I often had scratches and bruises when we were done. I knew that in a real fight it would have been much worse, so I didn't complain.

Isis and I stayed clear of each other during the day. Usually, I was so exhausted from hunting and learning to defend myself that I slept most of the time.

Life went on like this for a month and then my new skills were put to the test.

We were hunting, deer again, close to the same area where we'd seen the stray werewolf. We saw him again and this time he wasn't alone.

We'd just slaughtered a huge buck and three little does when Kirk spotted them. This time the entire pack was standing at attention and snarling so I did the same.

It wasn't long before five werewolves came out of the forest to surround us. Kirk and Isis barked a vicious warning, making it clear that if they didn't back off, we would attack.

When they kept advancing, snarling and growling back, Kirk stood on his back legs, standing to his full height, and roared before charging the head male of the opposing pack.

Isis spun to her left and swiped her claws at the head of another attacking male and the rest followed suit. I leapt over a small female that charged at me. Spinning swiftly, I bit her rear right flank, sinking my teeth in until I tasted blood. She yipped in pain and howled in frustration. I released her and circled around her slowly. With the injury, she couldn't maneuver well or jump.

I charged her side, knocking her to the ground. She managed to swipe my chest with her claws as she fell but the pain only angered me.

Pinning her to the ground, I clawed at her face until she lifted her chin. Once I had the opening I was looking for, I lunged forward and ripped at her jugular. Blood spurted everywhere as I tore her neck to shreds.

When she went limp, I glanced around to see if the others needed help. Angela and Frank were having trouble with a big male, so I went to assist.

The three of us circled him, growling, slowly moving in closer. He leapt forward and tried to claw Frank just as Angela and I pounced. We latched onto his sides and he reared back, roaring in pain. We bit down on the tendons in his shoulders, tearing them from his body. His front legs went limp and he fell face down on the ground.

Frank gripped the fallen werewolf's head between his massive paws, twisting and pulling violently until he ripped it off. Holding it over his head, Frank let out a roar of victory.

Frank dropped the head and we turned back to the battle. Simon was just finishing off another small female and Isis and Kirk were fighting the lead male together.

I winced when I saw blood fly through the air as Kirk was slashed across the chest. Isis jumped at the attacker, seizing his arm in her teeth and shaking violently. Quickly, we surrounded the only remaining wolf of the rival pack. With all of us working together, we soon brought him down.

It quickly became obvious that Kirk was seriously hurt. It took all of us to get him back to the house. For the last mile we had to take turns dragging his unconscious body.

We licked his wounds clean and pressed bandages to the gash on his chest to try and staunch the flow of blood before we tended to ourselves. We lay around him, cleaning our wounds and looking at the sky, whining. This was one night that we all wanted to come to an end. The need to be in human form was great for only then could we help Kirk.

Dawn came just in time, and ignoring our nakedness, we moved Kirk to his bed and began tending to his wounds. Isis stitched up the laceration while the rest of us bandaged bites and cuts on his arms and legs.

One by one, we left to get dressed, relieving someone else to let them go when we returned. By the time we were all clothed, Kirk was taken care of. The five of us just stood and looked down at him. He was almost as white as the sheets he was laying on.

For over thirty-six hours he was unconscious. When he woke, I was with him, lying on the bed beside him, trying to stay awake.

I hopped up and rushed to the door to call for Isis. She came running and I let them have a moment alone while I phoned the rest of the pack to let them know he was awake. Most said they would be right over.

When I returned to Kirk's room, Isis was helping him get a drink of water. I stood in the doorway and watched.

When everyone arrived, I snuck off to get a little bit of sleep. Hunting at night and then staying awake most of the day to watch over Kirk had worn me out.

In a less than a week, Kirk was up and almost back to his normal self. The lesser injuries had healed, but his chest was taking longer, and he didn't hunt with us for an additional week. It wasn't the same without him and there was always something missing in his demeanor when he ate what we brought back for him, as if he didn't take pleasure from ingesting something that he hadn't taken a part in slaying.

When he was back with us and we were tearing through the woods after what would be that night's meal, something occurred to me.

It wasn't just the force we created when we hunted and fought together, but also the caring for and protecting of each other that created the strength of the pack.

Something that I was now a part of.

THE TRI-BEAST

JESSY MARIE ROBERTS & ANTHONY GIANGREGORIO

Sarah twisted off the cap of her canteen and drank the final swig of purified water left on Exodus. Night was falling, and in the distance, a three-headed wolf howled to the three red moons—and she was out of supplies.

Without food, water or shelter, she doubted she would survive until morning.

She tossed her backpack onto the hard ground and unraveled her worn, thin sleeping bag. Lying down, she closed her eyes and shifted position every couple of minutes to get comfortable. She was exhausted and needed to sleep, but was aware that with each passing moment, the wolves crept closer...and they were as hungry as she was.

As sleep flittered just out of reach, she thought back to how she had ended up alone, hungry and tired.

Life as she knew it had ended when the Central Computer System crashed. It wasn't unexpected; after all, it couldn't last forever without maintenance, something she had no experience with. She was lucky it had lasted five years before succumbing to age and neglect. Soon, rationed food wasn't dispensed and the water filtration system stopped operating, leaving her with little option of what to do next.

For the first time since the Citizens had fled the planet, she felt truly alone.

She began to shiver, but not from the cold. It was always hot on Exodus, rarely less than one hundred degrees Fahrenheit. The Central Computer System had regulated the temperature inside the Village, an enclosed fortress connected by underground hallways and ventilation shafts.

The greenhouse was the only part of the Village with fluctuating temperatures. It was sectioned into regions that mimicked the weather patterns of Earth, the planet from which the early Citizens had fled thousands of years before she was born.

Sarah was unaccustomed to the blistering heat of Exodus and she was uncomfortable as perspiration soaked into her clothing.

It had taken three thousand years to find a planet capable of sustaining life on a planet other than Earth, and then one thousand years for the scientific community to prepare Exodus for human inhabitance. The genetic codes of all known living species of Earth were stored in the spacecraft's computer so that upon arrival, the new world could flourish.

But after ten years of the Great Drought, the planet Exodus was deemed inhospitable by The Council; there wasn't enough water to sustain them. There were two thousand and one people living in The Village, and Sarah's name had been drawn in a random lottery. It was unanimously voted that she would be the person to stay behind on Exodus to look after the Village, while the others evacuated.

On the day of their departure, Sarah left the Village to watch her friends and family board the spacecraft. Rain splashed her cheeks, washing away her tears for thirty minutes after the ship had taken off for destinations unknown. As the ship had disappeared into the sky, she knew she would never see them again. In many ways, her new position was like a prison sentence, one she would never be paroled from.

She could feel the wolves getting closer now. Every once in a while, she could see the glint of their six eyes in the streaming red-hued moonlight as they slowly stalked their prey.

Creating life forms from DNA was a difficult venture. One slight miscalculation in the lab and a new species was born. Rather than contaminate the Village with bio-hazardous waste, the scientists had disposed of the creatures by dumping them outside of the contained fortress, where many of the species survived.

Out of sight, out of mind.

But the creatures did more than survive—they thrived on Exodus, breeding and multiplying at an exponential rate.

The three-headed wolves were one such creature and she didn't know how many other mutated species were lurking in the darkness, just out of reach and ready to pounce.

She heard a low snarl to her left and snapped her head in the direction of the sound to stare into the fanged mouth of one of the predators. She bound to her feet, leaving her meager supplies behind, and sprinted further away from the perimeter of the Village.

She could hear the pack following behind her, their four legs having no trouble keeping up with her two.

She tripped on the uneven ground, her knees scraping open as she landed with a thud. The wolves surrounded her, their heads lowered, their maws dripping in preparation of her death. She screamed and covered her face with her arms, knowing she had only seconds left to live.

Suddenly, a loud retort cracked the air, causing her to cry out yet again.

The wolves, startled by the gunshot, abandoned their prey and retreated into the darkness. One stopped at the edge of the shadows, glared at her, its eyes glowing brightly, then it turned and loped off into the night.

Sarah laid perfectly still, only her beating heart filling her ears as she stared up at the night sky. She was terrified that whoever had scared away the wolves was even bigger, stronger, and hungrier than the creatures had been.

"Stay where you are, child," a hoarse voice demanded.

Sarah was too surprised to see another human being to so much as blink.

An old woman hobbled toward her, taking her time as she crossed the distance in a matter of a minute. A primitive gun was hoisted against her shoulder and when she reached Sarah, she stopped. She gazed down on Sarah's prone body, and just as Sarah was about to speak, to ask her who she was, the old woman swung the gun through the air in a vicious arc, conking Sarah on the head and making her head bounce off the ground.

For Sarah, the world went black.

*　*　*

Sarah awoke to an unpleasant, unfamiliar smell. Her head throbbed, and when she touched her fingers to the large welt on her hairline, she winced. Slowly, she opened her eyes, her pupils adjusting to the dim light of the one room, ramshackle cottage. In the center of the rundown room was a long table covered with bubbling glass beakers and glowing Bunsen burners. Smoke puffed from the beakers to hover in the air near the ceiling like small storm clouds as the foul-smelling liquid spit and sputtered. Here and there, boiling liquid escaped the clear tubes to splash onto the dirt floor like raindrops.

"I know you're awake, child," the old woman said from somewhere nearby. Sarah hadn't noticed her when she had perused the room, and when she followed the voice to its origin, the old woman crept out of the shadows, hunched over and using a bent wooden cane for support. Sarah recognized the gun the old woman had used to hit her leaning against the wall, barrel side up, in a far corner.

"Who are you?" Sarah asked weakly. She slowly sat up in the narrow, lumpy single bed and tossed the itchy blanket that was covering her.

The old woman hobbled toward her, balancing her weight between the cane and her wobbling knocked-knees. She was cloaked in a tattered, stained, once-white lab coat, the hem dragging across the dirt floor. The coat had probably been the correct length once, but time and age had scrunched the woman's slight frame, rendering her inches shorter than she had stood in her prime.

"I am Bethelehame," she said, her high-pitched voice cracking with the effort of speech. "I feared I would never see another human."

"Well, you have a funny way of showing it. Why did you hit me?"

"I am sorry about that. I panicked and shouldn't have done so. How did you end up being in such a dangerous situation? You would be dead had I not stepped in to save you from the tri-beasts?"

"I was left behind," Sarah explained. "Someone had to stay and watch over the Village, just in case they returned. But why are you still on Exodus?" she asked as Bethelehame moved closer to the cot she was positioned upon.

The old woman tipped back her sharp, bony head and let out a cackle, her long, pointy chin quivering with mirth. The sound was shrill and unpracticed, sending a shiver of panic down Sarah's spine. She realized that she may have been better off fending off the wolves on the vast, dry plain of Exodus than alone with the eerie old woman who resembled a crone in every aspect of the description.

"I was banished from the Village long before you were born, child. Taken from my lab and tossed to the mercy of this lifeless planet."

"I don't understand. I've never heard of anyone being banished before."

"The other scientists, and those confounding Elders, were not tolerant of my penchant for experimenting on children and babies. The young work best for creating new, sustainable species for Exodus. Nobody understood how important my work is! Exodus can be home to a variety of animals—I am creating a new creature, but haven't been able to complete the project because I needed human blood. My veins have retracted and I heal slowly as I'm so old, so I'm loath to extract it. But yours will do perfectly for my new DNA construct!"

Sarah scooted across the bed, her back finding the cold comfort of the uneven wall. The old crone's eyes gleamed with crazy zeal in the gloom, her rancid breath uneven with excitement and anticipation.

The old scientist raised a scalpel into the air, and then slashed down with a furious squeal. Sarah cried out as a large gash spewed blood on the underside of her ankle. Bethelehame spun the sharp, stainless steel instrument in the air, and this time, swiped the tip of the blade against Sarah's wrist when she tried to defend herself. The second wound cut deeper, and was more painful than the first. Blood poured out of Sarah's wounds, crimson rivulets streaming down the palm of her hand to trickle off her fingertips into a steel urn on the floor as the cut on her leg bled into the bed sheet

The old crone grasped Sarah's arm and twisted her skin above the cut on her wrist, the pressure causing the blood to flow out faster. Sarah was in shock, and instead of fighting, merely sat upright, watching as the old woman bled her.

After a minute or so, she leaned over and picked up the urn with the blood, then carried it over to the table that housed the experimental serums.

"I have brought life to this inhospitable world, creating new and wonderful creatures. And I will do so again. I will make a magnificent beast to keep me company in this world and beyond!"

Breaking from her fugue state, Sarah jumped off the bed and ran for the door that led to the wild, untamed plains of Exodus. Bethelehame cackled in amusement as Sarah struggled to open the door to the outside.

"That door is triple locked, child. And there are five more doors to get through after that one, my precious one. You will never escape—not until I have harvested every drop of your blood and thrown your dry, empty corpse out to the wolves!"

Bethelehame jumped across the room with far more dexterity and speed than Sarah imagined possible for a woman of her advanced age, still wielding the scalpel, slashing it through the air with a berserker's frenzy. Sarah stumbled backward, losing her balance, and fell heavily into corner of the room.

Too late, Sarah noticed the metal shackles hanging from a thick rope draped over a ceiling beam. Within seconds, Bethelehame was on her, snapping the chains around her wrists, locking them, and then hoisting Sarah high into the air with heavy grunts of exertion.

"You cannot escape! There is nobody to save you, child. You are alone on this planet! Well, alone with me!"

Sarah was now hanging in the air a foot off the floor and she shut her eyes against the pain as Bethelehame used her blade to slice open her arms and legs, her blood collecting in the urn on the floor placed beneath her.

In the distance, Sarah heard the howl of the three-headed wolves.

They were hunting her once more.

Bethelehame's ears twitched and annoyance flashed over her leathery features.

"They're coming for me, old woman," Sarah panted. "They can smell my blood, and they're very, very hungry."

The old crone snorted dismissively. "If they find you, they will kill you quicker than I, child."

The howls grew closer, and a whining canine cacophony surrounded the small cottage. Then Bethelehame spooned more of the blood into different beakers, and added other chemicals and ingredients.

Something scratched at the wall of the cottage and Sarah looked up from her suffering. She heard the four-legged creatures shuffling and sniffing as they wandered the perimeter of the cottage, searching for a way inside. There was a sudden silence, followed by the sound of dirt being shoveled by clawed paws.

"They're digging their way inside," Sarah whispered. Her heart pounded against her ribs, and sweat trickled down her face and the small of her back. "Let me go. I can help you fight them off."

"I'm no fool," Bethelehame hissed. "You will just try to escape if given the chance."

Sarah saw sharp claws peek in and out beneath the wall to her right, then the glimpse of a muzzle covered in wet soil.

"Grab your gun. Please," Sarah begged as the hole became larger. They were running out of time. The wolves would be inside the cabin within moments and already their grunts and growls filled the air.

Bethelehame looked from side to side, panicking as she realized her sanctuary was ebbing breached.

"Those mutants dare to attack my home? I am their creator— their mother! It was I that developed the first wolfen prototype on Exodus!

The scientist grabbed a set of keys from the table and hurried toward the door. Her hands were shaking, and she couldn't fit the key into the keyhole.

"Take me with you!" Sarah cried.

The first wolf popped one head, two heads, three heads, underneath the wall and gained entrance to the cabin. It looked up at Bethelehame and jumped up on its muscled hind legs, then lunged at her, trapping her right ankle between the sharp teeth of its middle head.

The old woman hissed curses, and then dove for the gun in the corner of the room. She picked it up, brought it to her shoulder and prepared to fire at the left head of the beast. But as she squeezed the trigger, she was knocked off balance and Bunsen burners exploded in a fury of glass shards and foul liquids. The percolating putrescence oozed out of the ruptured tubes and pooled around the feet of the attacking wolf, scorching and burning the tender pads of its paws. The wolf shrieked with pain, backing up toward Sarah, and coming to a standstill beneath her dangling toes.

Bethelehame picked up glass jars filled with unknown substances, and doused the wolf with their contents, drenching its gray fur with sticky slime. The wolf whimpered, all three tongues on each head frantically licking off the foul goo. Sarah could smell the hair and flesh of the beast burning as the acidic brew ate through the wolf's coat and skin.

The wounded wolf staggered backward, falling against the wall where the rope that strung up Sarah was tied off. Some of the acidic liquid splashed onto the rope and it ate through the thick twine, the thickness of the rope unraveling, to then finally snap with a loud *thwack*. Sarah fell on top of the wounded creature, the acidic chemicals burning through her clothing. The wolf twisted, spinning Sarah beneath it, pinning her to the ground. The beast writhed in anguish on top of her, the hundred pound animal crushing her as it flailed about. She struggled to breath and tried to wriggle from underneath the wolf, wanting to drag herself into the corner.

Bethelehame grabbed another flask, this one labeled **TOXIC**. "Damn you, wolf!" she hollered, and then emptied the contents on the animal.

The wolf stopped moving, slumping against Sarah, as its three heads fell heavily, smacking onto the dirt floor.

"I have defeated the tri-beast!" Bethelehame exclaimed, swooping and swirling around the room in a demented jig. "I outwitted the three-headed wolf!"

Sarah could still hear the rest of the pack digging as they struggled to get into the cottage.

The wolf's body twitched in its death throes as steam rose off the carcass. Bethelehame stopped her victory dance and watched as the wolf's body began to melt.

"Get this thing off me!" Sarah shouted, thrusting her hips and body in an effort to heave the decomposing carcass off of her. The liquefied tissue of the wolf seeped into her pores and her skin burned as it absorbed the three-headed monster like a sponge to water.

Suddenly, her heart stopped beating, and she found she couldn't breathe. She pounded her clenched fists against the dirt floor in frustration as she trembled uncontrollably. Spittle collected at the corners of her mouth and dripped down her cheeks in foaming rivulets as her eyes rolled up and back into her head. She looked like she was having a seizure.

Bethelehame walked over to Sarah, craning her neck to check if she was dead when Sarah's eyes flew open. The once blue orbs were now tinted a dark yellow and as her heart began to pump again, quicker and harder than before, muscles popped out over her small frame and hair sprouted on her skin to cover her body in a smooth pelt.

"Wolf!" Bethelehame screeched, scurrying into the dark shadows of the corner.

Sarah flexed her arms and legs as she grew accustomed to her new form. She slowly went to her hands and knees and then stood. She stared at the claws protruding from her fingertips in fascination, and at the brown fur now covering every inch of visible skin. She raised her head and opened her mouth, exposing long, pointed fangs and let loose a howl that caused the old woman to cringe in terror.

Sarah had never felt so alive as the primal power of a wolf coursed through her veins.

She felt strong.

She felt vibrant.

She felt *invincible*.

Outside the cottage, the rest of the pack howled in reply, doubling their efforts at digging to gain entry. Within moments, seven wolves were in the shack, snapping and snarling at the hovering old woman.

In two great strides, Sarah was across the room and her right hand reached out and grasped Bethelehame's white stringy hair, pulling her to the ground in a heap of flailing limbs. The wolves circled the fallen scientist, their muzzles already nipping at her wrinkled flesh.

"Help me!" Bethelehame pleaded. "I can use my intellect to help you find your friends and family!"

Sarah looked around at the wolves filling the cottage, feeling an instant kinship with them as they sat on their haunches, waiting for the signal that it was okay to feed.

She nodded her head, giving them permission.

The wolves growled and attacked with all three heads per body, ripping and clawing at Bethelehame. The old woman cried out as her chest was torn open, her insides pulled out to be fought over, the choice morsels going to the strongest of the pack.

Her shrieks of dying agony went on for more than two minutes, but finally, her heart was torn from her chest and she was silent. Still the beasts fed, chewing at the glistening organs as blood stained the dirt floor red.

Sarah watched as one of the wolves pulled off Bethelehame's left arm and dragged it in the corner to gnaw the meat from the bone.

For the first time since Sarah watched the ship leave Exodus, she was unafraid. She was now part tri-beast.

And she wasn't alone anymore; she now had a new family.

As the old woman's body was torn apart, Sarah knelt down, joined the pack, and began to feed.

BORDER WAR

DAVID H. DONAGHE

I was down at the shopping mall doing some early Christmas shopping and my partner, Roxy Delaney, was at the other end doing some shopping of her own. Seems I was alone, I decided to step into Victoria Secrets to buy her something sexy for Christmas.

Who was I kidding? It would be a cold day in hell before she wore it for me, but Roxy was the kind of woman that a guy couldn't predict. Most of the time she keeps me at arms length, but then when the mood strikes her, she's all over me. Hoping to get lucky on Christmas Eve, I browsed the aisles, checking out the slinky negligees and feeling as out of place as a Nun at a nudist colony. I noticed several little black teddies, plus a few red and blue ones with little white balls of cotton where the woman's nipples would be.

Not knowing what to get, I finally stopped and looked at a little red piece of fabric that left virtually nothing to the imagination. On the hanger underneath the negligee, was a tiny piece of cloth that pretended to be a pair of panties. It had a miniscule V at the crotch and a thin piece of fabric that would run up the crack of the woman's ass and look like butt floss. The top part was see through, cut low in the front, and was so short it would barely cover the panties.

Visions of Roxy's large breasts straining the fabric of the sheer nightgown flashed though my brain and a big grin crossed my face.

"Can I help you?" a sensual sounding voice asked.

Almost jumping out of my shoes, I looked over at a pretty young woman with a cute smile and long black hair. She had a rack on her that stuck out like a sore thumb, her breasts straining the fabric of her slinky black dress, and she had a pair of long darkly tanned legs that any man would die to run his hands over.

"Ah...I'm looking for something for a friend of mine," I stammered.

"She must be a good friend," she said and then smiled. "Or you wouldn't be shopping here. My name's Andrea. Is there anything I can help you with, Mister...?"

"Monroe. Mike Monroe, and yeah, she's a close friend. I kind of like this," I held up the slinky negligee, "but I really don't know what size to get."

Andrea laid a hand over her heart but of course it just landed on her breast instead. "Is your friend big up top?"

"Yeah, she's big."

"How big?"

I closed my eyes and cupped my hands in front of my chest to mimic the size.

She laughed, stepping closer to me and touching my shoulder. "Is she bigger than me?"

I shrugged, holding up my thumb and index finger, then spreading them an inch apart. "Maybe, just a bit."

"Do you like this?" she asked and then stepped up next to me. Our shoulders touched as she turned to face the negligee, and then began to caress the sheer fabric. "It's real silk, you know."

"I don't know. There's so much stuff in here, it's hard for me to know what to get," I said as I wondered if it was getting hotter in the store.

"Your girlfriend is probably the same size as me," she said, then glanced around the store and took my arm. "I don't usually do this, but come with me."

She led me to the back of the store, through a set of black wooden slatted batwing doors, and motioned to a black leather love seat. "Have a seat. I'll go try this on for you." She disappeared into a changing room and I sat down on the love seat. A few minutes later, she reappeared and my bottom jaw dropped, my tongue fell out, and my eyes shot wide open. I felt something rise in my lower regions and I had a hard time catching my breath.

The sexy little nightgown was see-thru and revealing. Andrea's large round breasts, her dark erect nipples, her tanned skin and her long sexy legs were on full display. The tiny piece of material at her crotch was sheer enough to show a hint of pubic hair underneath and her long legs were muscular and tanned.

"Do you like it?" she asked with a smile.

"Ah...yeah. I'll take it," I stammered.

"Good. I'll gift wrap it for you," she said, while spinning around to reveal a heart shaped ass with a tiny piece of cloth that looked like a mere thread running up its center. A few minutes later, after my blood pressure subsided, she came out of the changing room fully dressed, gift wrapped the present, and led me back to the cash register.

"Thank you for shopping at Victoria Secrets. I hope you enjoyed the service," she said after ringing up my purchase.

"Oh yeah, and then some," I said, patting my chest with my hand to feel my heart beat finally slowing down. A big grin crossed her face and she looked down at the cash register. After paying for Roxy's present, I stepped back into the main part of the mall when my cell phone rang. This was the cell I used for work.

"Monroe's Paranormal Investigations. This is Mike speaking," I said.

There was a pause and then a rough sounding voice came over the line.

"Mr. Monroe, I'm Colonel Jack Casey with the California National Guard. We have a problem down here on the California/Mexico border and I was told by General Kincaid that you might have some experience with this sort of thing."

"What's your problem, sir?" I asked.

"There's a little town on the California side known as Santa Rosa Springs. About a week ago, a group of drug runners invaded the town and killed several people."

"It sounds like this is something your boys might be better equipped to handle, or maybe the police or DEA. I'm not into boarder wars."

I listened to dead airspace for a moment before the colonel responded.

"Let me explain further before you say no, Mr. Monroe. So the local police went in first, then the DEA, but they got slaughtered. They called us up and I sent in a RECON patrol and we found the patrol's mangled bodies scattered at the town limits in the morning when we did a fly over with a chopper. It looked as if they were ripped apart by some type of animal."

"It was a full moon last night, wasn't it?" I asked.

"Yes it was, though I don't see why that would matter."

My mind was made up; it looked like I had a new case.

"Okay, Colonel, send me the grid coordinates to the town and email me everything you've got to my cell phone. I'll head down there tonight."

"Good, very good. I'll also send you the grid coordinates to our command post. You can have whatever you need as far as equipment and support goes. We could just bomb the place, but that wouldn't look too good in the newspapers, so we'd like to keep this low key."

"Don't worry, everything I do is off the radar, sir," I said.

After coming to an agreement with the colonel about my fee, I logged onto Google Earth with my cell phone and did a GPS RECON of the town—man, you've got to love technology. I have an updated program that is unavailable to the public and can zoom in so close that you can see a pimple on a fly's ass. Upon googling Santa Rosa Springs, I saw a sleepy little village with a stone fountain located out front of a main street lined with rustic wooden buildings, and on the screen, I saw light coming from a cantina. Logging off the internet, I called up Roxy.

"Hey, baby, where are you right now?"

"I'm at Penny's trying on bras. What's it to you?"

"Bras? I don't think I've ever seen you wear a bra the entire time I've known you," I said in utter shock.

"I didn't say I was going to buy one, I'm just trying them on."

"But, I didn't know they even made bras that big?"

"Yeah right, don't be a jerk. What do you want?"

"Duty calls, darling. We got a case."

"Where to now?" she asked.

"We're going to a little town on the Mexican border called Santa Rosa Springs."

"That's great. What is it this time? Vampires? Zombies? Sasquatch? What?"

"From what the National Guard colonel tells me, we're looking at a pack of werewolves. That's good for you as you haven't been on a case with werewolves yet," I said.

"Werewolves? Seriously?" she asked.

"Wow, Roxy, I'd think that by now nothing would surprise you."

"Not where you're concerned anyway," she jeered. "So when do we leave?"

"Right now. I'll meet you at Penny's and then we'll take my car to the KOA camp. I think we'll use my motor home on this one."

"It'd be nice to have some comfort for a change, but you'd better keep your grubby little hands to yourself, mister," she warned me.

"You didn't think they were grubby last night?"

"Last night I was in a charitable mood. Tonight I'm tired."

"You can sleep while I drive, and I'll keep my clean, ruggedly masculine hands to myself," I said and cut the connection.

I waited for Roxy in front of Penny's while she went through the check-out line. Gazing through the window, I took in her hourglass figure, her large breasts covered by a thin cotton t-shirt, and the sexy little black leather skirt that was almost not there. I took in her long shapely legs and her flowing blonde hair that cascaded down the sides of her bountiful breasts. When she stepped from the store, my eyes dropped to her chest, noticing her nipples pushing up under the cotton.

"What are you looking at, pervert?" she snapped as she walked up to me.

"Only you, darling, only you." I put my arm around her and we hurried through the mall. Halfway to the exit, I let my hand drop to her ass, but she promptly gave me an elbow to the ribs. Outside, we jumped into my 1984 Mustang with its 5.0-liter V8 and roared out of the parking lot.

After swinging by my place to gather some things, we did the same for Roxy so she could change and gather what she'd need. Then we headed over to long term parking where I kept my motor home. The Winnebago is my home away from home and I use it whenever possible.

Soon, we were driving north on the freeway, headed south. Forty-five minutes later, with Roxy sitting in the passenger seat with her long sexy legs propped up on the dashboard, my eyes began to wander, wanting to take in those Daisy Duke shorts she now wore that always drove me wild.

"Keep your eyes on the road, bud," she said and then noticed the bag from Victoria Secrets in the back seat. "What's this?"

"Stay out of that. That's your Christmas present."

"Victoria Secrets! How sexy. Let me open it," she cooed, letting out a giggle.

"No way."

"Oh please, let me," she begged.

"I said, no."

"I'll make it worth your while," she said, pulling up her t-shirt to expose her left breast. I swerved, almost hitting a car while I watched her tease the nipple.

"Jesus Lord Thunder, put those things away before you get us killed."

"Can I open it? Pull over. We could go in the back."

I could never say no to her for long and she knew it. "Fine! Go 'head and open it."

Pulling the negligee out of the bag, she let out another giggle.

"Did you really think I was going to wear this thing?"

"I can only hope."

"Okay, pull over. A deal's a deal."

"We're on the clock, darlin'. Any other time and I'd be back there quicker than a dog in heat, but we have people waiting for us," I said, letting out a heavy sigh.

"All that equipment you have back there. The silver bullets, the silver Saint Christopher's medal you made me wear before, and those canes with the silver goose heads on them. Do you really think that stuff will work?"

"Yes," I replied nodding my head. "I believe they will. It's about belief, baby. If you believe something strong enough, it's true. Some people call it faith."

She was quiet for a few minutes and then said, "I wish I could believe that."

"You have to have faith in something, Roxy. What do you believe in?" I asked.

Silence filled the cab of the motor home, but then finally she said, "I believe in you. If you say it will work, then I believe it."

I nodded and a smile crossed my face.

"That's a start. We've got a long ride ahead of us so why don't you get some sleep?"

"I think I will." She stood up, but I hit a bump in the road and she fell into my lap my free hand finding her breasts. "You're such a pig," she said, pulling my hand away, and then laughed.

"But you love me anyway," I said and with Roxy grabbing some shut eye, I concentrated on the road.

Pulling off the highway three hours later on the outskirts of San Diego, I took another two-lane highway heading southeast. An hour later, I pulled off onto a poorly maintained dirt road that led toward the border. After bouncing over the rocky dirt road for almost another hour, I saw lights in the distance. A sentry, standing guard on the road, stopped me when I pulled up to his checkpoint.

"Excuse me, sir. This area is under quarantine. No one is allowed in or out," a young corporal said when I stepped out of the motor home.

"They're expecting me, Corporal. Contact Colonel Casey," I said as I handed the guard my ID.

The guard talked on his hand held radio for a few seconds and then said, "I've gotten approval to let you in, sir. HQ is down the road a quarter mile where all those lights are," the guard said while handing me back my ID.

"Thank you, Corporal," I replied and then climbed back into the motor home. Driving down the road, I pulled up to a large military command tent five minutes later.

"We're here?" Roxy asked, stumbling into the cab of the motor home, still looking groggy from sleep.

"Yeah, but you might as well go back to bed. I'm gonna have a quick briefing with the colonel and then I'll need to get some rest after all that driving. Besides, I'd rather not head into town tonight. I'd like to pull in there just before sunset tomorrow."

"Okay. Wake me if you need me," she said in a sleepy voice and then stumbled back into what was considered the bedroom of my motor home.

I stepped out into the cold night air, and Colonel Casey swaggered up to greet me. A blood-curdling howl split the night from off in the distance and he glanced around nervously. I couldn't say I blamed him.

"Hello, I'm Colonel Jack Casey. I assume you're Mike Monroe?"

"That's me, but call me Mike," I said, extending my hand. He took it and we shook.

"Okay, come into the command tent, Mike. I'd like to know what your plans are for the town," the colonel said and I followed him into the tent. He led me to his desk, showing me some aerial photographs, and offered me a seat. Looking at the photos, I noticed the same large stone fountain in front of the buildings in what seemed like the hub of the shabby little town. Across from this, I saw an empty area similar to a large parking lot.

"What's this?" I asked, pointing to the fountain.

"That's the town's only water supply. It's fed by an underground spring," he said and then pointed to a building in front of the fountain. "This is where the targets hole up most of the time. During the night, they go on the hunt and anyone out is in danger. They attacked us once, but we managed to drive them off. So, what are your plans?"

"I'd like to go in there tomorrow evening just before sundown. I'll need some equipment and I'd like a helicopter fueled and ready to fly, plus I'd like a squad of soldiers on standby," I replied.

"You can have whatever you need, Mike. We've got choppers here plus enough troops to fight a small war. Make out a list, and I'll see that you get what you need by zero six hundred tomorrow morning."

Taking a pen from my pocket, I made out the list and handed it to the colonel.

He scanned it quickly and nodded, then asked, "Is there anything else?"

"No, sir. Right now I plan on getting some sleep and I'll go over my equipment in the morning."

"Come to the command tent at 0700 hours. My cook makes a mean breakfast."

"I'll do that," I replied and then stepped out into the night. In the distance, I heard another howl, and then someone opened up with automatic weapons. A cold chill shot down my back and I wondered if these weekend warriors were up to the task of defending themselves against a pack of hungry werewolves. Walking to the motor home, I went inside, took off my clothes and climbed into bed next to Roxy.

I was fast asleep as soon as my head hit the pillow.

We woke early the next morning, had breakfast with the colonel, and spent the day getting our equipment ready. After cleaning our weapons, we packed our gear and I made sure that Roxy had her Saint Christopher medal on; after that, we spent the rest of the day resting up for the night's adventure and around six p.m. that evening, I made one final equipment check.

"I'm going to take a quick shower before we leave," Roxy said.

"Okay. Make sure you put the medal back on after you're finished. You'll need the protection."

"Yeah, yeah, I'll put it on," she replied with a wave.

"Do you need someone to wash your back, or maybe your front?" I called after her.

"Nice try," she said and then slammed the bathroom door.

After she finished in the shower, we suited up, putting on our body armor, and then slung our rifles so they were hanging across our chests.

"Is all this armor really necessary?" Roxy asked.

"Yeah, it is. Those hairy bastards mean business, but as long as you have the armor and your Saint Christopher medal, you should be all right. You did put the medal back on, didn't you?"

"Yeah, yeah. I got it right here between my boobs. You know, the ones you can't keep your eyes off of."

"Good. Let's try on your coat. When we go into that cantina, I want to look like an ordinary couple coming in for a drink."

She put on the long fur coat that concealed all her hardware underneath; I stood back and gave her a thorough inspection.

"Good. You can take off the coat for now. But we'll keep the armor on, that way we'll just have to put on our coats when we get down there."

We pulled out of the military compound heading south with Roxy resting her feet up on the dash on the passenger side of the Winnebago. She wore a pantsuit, looking rather conservative for her, and a pair of low healed shoes, and other than for the body armor, she looked like your average businesswoman on vacation. The closer we came to Santa Rosa Springs, the worse the road became, and when we pulled down the dusty main street, not a soul stirred except for the whispering wind.

Pulling the motor home into the parking lot across from the fountain, I turned off the engine and cased the town with my binoculars. Noticing a small Catholic church a few doors down from the cantina, I saw a silver crucifix hanging from the front door.

"Check out the church," I said, handing Roxy the binoculars. "You can bet that's where the town's survivors are holed up."

"What's with the crucifix? I thought that only worked with vampires."

"That all depends," I said. "Werewolves don't care for silver. But if the priest is a true believer, he blessed that crucifix and put holy water around the doorway, it should keep them at bay. Of course, guns and silver bullets work good, too."

We got comfortable and waited, and when the sun went down, we were ready to go. Roxy put on her fur coat and I put on a long leather duster that covered my Bush Master AR-15. Picking up my cane with the silver goose head mounted on top of the handle, we left the RV.

Roxy took my arm as we crossed the dusty street. Passing by the stone fountain, we stepped up onto a rustic wooden boardwalk and entered the wolf's den of the bar.

The second we walked inside, all eyes turned to us, and silence wafted across the bar room. Outside, a full moon rose into the sky and I paused to take in the bar's patrons. They looked like the grubbiest band of filth that I had even seen. Several men lay slumped over tables, and a few shabbily dressed men sat at the long wooden counter, while several worn-out looking women served drinks.

But then things changed. The drunks at the tables began to stir, and a hungry grin crossed the faces of the men sitting at the counter as the change came over them.

"Look amigos. Here's supper," one of them said and chuckled.

One at a time, their clothes split down the seams, their flesh rippled and they sprouted long course hair that covered every inch of their unwashed bodies. Fingernails changed into claws, teeth into fangs, as their bodies began the transformation of becoming a werewolf.

"Well, boys, I guess it's time for silver bullets and double eagles," I said while tossing a silver dollar into the air. Their eyes watched the coin rotating in the air while I pulled my AR and sprayed the bar with silver bullets. Roxy pulled aside her coat and opened up with her Mini-14. We cleared half the room, but the biggest one of the bunch, who I figured for the alpha male, shot across the room and hit Roxy in the chest, knocking her to the floor.

I had my hands full with another hairy bastard, so I pulled out my .45, put a silver bullet through the werewolf's brainpan and then turned around to bash the one on top of Roxy with the silver goose head on top of my cane. He let out a roar and then dived aside, the spot where the goose head had touched him stinging like he'd been burned.

Blood soaked the front of Roxy's clothes, so I pulled the top of her pantsuit away, revealing deep teeth marks on her right shoulder.

"Damn it, Roxy! I thought you said you were wearing your Saint Christopher medal?"

"I'm sorry. It just sounded so silly," she said in a quiet voice. Her face looked ashen, and I thought she was about to pass out from losing too much blood. Already she looked as if she was going to faint from shock. I knew it was time to retreat to fight another day.

Firing my AR at three werewolves leaping toward us, I picked up Roxy using the fireman's carry and charged out the batwing doors.

I ran down the street with several werewolves hot on my tail, so I spun around and fired a burst of silver bullets and then charged up the street to the Catholic Church.

"Let us in!" I yelled as I banged on the front door.

"Go away. Evil has no place here," a soft voice said from within the church.

"Let us in! The hairy bastards are right on my ass!"

"I beg you to go away. I told you, evil has no place here."

"I'm not evil! I stand under the power of the cross and I'm the one trying to save this sorry little town, now let us in before I blow the damn door down!"

The door squeaked open and a skinny white haired priest in a black robe peered through the opening.

"She's been bitten. She'll change," the priest said as I rushed inside and set Roxy down. The priest closed and locked the door.

"I know. I need a place where I can keep her so I can deal with these hairy SOBs." The priest nodded. "Come then. I know of such a place." He led us down the center aisle of the church. The townspeople filled the pews, praying softly, and I could see they looked scared. From their attire, they resembled common people of the land: farmers and ranchers mostly. Their eyes tracked me while I followed the priest who led me up onto the platform behind the pulpit and opened a trap door to reveal a dark shaft descending into the earth.

"A tunnel. It would have to be a tunnel," I said. If there's one thing I hate, it's tunnels.

"The tunnels have been here for years," the priest said. "The town once used them when the mines were active. At the bottom of the shaft, head to the right. There is a stone room with an iron gate. They used it to store dynamite."

"Where does this tunnel lead exactly?" I asked.

"To the mines out in the hills, but there is another shaft leading to the surface just outside of town in the desert. We have food stored in the mines. That's how we have survived since this evil menace came to our town."

"Okay, Father. When I get her stable, and locked away, I'll see what I can do about this situation. We've killed some of them already."

46

"Bless you, my son, you're doing God's work," the priest replied.

With Roxy over one shoulder, my gear bag and my AR-15 slung over the other, I descended into the tunnel. The survivors of Santa Rosa Springs had placed small oil lamps throughout the tunnel leading to the mines, so I wasn't without light, dim though it was.

My heart boomed inside my chest, my breathing accelerated, and the world pressed down on me, but after what seemed like an eternity, I came to the room that the priest told me about. An iron gate closed off the tiny little room and a bed and a table took up most of the available space.

Laying Roxy on the bed, I set my gear bag down and rummaged around in it while Roxy faded in and out of consciousness. Taking out a backpacking stove, I fired it up, poured some water into a small pot from my canteen, and then put it on the burner. I added some herbal leaves used in medicine and let it simmer.

While the concoction brewed, I took off Roxy's body armor and her shirt to examine her wounds. Teeth marks on her shoulder oozed puss, and the skin bubbled, giving off a rank smell, so I poured hydrogen peroxide on the wound. Roxy's skin sizzled and she jerked awake as the cuts foamed.

"What was that? That hurt like hell," she said as her eyes popped open.

"Just some peroxide. Here, drink some of this," I said, taking the pot from the burner and pouring her a cup.

After taking a tentative sip, she asked, "What is this stuff, it's awful?"

"It's boiled leaves from a flower commonly known as wolfbane and a small amount of colloidal silver. At least drink half of it if it tastes so bad."

She made an ugly face while choking down the potent brew, but she did as I asked. I poured the rest of the mixture onto her wound and she jerked, letting out a yelp.

"I got bit by a werewolf. There's no cure for that, is there?" she asked, the worry in her voice apparent.

"Maybe, if I can kill the alpha male, but if the virus progresses too far, you might have to deal with it for the rest of your life. There are ways to keep it in check, though."

"That's just great. Wow, Mike, you always take me to the best places, what's next on the menu? Maybe an erupting volcano? Just let me know so I can bring my sun block."

"I told you to wear your Saint Christopher medal." After bandaging her wound, I made her as comfortable as possible. "I'm going to have to leave you here while I deal with those furry bastards."

"Okay. You be careful though," Roxy said. "I'm not done with you."

I leaned over and kissed her forehead. "I'm gonna lock you in here while I'm gone."

"What? Why do you have to do that?" she asked trying to rise from the bed.

"Your body is going to change. You won't be able to handle it. It's for your safety, as well as mine."

"Okay. Just don't be too long," she said and then pulled up the dusty blanket at the foot of the bed. "I'll just get some rest while you're gone."

I closed the iron gate, barring it with a long metal bar that she couldn't reach from the inside if she tried to get out and then headed back up the tunnel. My breathing came heavy as my mind flashed back to that time in Haiti in the Tombs of the Undead and a shiver ran down my back. I kept expecting zombies to jump out at me from the darkness. After what seemed like an eternity, I came to a shaft leading up to the surface. I climbed up a rickety old ladder, dropped to a knee, and panned the desert with my night vision goggles.

The werewolves roamed the night, hunting for food, and when I looked back at the town, I could see several were clawing at the door of the church. Low crawling through the brush, I made my way to the edge of Main Street, took the military radio from my belt that Colonel Casey had given me, and called in to HQ.

"This is Casey. How's your situation, Mike, over?" the colonel asked over the radio.

"Not good. My partner got bit, but we managed to take out some of the targets, over."

"What can I do to help? Over."

"You know that stuff I wanted, were you able to get? I need it, over."

"We have it here now. I'll have a chopper drop it off to you immediately. Where do you want it? Over."

"Tell your pilots to drop it next to the stone fountain. I need about ten gallons of the stuff, over and out," I said and then ended the transmission.

Fifteen minutes later, I heard choppers in the air and watched them strafe the town, knocking down two werewolves that quickly jumped to their feet and ran off on all fours. Another chopper flew over, and I saw someone throw two objects out the open door through my night vision goggles. Then a parachute deployed and two aluminum canisters floated to the ground.

"The package is delivered," someone said over the COM-net and then the choppers moved off. Jumping to my feet, I darted forward onto the main street of Santa Rosa Springs, opened up the aluminum canisters, and poured ten gallons of highly concentrated colloidal silver into the water fountain.

I had just turned around to head back into the brush when a werewolf plowed into my back and sent me tumbling. Rolling over, the hairy beast loomed over me, raised its right foreleg to slash me with its claws, but stopped when it saw the Saint Christopher medal around my neck. Pulling my .45, I put a silver bullet through its head, splattering its brains onto the dirt. Leaping up, I ran out of the town with three more of the hairy beasts on my tail.

Spinning around, I fired off a burst of silver bullets with my AR and they fled into the night. Tripping over something on the ground, I landed on my face and then pushed myself up off the ground. Wondering what I tripped over, I saw a severed leg, an arm, a head and a pile of entrails. The stench was enough to make me lose my lunch, but I shook it off and ran back to the trapdoor. Pausing at the trapdoor, I watched the scene through my night vision goggles, and ten minutes later I saw several werewolves stop and drink from the stone fountain.

"You boys are gonna have a belly ache tomorrow," I laughed.

Several more of the creatures were clawing at the door to the church, and I wondered why the werewolves hadn't attacked through the tunnels, but then it hit me. The mines outside of town were silver mines and I bet that tiny flakes of silver ore covered the ground near the trap door and throughout the tunnels. "I'll deal with you boys in the morning when you've got a tummy ache," I said and then descended back into the earth, closing the trapdoor behind me, as I made my way back through the tunnels to check on Roxy.

"Mike, let me out," Roxy said when I returned to check on her. She was up and rattling the bars on her cage; she had taken off all her clothes and the wound on her chest looked better. The swelling had gone down and there was no more pus. "I know you want me," she said. "Open the gate and I'll put on that sexy little night gown you bought me. I'm so horny, baby. Come in and do me, Mike, please. You'll love it. It'll feel so good."

Then the change came over her and she began to sprout hair all across her body. As she transformed, she let out a mournful howl.

"Sorry, darlin'. I'm not into hairy women. You'll have to ride the night out by yourself," I said sadly.

She threw herself at the bars in a fit of rage, now fully changed into a massive wolf. She shook the bars and slashed at me with her claws but to no avail.

"You always did have a temper, darlin'," I said as I jumped back.

I spent the night leaning against the wall of the tunnel while trying to ignore Roxy's thrashing about; along with her animal grunts and growls. She kept throwing herself at the bars while howling in frustration as she tried to break free.

I dozed off after a few hours and at dawn, I looked up to see her back in her human form, fast asleep under the covers. I ventured outside, heading down the tunnel to the trapdoor, and climbed up to the surface. Taking in the situation, I saw that the werewolves, now back in human form, lay in the street, up on the boardwalk and against the buildings. They looked as if they'd come off a three day bender. Some of the men crawled on their hands and knees as they puked their guts out.

I got onto the radio, called in the cavalry, and soon a squad of soldiers bailed out of helicopters and filled the main street of Santa

Rosa Springs. Armed with silver bullets, the soldiers and I exterminated the now human werewolves where they lay. In their weakened condition, due to the colloidal silver in the fountain, they didn't put up much of a fuss.

I reentered the town, this time walking in instead of skulking through the brush to join the soldiers in mopping up the werewolves.

"These fur balls won't be bothering anyone anymore," I said after splattering the brains of the last werewolf with a silver bullet fired from my .45. "Let's inform the survivors that they can have their town back."

The people of Santa Rosa Springs poured out of the church and filled the street with smiles on their faces.

The priest came up to me and took my hand. "Bless you, my son. This town owes you a debt of gratitude."

"You don't owe me anything. I'm getting paid for this," I said.

"Even so, you're a true warrior of the cross. God bless you."

"Thank you, Father. I'll just get my partner and we'll be on our way."

"Let me send someone for you, my son, it is the least I can do."

I shrugged and let the priest fetch Roxy while I dealt with the soldiers and the remaining cleanup.

An hour later, I looked up from talking to a corporal to see Roxy step out of the church wearing a black robe that clung to her body; she looked tired.

"Let's get out of here," she said and took my arm. I led her to the motor home and five minutes later we were leaving Santa Rosa Springs behind. My job was done, Colonel Casey could deal with the paperwork, that wasn't my thing.

"So am I cured now?" Roxy asked.

"I hope so. I think we killed them all. I hope I got the alpha male, but who knows? He could have escaped."

"God I hope not. So what do I do, Mike?"

I patted her leg. "We won't know until the next full moon, but if you're not cured, the wolfbane should keep things in check. And make sure you wear your Saint Christopher medal from now on."

She nodded. "What do we do between now and the next full moon?"

"What do you think, Roxy the Wolf Girl, we go home and live our life."

"Shut up, Mike! Don't call me that!" she yelled.

"I'm just trying to make light of a bad situation. Don't be so touchy, darlin'," I said, letting out a chuckle as I pointed the RV back home.

Four weeks later, one of the maids was doing her rounds in a hotel in Las Vegas. As she reached the next room to be cleaned, she heard the sound of a chain clanking. There was a **DO NOT DISTURB** sign on the doorknob and she was about to turn and leave when she paused upon hearing an animal howl come from inside the room, and then a man yelled, "God, Roxy! You know I don't like hairy women! Control yourself! Haven't you ever heard of a bikini wax?"

"Tourists," the maid said as she shook her head, pushed her cart in front of her, and then continued down the hallway to the next room, while outside in the clear night sky, a full moon shone down over the city of lights.

A MAN ON THE INSIDE

DAVID BERNSTEIN

Mikel Konrad was handed over to the Special Sciences Division of the black-ops unit Red Works. He was caught on camera planting explosives in a New York City subway and apprehended in his downtown apartment. Three other men were with him when the F.B.I. raided Mikel's residence—all killed during the raid. Mikel's apprehension was kept out of the news. He was reported dead with the rest of his brethren.

"Is the serum ready?" Jax asked, a level four lieutenant for Red Works.

"Yes," the scientist said. "Tried, tested, and true."

"And the capsule, any problems?"

"No. I was able to implant it next to the patient's left ventricle as instructed."

"And the beast...is it still alive?" Jax asked.

"Yes, as long as we feed it, the creature will survive. Human hearts seem to be its favorite."

Jax smiled. "Quite a weapon we have on our hands, Doctor."

"Yes, it sure is," the scientist said proudly as he picked up a small canister—the syringe inside it—and handed it to Jax.

"Okay, I'm off to see our patient," Jax said as he took the canister to then exit the lab.

Commander Broderick waited in the hallway. "Is everything a go?" he asked.

"Yes, sir," Jax assured him with a grin.

Together the men proceeded along the hallway to the elevator. Jax pressed the down button and the elevator arrived at their floor within seconds, the doors opening smoothly. The two men stepped inside and rode the car to the sub-basement level.

They exited the elevator and walked down a brightly lit, white hallway to an observation room. Two high-ranking officials were waiting, both staring through a one-way mirror. The men turned toward Jax and Commander Broderick. Hands were shaken and greetings spoken before Jax left the room and entered the interrogation area.

Mikel was sitting at a table; his wrists handcuffed to a metal ring attached to the table's surface. The room had an overhead fluorescent light positioned directly above the table. Mikel's platinum hair seemed to be glowing. One of the bulbs flickered, but it was designed that way to give a sense of uneasiness to the detainee. The walls were painted a dingy tan and had cracks in them, purposefully created, of course. Compared to the rest of the state-of-the-art facility, the interrogation room resembled a forgotten relic.

Jax took a seat across from the combatant—the one-way mirror facing Jax's back.

"You're a small fry in all this, Mikel," Jax said. "An insignificant flea."

The prisoner's stare remained the same, looking off into space.

"We're letting you go," Jax stated.

Mikel's cobalt colored eyes met Jax's.

"That's right asshole," Jax said. "We're letting you go and not to my liking, but there's a condition."

Mikel took his eyes off of Jax, returning to his previously stoic state.

Jax placed the cylinder containing the syringe on the table and said, "We want you to take a message back to your people." He expected a reaction, but received none, the man hadn't moved. "Tell your people that the Defenders of Justice will crush every attempt made to destroy the United States or any other country we're aligned with. You and your terror networks' days are numbered. Before it gets to that point, and it will, we want to establish a communication with your regime." Jax paused, giving the words a minute to sink in. "Can you do that?"

Mikel remained motionless except for the rise and fall of his chest.

Jax stared into the terrorist's eyes. "I need to know that you hear me. Understand what I'm asking of you, if not, then you're going to spend the rest of your life in a room with fewer accommodations than the one you're in now."

"I understand, but your lies will never be believed," Mikel said.

Jax smiled. "I'll take that as a yes." He rose from his seat, the chair sliding backward. He picked up the cylinder and twisted it open. He pulled out the syringe and removed the orange cap on the needle. Mikel's eyes locked onto the needle like a heat-seeking missile. Jax smiled on the inside at seeing the trepidation in the man's eyes. He walked behind the prisoner.

"What are you going to do?" Mikel asked, his voice faltering. He followed Jax with his eyes until his neck could turn no further.

"Why, tough guy, worried?" Jax asked.

"You said I could go. You lied, infidel."

Jax sprang forward, wrapping his muscular arm around Mikel's throat. He plunged the syringe into the man's neck and injected the needle's contents. When the syringe was empty, he withdrew the needle, placing the orange cap back on.

Mikel was shaking; every muscle tensed as if an electric current was coursing through his body. Jax guessed the man was anticipating some kind of reaction. When none came, he seemed to somewhat relax.

"What have you done to me?"

"Nothing you need to worry about," Jax said. "You'll be escorted by private plane to Germany. From there you'll fly alone to your home country."

A guard stepped into the room, walked up to the prisoner, and shot him with a sleeping dart.

Mikel quickly slid into unconsciousness.

Forty-eight hours later, Mikel found himself back in his home country. It had been two years since he had visited. He was a low-level operative, sent as a sleeper to the United States seven years ago.

Immediately upon arriving on his native soil, Mikel suspected he would be tailed. After a few hours of waiting and observing the people that came and went, he realized he was alone. Had the operative for the Defenders of Justice been telling the truth? Mikel was given a message and was to deliver it to his superiors, but he had of course suspected it was some kind of ruse. He continued to wait outside the airport, watching, observing. Satisfied that he was truly on his own, he left by way of a taxi.

He informed the driver to take an out-of-the-way path to his destination; gladly paying for the extra miles. Finally, he arrived at his destination, a few blocks from one of the safe-houses he had memorized when he was in training. He hoped it was still in operation.

He walked down an alley and found himself at the door to the safe-house. With a few deep breaths and a quick prayer, he knocked on the door. The door opened a crack, to reveal a set of red veined eyes staring back. Mikel spoke the password; a code for operatives on the run.

"Back away from the door," the man told him. Mikel did as he was asked. The man then opened the door halfway and slipped out. He looked right then left down the alleyway. Once satisfied it was clear, the man ushered Mikel inside.

He was taken to a room, given some tea and bread, and told to wait. He spent the next eight hours staring at the walls and occasionally nodding off.

The door eventually opened by another man and Mikel was told to follow him. He was lead down a dark corridor, almost having to feel his way if not for the light coming from another open door at the end of the hall.

He entered a well-lit room. Two men holding automatic weapons stood to either side of the entranceway. Plush velvet couches lined the walls and there were men relaxing on them, talking silently. A video camera sat on a tri-pod in a corner, apparently not in use. Sitting in a chair in the center of the room was an older man. He had a long, but neatly trimmed white beard and a pronounced scar on his left cheek. He wore black fatigues—commando style, and hiding his eyes were a pair of mirrored sunglasses. Mikel was led to a chair placed across from the man.

"My name is Eborine Moharaz," the man said.

Mikel immediately knew who the man was; a high-ranking member of The People's Hand and a highly wanted international suspect. He'd been on the news countless times taking responsibility for bombings across the globe.

"Sir," Mikel said, bowing in his chair. "It's an honor to be in your presence."

The man gave a slight nod.

Mikel's palms were sweaty and he closed his eyes in embarrassment. "I'm sorry I failed The Cause, sir."

Moharaz laughed, stroking his beard. "You have not failed, my brother. You are here among family." The man's voice was reassuring and smooth.

Mikel opened his eyes. His heart was beating rapidly, but he felt more at ease. He'd seen enough to know when a man was doomed for death. But Moharaz, a vicious and deadly man, meant Mikel no harm. And why should he? Mikel had followed his orders to the T.

"Tell me what happened in the U.S.," Moharaz said.

Mikel told the man everything about his time in America leading up to his planting of the explosives and his time in the interrogation room, including the message he was to deliver.

The old man laughed when he finished. "The Americans believe they can defeat us, just like they believe they can eradicate the cockroach. We, like the bugs, will always exist, except we will strike back at their attempts to destroy us, bringing the Western World and its allies to their knees." Moharaz paused, his face somber. "It is true however. They have hurt our numbers and resources, but they have only strengthened our resolve. For they cannot kill what is in our hearts."

"Yes, sir," Mikel agreed. "But then why, great leader, would they let me go?"

"You are of no use to them. You are simply a member of a small cell. They know you have limited information and know nothing of the other cells in America or abroad. I do find it strange that they indeed released you, but it must be a new tactic. I truly doubt they meant to set up a meeting." The man pursed his chapped lips, appearing to be deep in thought as if he were a great scholar.

"I made sure I wasn't followed," Mikel said.

"We have men everywhere in this city. You were identified and watched at the airport. I was assured that you weren't pursued or I would never have let you within a mile of here if I knew otherwise." Moharaz eyes became menacing slits—murderous in their intent—but quickly returned to a more tranquil state.

Mikel let out a relieved breath as if a pressure valve had been turned. He truly did perform all of his duties well. He felt proud of his efforts, but was still angered at himself for botching the assignment in New York City.

"What is to be my new mission?" he asked.

"We shall discuss that in the coming months. You are most likely on every F.B.I. and inter-agency watch list so going back to America, at least for a few years, is off the table. We will find you a new task, in a new country—that, Mikel, I promise you. Come now," Moharaz said, rising to his feet. "It is time to pray."

The day passed pleasantly and Mikel had grown more comfortable. In a way, one he would never admit, the mission's failure had been a blessing. He was delighted to be home again. Fate apparently had bigger plans for him. What other man, having been in his position, would've been allowed to leave such a secret and powerful agency. The Defenders of Justice never let anyone go. God was truly looking out for him.

That night, Mikel slept as peacefully as he could remember.

The following day, he hung out with his new brothers. They all spoke about religion, family, The Cause, goals, and of course, their dislike of the Western world.

That night at dinner, Mikel began feeling as if he was coming down with a cold. The flu maybe, he thought. He began sweating, his thoughts swirling. The men at the table were eating, talking, and laughing, oblivious to his qualms. Mikel tried to fight his feelings and picked up his fork, but his arm filled with ache. His entire body burst into pain, as if it were ablaze. He fell off the chair and thudded to the cement floor, quickly curling up into the fetal position in pain.

The men seated at the table gasped and conversations ceased. Chairs slid along the floor in unison as the men stood, a few coming to Mikel's aid.

Mikel lay on the floor writhing in agony, thinking maybe he was poisoned—Moharaz deviousness after all. The men surrounded him; concern written on their faces. If it was Moharaz they certainly didn't know about it. Shouts of, "What's wrong?" and "Is it poison?" and "Get him up!" rang out.

Finally, four men picked Mikel up and carried him across the room.

"He must be sick," Moharaz said.

Mikel wasn't sure why, but he desperately wanted to be out-side—the night calling to him like a siren.

"Please, I need fresh air," he breathed.

"Bring him to the roof," Moharaz ordered.

He was carried to the roof by way of a staircase leading from the building's main room. The roof was flat like most of the build-ings in the city. A small garden was in one corner while chairs sat in a circle near the center.

The sky was clear, the stars twinkling brightly like holes punched in black fabric. Mikel's eyes locked onto the full moon and his pupils dilated. The small orbiting sphere was a thing of uni-maginable beauty. He reached out to touch it, the pain suddenly vanishing from his body.

The men carrying Mikel quieted; his sudden relaxed state alarming. They went to place him in a chair when he cried out in pain.

Mikel felt his bones ache as they began to stretch beneath his flesh. His jaw was elongating, protruding outward along with his nose. His fingers doubled in size and huge claws shot from his finger tips. Fur sprouted along his skin from every pore in his body. Within seconds, Mikel was no more, transformed into a beast—a werewolf.

The men screamed and began to flee, and a few who had guns drew them, aiming at the beast.

"The Western world's devil," Moharaz yelled, pointing an accu-satory finger at what had been Mikel.

The werewolf jumped up, and using its claws, ripped the throat from one of the men holding a gun before he could get off a shot. Another man with a gun took off running after seeing his comrade gruesomely killed. Everyone began heading back to the stairs, wanting to get away from the creature.

Within a few strides, the werewolf caught up with one of the fleeing men and sunk its teeth into his skull, removing a large piece of it along with a chunk of brain matter. Blood caked the were-wolf's snout, turning the brown fur into a glistening candy-apple red as it crunched the contents in its mouth like brittle popcorn.

As another man reached the stairwell's entrance, he cried out briefly as the beast's arm burst from his chest, a heart now held in its claws. The werewolf tossed the lifeless body aside before devouring the heart and galloping down the stairs after the other men.

Upon reaching the bottom of the stairs, the beast was met with a hail of gunfire from an AK-47. The werewolf howled in pain, but using its powerful legs, leaped sideways, bouncing off the wall. It flew through the air, tackling another man. The man with the AK-47 continued to fire, riddling his companion with bullets, along with the beast. As the machine gun finally clicked empty, the werewolf threw the dead man at the gunman as he attempted to reload, knocking him down. Men were running about, screaming.

The wolf leaped into the air, pouncing on the fallen gunman, tearing his chest open with its claws to remove his still beating heart. More bullets rang out and struck the beast in its side.

The bullets stung like annoying bee stings, but the werewolf charged in the direction of the gunman. The man tried screaming as the beast howled and brought its claws toward the man's head. Raking across the man's face, tearing the flesh away as if it were putty, the werewolf's claws caught in his open jaw, ripping it off. The man grabbed futility at his jawless face, his screams muffled by blood.

The bullet wounds along the beast's body were already healing as it quickly tore through two more men—the room falling silent. It raised its snout, sniffing the air—something was still alive.

The werewolf followed the scent to a large wall-cabinet. Running its nose along the crack where the doors came together, an overwhelming stench of urine, sweat, and fear assaulted its nostrils. The beast grunted angrily and then tore the doors off as if they were made of cardboard.

Curled up in a ball on the floor of the cabinet, Moharaz sat with his knees to his chest, crying.

"Stay away from me!" he shouted, his cheeks wet with tears.

The werewolf, a growl in its throat, lunged at the living meat. Using its powerful claws like a crude rib-spreader, it opened the man's chest and plucked the heart from Moharaz's body. It ate the muscle in one swift gulp, its claws and face glistening with crimson.

Wild and crazed, the beast raised its maw to the ceiling and bellowed a howl. It took off thrashing around the room, looking for a way out when it felt a burning in its chest. It howled in agony as it slumped to the floor. Its breathing grew shallow, vision fading, until death came—the beast transforming back into human form.

Back at the Red Work's compound, Jax and Commander Broderick stared at the heat signature of red dots on the monitor as each one faded. Finally, when all the dots were gone, Jax said, "They're all dead, sir. Including Moharaz. Our Intel stated he was inside when the attack occurred."

"And what about the creature?" Broderick asked.

"Also dead, sir. The silver capsule did its job upon remote detonation." Jax pointed to one particular dot just before it faded from the screen. "See, the red dot's gone, indicating a dead target."

"Wonderful. I want a team in there immediately. Make sure there's no sign of the beast. And I want this mission kept tight lipped."

"Yes, sir," Jax said while smiling widely. "It looks like we have a new weapon on our hands."

"Yes, Jax, it appears we do."

ONE NIGHT IN ASHMOUTH

JOHN ATKINSON

Julian ran as fast and hard as he ever had in his life. The thick, slimy mud, coupled with the torrential downpour, made it almost impossible to do more than lurch wildly away from the body. Tears streamed down his face as he screamed for help as loud as he could. The attack had come from nowhere and he was loath to leave Harry, but he knew his friend was dead and that the beast could still be out there.

His map had long since been stuffed, soaking wet, into a pocket which, in his haste, he had forgotten to button. He tried to draw it out now but it was little more than a ball of papery mush. He knew not if he had, in his malaise of panic and terror, waylaid himself and veered off the trail they had been following. He remembered that along this path, buried somewhere in the hills of this region, was the small, derelict town of Ashmouth.

Casting panic-stricken, wide-eyed glances behind himself, he hurried as fast as the treacherous ground would allow; the mud sucking at his boots as if attempting to pull him into the earth's embrace. He had no idea of his direction save that he was traveling steadily upwards and that, at least, he remembered was correct.

He hoped fervently that the sounds he heard behind and around him could be attributed to the rain pounding the side of the godforsaken hill. He struggled to keep hold of his sanity, as a man could have been driven insane by the sudden, unprovoked attack of the huge fanged beast that had torn Harry's still-breathing throat from his body and left him seeping his crimson blood into the wet, unclean earth. Some-kind of wolf, he told himself, but what would it be doing up here? In all the years he had been walking in the Peak District, he had never heard of a wolf attack.

* * *

The plan had been to walk from the small station in Edale, up to the summit of Kinder Scout, and across the Snake Road into the Hope Woodlands. From the Hope Woodlands they had planned to descend into Crowden, skirting around the oft-avoided town of Ashmouth—about a nine mile hike—not including the variations in altitude. The pace was a tough one, and only became harder when the rain hampered their spirits and the mud coated their boots. However, like the veteran hikers they were, they pressed on despite the adverse conditions and neither wanted to pitch their tent in the terrible weather.

They had successfully crossed the Snake Road and were deep into the Hope Woodlands moor when the attack occurred; a large beast the color of cold steel had risen from the shadows behind them to sink its teeth into Harry's neck. They had both been frozen in terror as the thing unfurled from its hidden crouch, but once Julian saw the blood, thick and red, run down his friend's neck and saw the foam, tinged crimson, at the muzzle of the huge wolf, his legs overcame their paralysis and responded to his brain's signals to carry him as far from the accursed place as possible.

* * *

Julian slipped on a rock, slick with the fallen rain and half buried in the mud, and fell into the thick, peaty muck that prevailed throughout the moor. He felt something give in his ankle as he collapsed, a sharp agonizing pain that slowly gave way to the dull ache of permanent damage. He scrambled in the mud, desperate to get further from the place of Harry's death. He looked wildly about, and in a brief lapse from the wind-driven rain in his eyes, he spotted a dim light in the distance, around half a mile away.

"Ashmouth," he breathed to himself. "It must be."

With grave and agonizing effort, he pulled himself to his feet and limped, dragging his injured leg behind him, towards the two-story house with the lit window.

As he entered the town, more of a hamlet to his eyes, he noticed that several of the wooden houses appeared deserted; indeed broken windows, shattered framework and swinging doors, un-hinged in gaping dark mouths of shadow suggested abandonment. He also noticed the smell, an underlying stench of burnt wood with an almost overpoweringly sickly-sweet smell of decay. He covered his mouth with his hand and struggled onward, through the deluge to the front door of the shadowy, unkempt construction that towered above the ramshackle husks that made up the rest of Ashmouth.

Julian raised his fist and pounded three times on the heavy wooden door. "Help me!" he yelled as he hammered away. "Oh, God, help me!"

The heavy blows and his shouts cut through the silence of the night, echoing through the town over the sound of the rain doing its own pounding.

The front of the house loomed high over him, the bulging eaves offering some slight protection from the downpour as he continued to beat at the rough wooden door. He heard a metallic sound, a sliding rasping noise, and realized it was the latch being drawn back on the door. This was confirmed a moment later when the door swung open, revealing a bent old man clutching a flickering candle in his left hand.

Julian was shocked into silence, his raised arm falling to his side, at the sight of the man. His walnut-like face, so haggard and aged, seemed both inviting and comforting. The man had a hard face, but a kind one, and with a crook of his finger, beckoned Julian to accompany him into the house.

The candle, flaring up brighter now that they were out of the wind, illuminated the twisted figure of the old man, his pallid skin wrinkled and weather-hardened to resemble pale leather. His hair was long, dirty and disheveled, his fingernails yellow, thick and encrusted with dirt and grime. He wore a gray cloak—protection from the icy cold draft that crept under the door—over torn, stained black trousers and a once-white shirt. His smile, however, seemed genuine and Julian followed him inside.

They stood in a large room, the wooden walls seemingly well insulated against the wind and the rain, only the door, hanging slightly crooked in its frame, admitted the draft. The floor was bare, the boards worn, a few disheveled rugs scattered about. A bookcase in one corner seemed packed with ancient, leather-bound tomes, and a high-backed chair sat nearby for the purpose of reading. There were more candles lit in this room, giving it a warm glow that was both inviting and comforting to Julian as he felt the panic begin to fade from his bones. All that remained was a confused numbness in response to the death of his friend.

Julian then noticed that they were not alone in the room.

An old lady, dressed in a gray cowl similar to the man's, sat silently in the corner, close to the dark wooden stairway leading to the second floor, her head high as if she sniffed at the air. When her head turned to face Julian, he wasn't surprised to see the milky cataracts that obscured her rheumy eyes, set in a face as weather-beaten, and yet as warm, as her husband's.

Nevertheless, it was she who spoke to him. "Come in from the rain, young man, we don't often get visitors anymore."

"You have to help me," Julian began but the woman cut him off with a wave of her twisted, arthritic hand.

"Oh yes, we heard you yelling for help. Tell us, what is it that ails you on this foul eve?"

The old man gestured for him to take a seat at the table in front of the old woman. Julian sat and began his tale. "We, I mean, Harry and I, oh God!" he lowered his face to his hands and rested his head on the worn, scuffed table. The sobs racked his body as the old man brought him a thick, rich smelling broth and some old, hard bread.

The man laid a hand on his arm and said, "Eat that, son, and when you've got the strength for it, you can tell us." The foul breath of the man washed over Julian and brought him to his senses. He realized that part of the knot in his stomach was hunger. He soaked the bread in the soup and devoured it, savoring the salty taste of the cured meat, while he continued his tale.

"There was a huge...*thing*. God, I have no idea what it was! It looked like a wolf but it was far, far too large! We were going to make our way over the moors, from Edale. But that's where it was. I didn't know what to do, so I ran! I ran and left Harry there!" He paused a moment to try and compose himself, taking another large spoonful of the broth, thick with beans and barley, into his mouth.

"We got lost; the rain and the mist and the wind, we just lost the path and our bearings. We carried on, relying on our map, compass and instinct; we'd been walking for years together." Julian's face grew pale and his hands began to tremble as he recalled the past. "And then from out of nowhere, we felt something behind us. We turned just in time to see a shadow rising out of the mist, and then it had Harry by the throat! A huge beast with coarse gray fur and long yellow fangs! What was it? What is it? It tore his throat out right in front of me!" He rose to his feet. "We have to go back. He could still be alive out there! We have to go and get him!" He started for the door.

"You're in no fit state to go anywhere, my friend." The old man blocked the door, holding a rifle in his wrinkled hands. Julian didn't know much about guns, but it looked well used and comfortable in the man's grasp. He stared wide-eyed as the man continued. "I'll go and see if I can find your friend, and if that beast shows up then it better have an iron hide to stop a .50. The only place you're going, lad, is to bed. Mary will show you to the spare room and we have plenty of blankets. They're a bit old and worn but I'm sure that'll bother you none."

Julian slumped where he stood, exhausted, the weight of responsibility taken, momentarily, off his shoulders. He realized he was achingly tired and his ankle still throbbed and pulsed painfully inside his boot. He nodded wearily and allowed the blind old woman to take his arm. In truth, it was he who led her up the stairs, a lit candle clutched in one hand, as the man buttoned an old, green, waterproof poncho over his gray cloak and slipped out into the howling wind and driving rain.

Unlike the single, large room below, the second floor had a central corridor and two doors leading off it, one presumably to the old couple's bedroom and one to the spare room. Mary led Julian up the corridor and stated, "The door is on the left, just up here." He managed to open the door and both of them entered the room.

Julian placed the candle down on the small table to the right of the narrow bed in the corner. The room was small and simple, but seemingly warmer than downstairs. The bed was a solid dark wood, covered in a stained blanket with equally blemished pillows. There was a small, lead-lined window set into the wall opposite the bed, through which Julian could see the slanting rain in the fading twilight. There was a wardrobe as well, on the other side of the bed, but one door hung open and Julian could see the sleeves of shirts and jackets through the gap.

"This was Billy's room." The old woman was almost whispering and Julian had to strain to hear her. "Billy's room be-fore...before..." She sensed Julian was watching her. "Before he went away," she finished, loudly. "Yes, this was our son Billy's room... before he went away. He went to the city to get work, you see. I don't like to think about it, my sweet boy all alone in that big city."

Julian gave the old lady a sympathetic smile she couldn't see, and she directed him to the stack of tarnished coverlets and spare blankets under the bed, then went off to get him a jug of water to wash.

He slipped off his boots and his socks, wincing at the angry purple bruising surrounding his right ankle. He felt around the bruise, pressing it to see where it hurt the most—nothing seemed to be broken. *Just a twisted ankle* he thought, *nothing that a bit of sleep won't help recover.* He slipped under the blankets to get warm, pulling another one over the top of himself. By the time Mary had returned with the washing water, he was already asleep.

* * *

When Julian awoke it was fully dark outside, the small pin-pricks of stars telling him the clouds had been banished from the sky. A full moon hung in the sky; bulbous and yellow, a harbinger of the horror to come.

He experienced a moment's panic at the recollection of Harry's attack. *But surely,* he consoled himself, *If there is any hope for him, the old man will see to it that he's set right.* He managed to wrestle the guilt that perhaps he had survived when his friend had not. It was now a numbness inside him that he resolved to deal with later, when he knew the full story.

He swung his legs out of the narrow bed and tested his swollen ankle. He could just about stand on it but would need a crutch to travel any form of distance. There was no chance he could leave this place without the mountain rescue service. He checked his pockets for his cell phone, but without much hope as he knew Harry had been carrying both phones in the rucksack strapped to his back, and he was sure he hadn't seen a telephone downstairs.

A scent wafted in through the slightly open door and filled Julian's mouth with a salivating longing. All he'd eaten was broth the previous night, and with the morning now here he was ravenous. He slowly eased himself out of bed, neglecting to put on his boots as he doubted his right boot would fit over his grotesquely swollen ankle. Limping, he made his way out of the room and began to descend the stairs. With each downward step, the smell became stronger but Julian could hear no noise of cooking, nor hear the crackle of a fire.

He paused at the bottom of the staircase and cast his eyes around the large single room.

Nothing.

Neither the old man nor the old woman was anywhere to be seen. There was no fire in the hearth and no meat anywhere to be seen, but the smell was unmistakable and stronger here than it was upstairs. He noticed with a start that the old man's green poncho was back on the hook by the door, his rifle leaning against the wall next to it. The poncho was smeared with a thick coat of blood. Julian couldn't tell if the blood belonged to the wolf-creature or if it was that of his friend. Surely though, they would have called him if his friend still lived? Perhaps the man had seen fit to give Harry a decent burial. Julian would have to find out where if that were the case; he was sure Harry's mother would want her son to have a proper funeral if, indeed, he was dead.

Or perhaps the man had found the creature, killed it, and was even now burning its foul body outside.

Julian hobbled to the door; unlatched it and poked out his head. The smell of roasting meat hit him hard, the fire and the creature must be out here!

He stepped out into the clear, crisp night, feeling the bite of the wind on his face. He cast his eyes around, conscious of the decaying husks of the old village that loomed up into the night sky. He could see no fire or smoke, so he started to make his way around to the rear of the house. He made a full circuit of the structure, unable to see flames or the grotesque creature.

On his second circuit, he noticed that the aroma of roasting meat was strongest at the rear of the house, and with eyes alert, he passed that way for a third time. Now that his eyes were focused and he knew where to look, he easily spotted the half concealed trap-door set into the ground. He got down on his hands and knees and inhaled deeply—the smell was definitely emanating from there.

Julian took hold of the iron ring that served as a handle for the trap-door. Heavy and pitted with rust, it was cold to his hand, the rotting wood of the door flaking around the handles. He pulled at the handle, straining and struggling as he tried to keep his weight off his right ankle, now regretting not at least trying to put on his boots, his feet now cold. The trap-door moved almost imperceptibly. Heartened by this, he dug deep into his reserves and pulled with all his might. With a squeal of rusty iron hinges the door swung open, revealing a set of stairs slanting down under the house; illuminated by an unseen light. The old man must have been stronger than he appeared if he had dragged the creature here, opened the trap door, and carried it down the stairs.

Julian descended the narrow, dimly lit staircase. This entire situation began to feel strange to him but he proceeded at a slow, almost creeping pace, the sweet smell growing stronger as he progressed. The passageway that began where the stairs ended seemed cut right out of the limestone, as if a system of mines had been built below this strange town, tunnels that branched off in all directions.

As far as Julian was aware, no such mine had ever been present in this part of the Peak District. So what was this passageway? Why go to all this trouble?

As he made his way down the passage, Julian could hear voices; they seemed to be chanting in a dull, low monotone. As he rounded a corner at the end of the next passageway, he could see a large fire with three figures silhouetted against the roaring flames. He edged closer until he could see that the three figures were indeed the old man, his wife, and something that resembled a dog but was hidden in the shadows, the old man and woman both hunched over the fire. They seemed engrossed by the something they cooked in the crackling flames, laughing as they consumed its bloody, dripping flesh.

The next thing Julian saw paralyzed him with fear; his legs freezing and the terror he had hidden inside himself rising, unbidden, to manifest itself as a scream of pure horror. For what Julian had seen was the huge creature that had attacked his friend. It was leashed on a long thick chain affixed to the cave's wall and was feeding on something; a hunk of meat was his first guess. The beast's eyes blazed in the firelight as it lifted its huge, shaggy head from its meal to stare, growling at Julian. Then it raised itself up on its hind legs, its head scraping the low ceiling.

As he took another step closer, Julian's eyes glanced down at the beast's meal, his eyes growing wider in panic as he noticed the blue piece of fabric, so similar to Harry's fleece jacket, that seemed to hang over the edge of its bowl.

Julian must have screamed then, for he heard his voice echo as the pair turned away from the fire.

The old man turned his head towards the large wolf that stood on two legs like a man, as the old woman set about unfastening its chain.

"Come on, Billy," the man called to the werewolf. "Another one for you, my son."

Julian remained paralyzed, his eyes now fixed on the form of his friend Harry as the limbless, headless carcass slowly turned, roasting over the open fire.

Then the werewolf pounced, and the last sight Julian saw were the large teeth as the beast tore out his throat, his screams once more reverberating off the tunnel walls.

THE HAIRS ON YOUR HEAD

DANE T. HATCHELL

The woods were black in the night, the stars shining above, and a full moon hung on the horizon. A creature defined both as neither man nor beast crashed through the brush, and small nocturnal animals scurried for cover. Folklore had given it the name of werewolf, and it was deemed to be just a nightmare of men. But tonight was no dream, and the beast was on the prowl.

The cool moist air filled its lungs, and its clawed feet ripped into the ground below it. Like a young buck in rut, it frolicked through the woods marking its territory.

Fear, like good and evil, was buried by the inhuman hormones flowing through its blood. And like any other carnivorous animal, a successful hunt was what its raw instinct demanded most.

A glow in the distance from a farmhouse caught its eye. It stopped and tilted its head, flexing its nostril to the wind. The scent of food was strong, and its salivary glands brought moisture to its mouth. The beast slowed its pace and made certain to quiet its approach as it headed toward the house. It traveled upright, using the rows of corn for cover, dropped to all fours, and ran when the rickety old barn came into sight.

It silently moved to the fenced-in area behind the barn that protected thirty hens. They were all snug in their coops, roosting for the night.

The werewolf rattled the fence and ran into the barn, spooking the horses. The chickens went wild with cackling, but the horses didn't go berserk until they picked up the predator's scent. The horses neighed frenziedly, and bumped and kicked, trying to make a break out of the barn.

The beast had set the trap. It ran away from the barn and behind a fresh bale of hay.

A light came on from the rear of the farm house and a man exited, struggling with the strap on his overalls. He carried a shotgun in one hand and held a flashlight with the other, as he made his way to the barn.

"Damn coons! Get outta here! Heyaaa!"

The man entered the barn and quieted the horses first; chickens were cheaper to replace and he didn't want his barrel horses to injure themselves. He had never seen his horses act like this before, and wondered what had happened to make them so upset.

The horses calmed down to his soothing whispers and he gently stroked their faces until they were reassured. Satisfied they were content, he left them, walked the perimeter of the chicken yard, and found that the fence was secure. He expected to find a pile of feathers and a few less chickens, but he didn't find any reason for the ruckus.

The full moon's glow above was enough for him to see across his property all the way to the surrounding woods, but nothing unusual caught his eye. The man turned and walked back towards his house, the muzzle of his gun pointing at the ground.

Not more than twenty steps were taken when a noise from behind sent a cold chill down his spine, and the hairs on the back of his neck to electrify. The farmer spun around and the last picture his mind would ever frame was of a man-beast silhouetted against the orange moon above.

The werewolf was an efficient killer; it held the man's throat in the death grip of its jaws until the farmer's life force ceased.

With victory came the spoils of the hunt, and the satisfaction of a full belly.

Four weeks later, Sheriff Landon Richards and Deputy Barbe were starting their morning, having coffee and reading the local newspaper.

The headline exploded, **Fear of Full Moon Weekend**.

Richards winced when he first read that. He felt it sensationalized what the people of Jasper County were going through. And it did nothing to help him and his police force solve the mystery.

"Well, Sheriff, did you get that call from the State Police?" Barbe asked.

Richards sipped his coffee, not taking his eyes from the paper. "Yep...sending four cars and eight officers, and we'll be doubling our shift Friday through Sunday at night."

"You think something's going to happen again?" Barbe got up from the table and poured a fresh cup of coffee.

"Might not, with all the publicity this has been getting. Whoever's doing this might lay low this time."

"You know, Sheriff, you're one of the few that think people are responsible for this. Most think that a cougar is running wild out there."

"No, I don't think so…they're just trying to make it look like an animal," Richards retorted.

Barbe walked to the window and watched the passing cars ferrying their drivers to work. "There have been six incidents in six months…but I hope you're right. If this is an act of a man, I do hope they lay low. It might buy us some time to track them down before they strike again." Barbe sipped his coffee. "Say, Sheriff, she's out there again."

"What?"

"I said that she's out there again, Mrs. Mendoza. She's across the street. Just staring over here with that same blank look on her face."

"Sonofabitch," Richards tossed down the paper and walked to the window. "It's them I tell you, those damn Gypsies. They're behind all of this somehow, they're nothing but trouble."

"Sheriff, The Mendoza's aren't Gypsies, they're Mexican."

"Don't matter, they live like Gypsies. Moving from town to town, living out of those travel trailers."

"They're responsible citizens," Barbe added. "They bought that old campground and moved a single wide on it; they pay their property taxes. They're hard workers, they have green cards; they're legal. Sure they have to travel to where the work is, but Sheriff, what would our strawberry crop be like without people like them?"

"Trash, nothing but trash, and a bunch of Satanists, too."

"Satanists?" Barbe was taken aback, "The Mendoza's are devoted Catholics."

"That's just what they want you to think. You remember when we found a bunch of old books on the supernatural when we did the investigation on Mrs. Mendoza's missing kid? We found knives made of pure silver, and that stuff we didn't recognize turned out to be wolfbane. I tell you, they're into some type of godforsaken rituals. The daughter probably ran off to get away from them."

Barbe thought a moment and said, "Well, she did go missing about a month before the animal attacks, but I don't see any connection between the two."

"I think they're harvesting human organs for their rituals. I've been reading some strange shit on the internet about what these Satanists do. I bet they maul up the body to make it look like an animal attacked it."

"Sheriff, look at the poor old woman out there. She may come from a different culture, but she misses her daughter. All she wants is for us to find her."

"No, she blames me 'cause I'm the sheriff of this county. This is my town and these are my people. She thinks that I'm protecting somebody. Hell, that's insane! My boy is still torn up over her daughter being missing. He was going to take Maria to the prom; he told me he loved her. I told him she was trouble, but he was thinking with the brain in his pecker and not the one in his head and didn't listen to me. Now the boy is on prescription medication for depression. Some mornings I can't even get him out of bed to go to school. That old woman needs to blame herself and her family's lifestyle for making her girl run off."

"I know, Sheriff, I know.....there's a whole lot of hurtin' going on in our little county these days." Barbe picked up his gun off the desk and put his hat on; it was time to make his morning patrol.

The Sheriff looked on at the old woman, swallowed dryly, and shook his head from side to side.

The face of the moon showed full again, its white light brightening the cloudless sky. The people of the town were all too aware of what the next few nights could bring.

The local businesses were feeling a financial pinch as the full moon had cycled on a weekend last month, too. Restaurants were advertising nightly specials and extra security was hired to patrol parking lots. No one really wanted to be a prisoner in their own home, so they were looking for an excuse to go out and have a good time. Plus, the human rational is that bad things only happen to other people.

Greenwood Cemetery was the county's largest and oldest burial ground. It was also the site of the county's first established church, which dated back to 1880. Over the years, the church's congregation had outgrown the old church, and a new place of worship was built at a new location. The old building was lost to termites and torn down, but the cemetery continued to serve the needs of the townspeople.

Albert Green was in his late forties and a retired sergeant from the U.S. Army. His wife divorced him many years ago, the strain of military life being too great. She and their two grown children lived elsewhere, and none of them stayed in contact. The town of Jasper had been his home for a few years now. He defined himself as a man of simple means, enjoying a beer or two at night, and being an avid fan of basketball.

Albert received a monthly check from the U.S. Government, his pension for his twenty years of service to his country. It wasn't a lot of money, but it got him by.

A few months ago, Albert picked up security duty at Greenwood Cemetery. Vandals, kids, or thieves had been stealing metal urns and markers, probably to sell as scrap metal.

Working the night shift in a cemetery comes with its share of concerns; most based in superstition. The last time he worked night duty had been in Baghdad, so he didn't see his new job as much of a challenge. His job was routine and mundane; about twice an hour he would hop on a golf cart and patrol the cemetery. The rest of the time he was inside the kitchen area of the main building, drinking coffee and watching television.

He looked at his watch and set up the microwave to heat his frozen dinner, knowing it would be ready for him by the time he returned. He picked up his 6 D cell Maglite flashlight off the counter and headed for the cart. The Mag was big and heavy for a light, but its secondary purpose was to be used as a club.

The cart hummed in the night air along with the crickets and frogs, and leaves and twigs crinkled and snapped as the tires rolled over them. Albert steered with one hand and shined his light about with the other. Two old mercury vapor lights on the property cast a dim eerie glow on the grave sites below.

He was mindlessly shifting his light left to right, but his mind was on his chicken dinner. A scratching noise caught his attention and he slowed to a stop and focused the beam to investigate.

There had been a funeral earlier that day, and this was the burial site. His light revealed fresh flowers strewn around the area, partially covered with fresh dirt. As Albert looked on, more dirt came flying out of the hole.

Gravediggers!

He reached in his pocket for his cell phone, but remembered he'd left it in the charger in the kitchen. He wasn't licensed to carry a gun, but he always carried a backup in an ankle holster. "Better to be judged by twelve than carried by six," he'd always said. He didn't want these ghouls to get away, especially since he had known the man buried earlier.

He turned off his light and unstrapped his Charter Arms Undercover .38 caliber revolver. It only held five bullets, so he had it loaded with +P ammo for superior knock down power.

Dirt was still flying out of the hole when he approached with his gun drawn. Ready to pull the trigger, he pointed the flashlight into the hole, and turned it on.

"Freeze!"

The light lit up the hole and staring back at him were two glowing green eyes, a dark face covered with hair, and a gaping mouth sporting one inch fangs. The beast roared a bloodthirsty growl, and Albert screamed and dropped the light. He blindly fired twice into the hole, then turned and ran away.

He had been in many firefights in Iraq, and had even caught his share of shrapnel. Nothing had ever scared him like what he'd just seen. The senses that now controlled him were primordial. The fear that gave him flight had its origins at the dawn of time. His heart pounded hard in his chest, and his lungs strained for more air as he ran towards the main building.

The beast was at his heels in no time. It leapt onto his back, and rode Albert to the ground. He tried his best to roll over and fight, but the strength of the werewolf was equal to that of three men. He felt jaws of iron clasp down on the back of his neck and he screamed. Intense pain traveled to his brain, and mercifully snuffed out his consciousness.

The satisfaction of victory was a warm feeling to the werewolf, each bite sugared with the sweetness that only human flesh could provide. The beast tore ferociously at the meat of the arms and legs, cleaning the bones and tossing them aside. But nothing pleased its animalistic palate more than the warm blood that filled the heart of its kill, and the savory goodness found in the liver.

When the werewolf was finally satiated, it wiped its mouth with the back of its hairy hand. The moon above bathed the beast with life giving moonlight and it raised its head and howled to the stars.

The werewolf left the cemetery the way it had entered, not knowing where the night would lead next.

Almost another four weeks had passed; rumors were that the FBI was just about to come in and run the operation. Sheriff Richards didn't like the sound of that. He didn't want to lose control of his town. Wildlife and Fisheries had set multiple animal traps and placed digital motion activated cameras in the areas where cougars and bears were most likely to be roaming. Nothing of any interest was caught by the cameras so far, but the deputies now ate barbecued raccoon on a regular basis thanks to the traps.

The sheriff was sitting behind his desk with a stack of mail to one side, and a pile of suspect profiles on the other. His face was pasty white underneath a two day growth of a salt and pepper beard. His shirt looked a size too big, and he had lost about thirty pounds over the past several months. His increased anxiety had reduced his sleep to something less than three hours a night. But his problems didn't end there; the horrific events that plagued his town jeopardized his re-election. And what was left of his family life wasn't much better. His son was growing further away from him and he was out of ideas on how to reach him.

His office door slowly opened with the squeak of a rusty hinge, and a lone figure hesitantly made his way in.

Sheriff Richard's trance was broken by the presence of a young man standing before him. "Will...what are you doing here?"

"I didn't go to school today, Dad. I...I just don't see the point," Will said softly while looking down at the floor.

"Son, the point is that you can't go to college unless you graduate from high school. You've got your whole life ahead of you, you just can't throw it away now." Sheriff Richards felt that he had said these same words a hundred times. "Did you take your medicine this morning?"

"Yeah, but drugs can't change the things that have happened in my life."

"You're right, drugs can't change things. Only time and you and me can change things. Time has to pass, and time has passed. It's up to you now to make the changes in your life. You've got to snap out of it, son. You owe it to me, you owe it to yourself, and you even owe it to Maria."

Will's eyes lit up. "What do you mean? You act like she's dead. Do you know something knew, did they find her?"

"No, son that's not what I meant."

"Dad, you're the one that said she might have run off with her old boyfriend from Carroll County. I thought she might still be alive. So what do you know?"

"Look, son...I don't know anything. She's been missing for months now, nothing has come across the wire, and I'm now thinking she may be dead. And if she is, she would want you to move on in life."

Will's face blushed and tears started to well up in his eyes. The pain of her loss was as fresh to him as when she first went missing. Will stood in silence, the void in his soul growing larger.

The sheriff picked up a report from his desk and pretended to be interested in it. He tossed it down and pulled out a pocket knife and shaved off a hang nail.

Will stood in silence; alone inside himself.

Sheriff Richards closed his knife and picked up a brown envelope from the mail pile on the corner of his desk. He tore it open and spilled the contents out as a chill ran down his spine. Will stood unmoving, but his eyes were now focused on the contents of the envelope.

A silver crucifix and a broken chain lay next to a bronze name tag with some torn brown clothing stuck to the pin of the name tag.

The crucifix was small, but the figure of Jesus had a good amount of fine detail.

Will picked up the crucifix and gently examined it. "Maria had one like this," he said, closing his eyes as if trying to recall a memory.

Sheriff Richards picked up the name tag; he already knew what was written on it—it was his.

"Dad, is this Maria's?"

"I don't know son," Sheriff Richards said dryly.

"Why was your name tag in that envelope?" Will asked, his face twisted with confusion.

The sheriff's heart raced, but he knew he had to master his emotions or he might lose his son forever. An uncomfortable silence passed then he stood up and looked his son in the eye.

"Will, I get stuff like this in from time to time. You know we have officers and volunteers that are constantly searching for clues to help us solve these crimes. Somebody sent this to us in case we might find them useful."

"What about your name tag?"

"I lost that a while ago. I tumbled down a hill chasing after a drunk that thought he could out run me after I pulled him over. I got all torn up in the brush and the name tag got ripped off my pocket."

"But why is there just the crucifix and your name tag? Who sent it?"

"Well, I don't know. They probably forgot to put the evidence report in the envelope. Probably was Barbe. That man would forget his head if it weren't attached to his head."

Will again looked down, as if the answers to all his questions would somehow spell themselves out in the pattern of the tile floor. He'd been disenchanted from reality ever since Maria went missing; lost, adrift as a ship on a cloudy night. A light was shining somewhere in the peripheral vision of his mind, but he was too tired to think through it right now; it had been a bad morning.

"I...uh...I think I'll go home now." Will never looked up as he turned to leave.

"Okay, son. Say, why'd you come here in the first place?"

Will stopped and tuned back to face his father. "I don't know, well, I guess I was a little scared. I was scared and depressed...this is another full moon weekend, you know."

Sheriff Richards pulled out a twenty dollar bill from his wallet and handed it to his son. "Will, no one has ever been attacked inside a house or a business. You know that I won't be home tonight, so just stay in and rent a pay per view and order some pizza before it gets dark. Keep the doors locked, and I'll be home in the morning. You know where I keep the shotgun, right?"

Will nodded and set the crucifix carefully down on the desk; it held his gaze for several more seconds, as if he didn't want to part with it. There was so much more for him to consider now. His life was no longer on hold. He left from his father's office without saying goodbye. The squeaking hinge of the door closing sang through the silence between them.

Sheriff Richards picked up the crucifix and chain, put it back in the envelope, and locked it in the top drawer of his desk. He knew what he had to do, and he had a plan that he thought would work.

It was risky but he had no other choice.

Another full moon brought another transformation from man to beast, the werewolf once again unleashed into the night. The cells in its body had grown accustom to its lunar metamorphosis; and it was maturing as a hunting, killing machine.

The beast ducked under low hanging limbs, and the scent of pine filled the air as it ran through the forest. The moonlight reflected off a small pond and reminded the werewolf of its thirst. It ran to the water's edge and knelt down, lapping the water like a canine. When it finished, it lifted its head to see its reflection staring back.

The beast knew that it was looking at itself, and not some other animal for it was self aware, and the spark of humanity inside it was aware that it was more than an animal. And this night, it knew, would prove it.

The town was in total lockdown, all of the businesses closed before nightfall. Sheriff Richards had set up eight different patrol areas to cover the heaviest populated areas and the State Police had doubled their force for the weekend with men and vehicles.

The sheriff was riding alone in his Crown Victoria police cruiser. For his plan to work, he had to keep tabs on the various patrols throughout the night. At ten p.m., Richards made his hourly checks on the radio, and all reported 'all clear'. His plan could now move forward.

Driving on a two lane road at the northern most point of the county, he slowed his vehicle and turned at an old broken KOA sign, then continued down a dusty gravel road. He turned off his headlights and eased down the road until he could see a dim light coming from a trailer. He stopped the car and turned off the engine, then keyed his radio mike. "Mabel, this is Richards, over."

"Go 'head, Sheriff, over."

"Look, I'm going up north to visit Mrs. Mendoza. The rest of her family is away working in another county. She's up there alone watching the place. I'm going to check on her and make sure she's okay, or if she needs anything, over."

"That's real nice of you, Sheriff, I'm sure she'll appreciate the visit, over."

"Yeah, well, it'll take me about forty-five minutes to get there. I'll call when I'm finished. Richards, out."

"Roger, out." The radio went silent and Richards was ready to put his plan into action. He had forty-five minutes to kill Mrs. Mendoza, dispose of her body, and return to the campground. He would then radio in that her trailer had been broken into and robbed, and that Mrs. Mendoza was missing.

He had a body bag in the trunk and he was confident his plan would work; it had worked before. He opened his cruiser door and exited quietly, then gently pushed the door closed. He removed his police issue Glock and slowly made his way towards the trailer. He didn't plan on shooting her, wanting to knock her out and then suffocate her to spare her pain, but he would fire on her if he had to make that choice.

The frogs and the insects were singing in the night as the sound of gravel crunching softly under his boots came to him as he approached the door to the trailer. He cautiously peered through the tiny door's window, the drapes thin enough for him to see inside.

Mrs. Mendoza was sitting on a couch with her back to him. She was alone, reading by the light of a small table lamp. Richards placed his hand on the door knob and slowly tried to twist it open but it was locked. The door was so cheaply made he knew he would have no problem kicking it in if he had to.

Suddenly, the sound of crunching gravel sounded from behind him, telling him of the approach of someone running towards him. Richards turned and saw a dark man-like creature covered in hair leaping through the air at him. He raised his left forearm in defense as the beast crashed into him and knocked him to the ground.

The werewolf was on top of him and it sank its fangs deeply into his forearm, causing Richards to scream in pain. He still had his gun held tight in his grasp, but it was trapped between their two struggling bodies.

The claws of the beast lashed out and scratched the left side of his face and four rows of torn flesh spilled blood down his cheeks. He was on his back with the werewolf's body pressing into him and he knew he couldn't take much more before suffering a killing wound.

Richards thrust his pelvis into the body of the beast, allowing him to wiggle his gun hand free. The gun rang out with four quick bangs and the werewolf let out a horrific howl. The hairy monster rolled off the sheriff and stumbled off while clutching its side. Richards quickly righted himself and fired three more times, this time missing his target. The beast howled again, turned, and disappeared into the darkness. He ran to the trailer door to see Mrs. Mendoza's eyes meet his through the small window.

"Open up, damn it! Open up! Open up or I'll break it down!" he demanded while pounding his fist on the thin aluminum door.

The door unlocked and he pulled it open, and as he charged in, he knocked Mrs. Mendoza to the floor. He quickly closed the door and locked it. Mrs. Mendoza was on her backside with her hand to her mouth in shock but Richards ignored her and went to the kitchen, grabbed a rag from the counter, and wrapped it around his bleeding forearm.

"What in the hell was that?" he screamed at her. "What's wrong with you people? What in the hell do you have going on around here?" Blood was still running down his face to splatter on the kitchen floor of the trailer.

Mrs. Mendoza sat up, her entire body shaking.

"Answer me, damn it!" he commanded.

Mrs. Mendoza raised her right hand and pointed a finger at Richards. She slowly stood up and took two steps towards him. "My people are good people," she said, her voice weak and quivering. "Yes, our family is cursed. But God helped us, the Blessed Virgin helped us....we took care of Maria during the times of madness. She never hurt no one, not ever, no one."

Richards face was white as a sheet and shock was starting to creep in. Mrs. Mendoza continued to point at him and her finger shook more and more.

"My daughter was a good girl. She respected her family and loved God...until your son came into her life." Her voice was getting stronger and resolve filled her eyes. "Your son put bad thoughts in her head, rebellious thoughts, and she disrespected her family for him."

Richards was trying to follow her story when he remembered why he was there in the first place. Mrs. Mendoza knows what he did to her daughter. He needed to get rid of her now for time was running out. He hoped the creature outside was dead or dying somewhere. He didn't know how he was going to explain the creature to the FBI, but he might be able to use it in 'explaining' the disappearance of Mrs. Mendoza.

"Look, I don't know what you're talking about. My son had nothing to do with your family's problems. Vagabond trash is just vagabond trash."

"Where is my Maria, Sheriff? I found her crucifix and your name tag in the same place while searching for her. I know you had something to do with her disappearance, I just can't prove it yet. So, tell me now, what have you done to my Maria?" She charged forward and Richards grabbed her right wrist and forced her to her knees. "Where is my Maria? She never hurt no one, what did you do to her?"

Richards squeezed tighter. "Stupid woman, your daughter was pregnant. My son got her pregnant and wanted to marry her and not go to college. I couldn't have that. I couldn't have her ruin his life."

Mrs. Mendoza's eyes widened, swelling with tears. "Maria, my Maria....tell me where my Maria is, please."

"She's is at the bottom of a well...and don't worry...you'll be joining her shortly!" Richards pushed her down to the floor and pulled a small silver knife from his back pocket, opening it with one hand. His plan wasn't going as he'd hoped but it could still be salvaged. He had owned the silver switchblade since he was a kid and it seemed fitting that he would use it now to save his hide.

"I'll leave enough blood that they'll think that beast killed you in here and then carried you off. No one will argue the evidence." He raised the knife and Mrs. Mendoza closed her eyes and prayed.

But before he could bring the knife down and end her life, a loud thud hit the door and Richards spun around. The door was hit again and burst apart as the werewolf sprang forward, its claws going for Richards' jugular.

Richards was startled by the assault but managed to raise the knife in defense and he pierced the rushing beast directly in the heart. The werewolf screamed like a hound of hell, its momentum knocking Richards to the floor, the knife pulled from his hand as it was embedded in the creature's chest. The beast fell on its side, writhing in pain and anger. One loud last gasp and a long breath exhaled out, and then the werewolf went limp on the floor.

The sheriff slowly rolled to his knees and pulled out his Glock. Standing up on weak legs, he kicked the man-like figure to check for signs of life, then rolled it onto its back. This wasn't a cougar or a bear, or nothing that God could have ever created. Hair grew from every pore of its skin. Its teeth stuck out from the mouth even though it was closed, and the black nails looked sharp enough to cut through cowhide. The face resembled that of a wolf, the nose wet and black.

Richards looked around, accessing his situation. Mrs. Mendoza was holding a rosary, still on her knees as she prayed softly. He needed to act now.

He turned to the body to pull out his knife and he stopped cold as the body began to transform before his eyes. The hairs were returning inside the skin, the face was shrinking from wolf to man, and the teeth and claws were retracting. The beast was transforming back to its human form. The frightening animal characteristics of the form softened, revealing the dead body of a beautiful young man.

"Oh no...God no...Will?" Richards whispered as his world crashed down around him. His little boy that had grown into a man was dead, and he had been the one who killed him. Tears streamed down his face and he fell to his knees next to his son.

Mrs. Mendoza stopped praying and moved over to him. "My ancestors were cursed many years ago, for what, I do not even know. But your son chose the curse. He wanted to be like my Maria."

Richards knelt in silence, his hands over his face.

"My Maria's curse is gone, and your son's curse is gone. But you...your curse is just beginning!"

Large beads of sweat formed on Richards' brow, and liquid fire ran through his veins. The wounds on his face and arm healed from the inside out and his entire body felt inflamed. His teeth suddenly felt too large for his mouth and hair began to push through his skin to coat his body.

In the night sky, the full moon cast its pallid glow onto the trailer as Mrs. Mendoza's scream pierced the darkness, followed by the howl of a savage beast.

As the howl echoed through the forest, the frogs and the insects went silent, and the nocturnal animals of the woods hid in fear.

THE CAPTIVE

SPENCER WENDLETON

Gerald Kerre studied the man outside the iron bars of his makeshift cell. The stranger had recently entered the room through a steel reinforced door. He carried a stocked plate of food in both hands, walked to the table near the cell, where he seated himself without a word.

Gerald had woken up ten minutes ago, alone, in what appeared to be the cellar of a house; asleep on a cot without a mattress or blanket. Whether knocked out by narcotics or brute force, he didn't remember, but he understood he'd been kidnapped because he was still wearing his hospital gown. How he arrived here didn't matter because he refused to be scared; he'd been through worse in his sixty-eight years of life, the worst as a P.O.W. in Vietnam.

Despite his ability to keep calm, he studied his enemy's next moves.

The man, in his early forties, was clad in a loose-fitting white button up shirt and dirty black slacks. Sensing Gerald's eyes on him, the man averted his gaze from his meal. The man sized Gerald up, casting an expression as if accusing, *Why is this man not scared of me yet?*

Gerald dared to ask a question with the air of friendly conversation, wanting to test his jailor's demeanor, "What are you eating with? That's not any kind of silverware I've ever seen before."

The man raised two stick implements of shaved wood, possibly random sticks that had fallen off of trees to scatter the ground. The tips were sawed into dagger points. The man inspected his tool, as if he too, just realized how odd their use would come off to others.

"I detest silverware," he answered testily. "I can't bare the taste of the metal, and it causes other problems, too. I guess these sticks are going back to nature for me and the pack would've approved if I hadn't shunned them first."

The pack? Going back to nature? These were ideas he couldn't understand, but he remained composed. He stayed collected in the face of a life and death matter. The man couldn't hurt him without opening the cell, he reasoned, and when he did, Gerald knew a number of fighting tactics to protect himself.

Knowing this, he quizzed the man some more, while he returned to stabbing his plate of a mountain pile of meat, spearing into a flap of rare roast beef. The man turned over the impaled meat with a squish. The color of the meat kept troubling Gerald; it wasn't brown or red, but instead a fleshy lard-white.

"Why would regular silverware cause you problems?" Gerald asked him.

Chewing on his food, the impolite man replied, "It's because I'm a werewolf that silver coating bothers me, if you must insist."

He bit down on a wad of meat with a crude pop of juices, dismissing the question as ridiculous and obvious, and with a deep purr from a bestial throat, he returned his attention to his plate, saying one last thing before becoming completely enraptured by his meal, "If you don't mind, I want to finish my leftovers before they get cold."

Gerald watched in stunned silence as he learned what was really on the man's plate. The layers of meat were piled as slick vestiges on top of each other, the tender juicy pieces cooked off the bone. The modified sticks turned over a section of meat where strands of hair and a series of moles speckled the skin.

This was human meat, he easily deduced.

Underneath the flesh folds, a pale purple heart was hidden, undercooked and oozing watered-down blood. There was so much meat—a feast for five men—on the buffet-sized plate, but the man kept working on it, seeming to become hungrier with each bite.

The curious man's teeth gnashed and tore at grains of flesh audibly, the incisors and canines shifting in his mouth and extending like jig hooks in a show of horror, the gums muscles working to reset the teeth as new meat crossed his pallet with differentiating tenderness.

Other than the man's long teeth, the rest of him remained the same, though his jaw was much too tight, formed snare-tight with bulging lean muscles. The same muscles flexed at his fingers and arms as if a stronger vessel was hiding within the temporary shelter of unassuming flesh.

After twenty minutes of witnessing the man masticate and slobber and defile dead human flesh, all that remained of the plate was a circle of grease and the same pale, pink blood that colored the outside of his mouth.

Now that the leftovers were finished, the man's eyes glowed yellow, and the unreal orbs suddenly cased Gerald with renewed interest.

"You don't believe I'm a werewolf, do you. You're thinking this guy's a cannibal who validates his actions by saying he's a werewolf. I normally wouldn't care what you think, Mr. Kerre, but I need something from you. Despite my strength and my abilities to rip a body into shreds, I can't—or let me rephrase this—I won't, enjoy mutilating you unless you're terrified. I want your blood boiling with fear. When that happens, your adrenalin races, and the quality of your blood changes. Instincts and hormones and pheromones start mixing together, and the meat tastes so much better that way; it's so succulent how the body tenderizes itself."

Gerald said nothing, just stared at the man.

"Ah, but you don't even flinch when I tell you this. You're not scared of me one iota. This is the problem, Mr. Kerre. I guess I didn't think about it when I took you from the hospital and noticed the tattoos on your body and caught on to how you were in the service. Whatever war or bullshit brigade or section you were in, I don't care. It won't help you now."

Gerald crossed his arms over his chest but remained silent.

"But I'll get you scared, don't worry about that. I'll have my feast. It's why I built this cage. It's why I don't hunt people like the other werewolves do. I like the fear to build and gather up in their veins. I want your blood to burn in my name. Your skin to quiver in my presence; you understand me? I busted my ass sneaking into St. Anthony's General Hospital and carrying you out through the back way."

Gerald's eyes creased but he held his tongue.

"This is how I get most of my victims; the best victims, in my opinion," the man continued. "The sick are always more suscepti- ble to panic. It's easier to steal patients than you think during the late evening hours. Of course, none of this matters because I'll get what I want from you. I will feast on your flesh, and it will taste the way I please."

Another hour—or was it two? Gerald had no way of knowing; cornered in the over-lit basement cage with no windows. Upon finishing the speech, the mail departed without an explanation or further comment.

Alone, Gerald considered how he'd never tell this crazed 'were- wolf' man in depth that he'd been a P.O.W. during the Vietnam War, and how he'd suffered deprivation torture for eight months. During that isolation, he'd gained the ability to wander outside himself, even during life-threatening moments, and find his 'happy place' which was a feeling of nothing. 'Numb body,' he'd called it, his body a collection of anesthetized nerves, numb everything, and he could turn it on and off at will.

He was an anomaly to his co-workers on the Ford assembly line when production quotas weren't being met and they had to work longer and harder, and he was chewed out by his supervisors because he didn't shift his expression or sweat a single drop during his reprimands. Nothing could penetrate his steely resolve, not that he'd tell the werewolf any of this.

More than half a day had passed and he'd done his best to in- spect the cell for security flaws. It was a homemade set-up; the iron bars had been placed into the floor and sealed in cement and cut through the wooden rafters in the ceiling. He attempted to pummel through them, but after ten minutes of scissor kicks, his heart burned in his chest; the very reason for his hospitalization.

He'd experienced electricity up his right arm while mowing his front lawn less than twenty-four hours ago, and the next thing he could recall, he awoke in the hospital to a doctor telling him he'd need a triple bypass. His body couldn't take much physical work, though kicking through the bars was useless anyway; they were strong and impenetrable.

Outside the cell, there was a vast amount of open space, though the very back of the room was cast in darkness. A garden hose was meticulously coiled up and hung on a rack on the far wall. A mop bucket and a shelf of cleaning items were the only other noticeable items in the basement, as was the steel door right across from his cell. Perhaps it was sound-proofed, and even if it wasn't, he could be out in the country where nobody would hear his cries for help.

No way out.

Nobody around to save him.

He'd have to wait for the man to return for a chance to negotiate his escape.

The man was obviously a murderer and a cannibal, and possibly a psychopath, too. How his eyes glowed was a mystery, as it wasn't by using contact lenses. They had changed from hazel brown to a weak gold on their own.

This wasn't a normal man, Gerald finally decided, but a monster.

He'd encountered one such creature before in his lifetime, over thirty years ago, and he had prevailed that time and he knew if he was patient, he would win this time also.

He just had to bide his time.

Gerald had nodded off out of sheer fatigue, and when he woke to the sound of sniffing, he opened his eyes, but didn't panic. The numbness came over him; he was in control, an automatic failsafe of cool headedness.

Gerald spotted the man crouched on all fours with his head cranked upwards and his nostrils puckering open and closed as he smelled him through the bars, memorizing his captive's scent. The man was still human and wearing a checkered flannel shirt and beige khakis.

The room stank of urine, the tang reminding Gerald of burnt orange peels, and he caught a puddle of dark yellow urine on the floor near the steel door.

After a few minutes of the man sniffing the cage, he ran out of the room, throwing shut the steel door behind him, infuriated for no particular reason.

"I can make you scared of me, Mr. Kerre. I'll show you what I'm capable of, and then you might change your mind. You don't believe I'm a monster but I am, I assure you. I thought being trapped in a cell would get you going, really freak you out. But being a veteran must have taught you some tricks if you were ever captured. You were probably taught breathing techniques to get you through sticky situations, or some bullshit along those lines. You look just as calm now as you did sleeping in your hospital bed, and I don't know why."

Gerald said nothing.

"Let me remind you, I can make your heart stop, but then you'd be dead, and I prefer my prey to be alive. Then what's left of you after you're mutilated, I'll eat later; you know that much is true, you saw me eat that heaping plate of meat yesterday." He smiled, showing his sharp teeth.

"I was born a werewolf, Mr. Kerre, by birth. And no, I don't howl at the moon, if you care to ask—you can ask me questions if you like. You don't care to ask me anything, do you? You haven't spoken a word to me in days. Probably a military thing, too. I'll tell you about myself, anyway; I turn when my blood craves iron— it's a physical reaction. I can't help myself, and unlike many of my pack, I don't wait to turn and hunt in the city or in the country where I can get caught or blasted by some NRA-totting gun nut. I already have a body ready, you see, and I stay here, and I eat my victims like I'm going to eat you. But you're a tough case. I will conquer you, Mr. Kerre, and your meat will be that much sweeter."

Asleep again after being alone for hours on end, Gerald was disturbed by the shadow that stayed over him long enough to make his skin cool beneath it.

The man was standing up straight with no expression on his face, unflinching and focusing on Gerald's body. Then, without an explanation, from his hairline, thick rivulets of blood coursed down his features, splitting them into red cross-sections. After bleeding from an unknown infliction for many minutes, threads of blood parted, and up through the harsh color, course steel wool hairs sprouted from the flesh until the man was completely covered in copper-colored hair that accelerated into a rough patchy fur coat. Then the man's eyes morphed into a resplendent crimson-yellow color.

A werewolf.

Snarling, the beast's jaw broke in four places as it extended into a narrow muzzle, to completely change the shape of the face. The beast's jagged talons slashed at the bars to reap sizeable sparks, and beating at the iron slats, the werewolf issued an ear-piercing howl as it smelled Gerald.

It finally backed off with a huff and retreated through the metal door, its lust for fear un-satiated.

Naked, the man was colored in blood upon returning to the basement after an hour's absence. He was in human form again and he faced Gerald unabashed about his nudity. The staggered silence was broken when the man's patience evaporated, and he shouted the question, "Why aren't you afraid of me? What's so special about you, Mr. Kerre? You old bastard, you can't beat me! I'll win in the end, you son-of-a-bitch. YOU—WILL—FEAR—ME!"

Minutes after the verbal lashing, the man dragged down a mauled corpse of a young woman, a teenager, though she was unrecognizable after suffering the slashes that were bone deep. There were bloody wounds down her back and along her face, the eyes, nose, and lips shredded into a pink mess resembling mashed fish guts.

The man calmly plopped down into a chair clasping a knife and cut apart the victim's jeans and then removed her jacket, until she was completely unclothed. The next step, he sawed into her body, starting mid-pelvis and dragging the edge up to her chest in a straight line, and using the open skin flap, he stuck his hands in and removed the organs, slapping the wads onto the concrete floor in a slimy pile. He then produced an axe stored in the cellar and slammed the blade down to dismember the dead woman's arms, then the legs, and then the head, each swing committed with methodic callousness.

Carting the pieces, clutching them like firewood, he smiled at Gerald, "These are going in the cooker to smoke. I'll shove the torso into a bigger cooker, and add an entire six-pack of beer for flavor to let it simmer."

He slipped up the stairs to go about his work, but he peered back at Gerald one more time, the fool's gold hued eyes searching for the reaction he desperately craved, and added, "I've got my eyes on that meaty belly of yours. I think I'll need a whole twelve pack for your torso, Mr. Kerre. When the time finally comes to eat you, too, that is." He grinned widely. "Terror is a pheromone that leaks out of your skin, and when I smell it, I turn into an alpha dog that wants to jump on a bitch in heat. Right now, your pheromones run cold, Mr. Kerre, but I won't quit tormenting you until your nerves boil!"

It happened in minutes, his captor strapping the newly acquired, middle-aged woman into a chair with leather belts; she had flowing auburn hair and a naturally smiling face that had turned south in the presence of the man who was undergoing his transformation from human to beast.

She screamed in horror as the elongated fingers tipped with talons, much like the edges of box cutters, slashed down the side of her face, scraping deep. She quivered and suffered spasms of agony and failed to pass out before the wolf's snapping jaw ripped off the top half of her skull and tore the scalp back.

Ready to create more violence, the wolf kept chomping down, the sharp teeth grating against bone and gray matter, and the last thing Gerald saw before he refused to watch a second longer, was the poor woman's jaw had somehow ended up in the beast's mouth, suddenly snapped in half by the powerful teeth, the action sending the beast towering over the half-headed corpse and defiling the rest of her in more ways than just consuming her.

"You keep mocking me, Mr. Kerre! I will not be mocked by a piece of shit like you! Why aren't you afraid of me damn you?"

Eight victims' blood was seeping into his cell, each of their remains piled up in a macabre heap a few feet away. Gerald had witnessed each of their grizzly deaths. He couldn't help but study the pieces, feeling guilty, somehow wondering if he was responsible for their demises though it was obviously untrue. He was confused, trying to separate one body from the next, believing he was looking at an elbow and it turning out to be a knee. Everything was a jumble, a broken neck actually a fingerless hand, a fingerless hand actually a head without eyes, and a set of legs was actually—he gave up, pointless to trace any of the gory mess for recognition.

The werewolf hoped to gain his detestable wishes, to earn Gerald's fear by putting on the murder show. But the beast couldn't harm him, Gerald kept telling himself, the assurances heavy with meaning and keeping him strong.

He was hungry and near starvation, but he lapped water from the small sink installed in the cell to abate the hunger pains, and he knew no matter what, it was only a matter of time before the wolf would lose.

"You were sent to infiltrate me. That's the only way you're not folding to me," the man said angrily. "The FBI or some other branch couldn't believe I was a werewolf, or they were too chicken shit to catch me themselves, so they had you placed in the hospital, knowing I'd take you. You're like some scientific kamikaze here to study me. Is that it? Are you here to figure out my shit? Who are you, Mr. Kerre? Who are you, really? Tell me, goddamn it!"

Gerald just stared at the man.

"You have to be hungry. I won't feed you, though. I'll let you starve. Then I'll have what I want. All you have to do is be afraid, and I'll devour you. I can end your pain, Mr. Kerre. Just give in to me."

Crouched in the corner in a ball, nude and slathered in his latest victim's blood, the man beckoned to Gerald, opening up to him. "My family shunned me because I refused to run amok in the country and cities with them. I wanted to play it safe, and they didn't like that. But I still have fun, though they don't realize it. That's why they're all dead; careless idiots, shot dead by people refusing to be victims. But I'm still here. They said I was dishonorable in going against our nature. I didn't care. I wanted to live and not be hunted like a scampering buck in the woods. I've dealt with being ostracized by my own kind. I've come this far, Mr. Kerre, and I won't let you defeat me. I will find a way to break you, regardless of your rare determination."

Gerald remained silent.

"You're a werewolf, aren't you? Or maybe you're another monster altogether, huh? Answer me, Mr. Kerre, or I'll rip that head off from between your shoulders and shit down your throat." He dashed towards the bars, Gerald only two feet from the man's face.

"Oh, incredible—fucking impossible—you still don't flinch, and I'm right in your face. He snapped his fingers. "You do hear me, don't you? Yoo-hoo. Oh, you blinked then. You are hearing me. What is it you're hiding from me? No, you're not a werewolf. You would've needed to eat something by now, or your iron would be so depleted that your body would've turned. No, not a wolf. Maybe a vampire. Do vampires exist? Do they, Mr. Kerre? You'd know, because you are one." The man sprinted to the darkened part of the basement and parted a curtain. A square of shaft of light filtered into the cell, bathing Gerald in rich sunlight. "There! You should be burning! Burn you bastard! Burn you bastard! *Burn!*"

Gerald merely squinted from the glare but otherwise was fine.

"So, not a vampire, are you? Okay, where do we go from here? You're a human being because you were checked into a hospital for heart problems—how fucking ironic, Mister Faint Heart. You're handling me with no problem even when you need a triple bypass. You're as happy as the day before you met the likes of me, so what are you hiding from me? How are you not terrified of me?"

The man creased his eyes as he squeezed his hands into fists.

"I've met your kind before, Mr. Kerre, and you'll die the exact same way they did when they tried to kill me." Without waiting for a reply, he turned and left the clear, slamming the metal door upon his exit.

The severed head on a stick clutched in the man's hands belonged to an older woman. She looked to be in her seventies, the garish makeup giving the appearance of a bleeding mime's face the way the blood and pale skin mixed with the cosmetics. Like the head was a giant candy-apple, the man kept chewing on the cheeks and neck stump, desperately holding out hope for any expression on Gerald's face, even one of disgust or mourning, and all he got was a man sitting on his cot in subdued quiet.

"You asked me about my special silverware before. You've got a heart condition. You were in some war. I'm trying to piece you together, Mr. Kerre. Everyone else I capture pisses and shits themselves after my eyes start changing and I start slaughtering people in front of them. You've shown me nothing. I can hear your heartbeat, and it's relaxed. It's impossible you're so mellow. I don't know what to do about you, Mr. Kerre. Maybe I will have to kill you anyway. But I have to think about this first. Yes, I may have to kill you anyway."

Six hours later, the man stomped down the set of stairs, shouting in a rage as he charged into the cellar. "Well, saying I was going to kill you anyway had no effect on you. Fuck this shit. Fuck you, Mr. Kerre. I've had enough of these games; I'm coming in after you!"

He moved to the cell.

"Now it's your time to die. Come in and get me!" Gerald yelled as he took a step away from the bars.

The transformation was instant, the spraying blood flecking Gerald through the bars as razor-sharp blades of animal fur ripped through the changing man's flesh, giving birth to the feral beast that peeled back the iron bars and bashed an entryway to reach in and clasp him by the neck.

The werewolf shook Gerald like a rabbit in a bear's jaws, and he couldn't breathe, couldn't see, as his vision was turned into blurry lines of motion.

Next, he was forced down onto his knees in a bow of mercy. The werewolf howled and screeched and slashed divots and trenches into the concrete around him, desperate to gain victory over Gerald and force the slightest hint of fear from him, and upon failing, the incensed werewolf's jaws clamped down on the top of Gerald's head, ready to reap his kill by tearing his skull in half.

As the teeth sank into Gerald's skull, suddenly the beast halted as if shot and released its grip on his head.

Shaking in a spasm, the werewolf dropped to the ground and curled into a ball, its contorted face one of utter agony

Half-human and half-wolf, the combination resembled a rain-soaked dog, shivering with its diminishing arms curled around its chest, and its bent, knobby legs posed to shield itself from incoming harm.

Gerald stood over the deteriorating beast to watch it die as thin rivulets of blood seeped down the sides of his head where the teeth had penetrated his scalp. The wounds weren't deep and would heal easily.

The werewolf's jaw was a set of bleeding gums now, the teeth shattered, the tongue melting and evaporating as vapor exuded out its snout and partially opened mouth. The death continued out its throat, chest and guts as a red caramel-heavy mess sizzled through its flesh, the werewolf's fool's gold eyes going dim.

But not before Gerald leaned over the dying beast and whispered a secret into its ear.

Gerald walked up the stairs behind the steel door to make his escape. Upstairs, he used the phone in the kitchen to notify the police. After making the call, he stood outside the unassuming house secluded in the country to await an ambulance. He was starving, and on the verge of exhaustion, he sat on the front porch, repeating the words in his mind that he'd spoken to the werewolf before the beast's timely demise.

You're wondering why you're about to die, aren't you? Why I wasn't scared. It's called confidence. It's also called experience. I've had a metal plate in my head ever since my first year in Vietnam. The silver alloy plate also killed another werewolf that tried to slaughter me during one of my crazier tours of duty.

MOTOR CITY WOLF

DAVID PERLMUTTER

The whole thing really began when Carla and I came across that dead body in the apartment. Nothing unusual about that, you say? You think eight year old girl scouts come across dead bodies every day in Detroit? Well, we do, sometimes. But we didn't expect to find what this one would lead to...

* * *

Through what I still consider to be a rather fixed drawing of names by rote, Carla and I were selected to be the ones to be the representatives of the Wayne County Firebirds—the troop and organization to which we belong—for our annual cookie fundraising drive. Mostly 'cause I think the rest of 'em don't wanna waste time dragging a pulley full of cookies up and down Woodward Avenue for a whole day! Be that as it may, we were in the process of trying to earn some cash through this systematic method of distribution when the strange things began happening. And, even for Detroit, I mean strange.

You, no doubt, are acquainted with this custom wherever you may live, because there likely are scouts like us who live there, too. And they probably use some variation of the sales pitch which we employ, which runs as follows:

Good morning/afternoon/evening, sir/madam. We represent the Firebird Scouts of [Wayne County], and we are offering today, for your enjoyment, this hand made assortment of cookies, which we hope will meet with your approval...

Unfortunately, that's usually about as far as I get with the pitch before my potential customer says "No!" —or more profane words to that effect—and abruptly slams the door in my face. The rest of the pitch, by the way, is the standard boilerplate about how "really good" the cookies are, and it would give me further opportunity to show off my charm and good looks. If I ever got a chance to say it!

Anyway, where was I? Oh, yeah! The dead body...

Well, it happened like this. Carla and I, in our matching and form fitting yellow/brown blouse/skirt/sash/beret/shoes uniforms, had come across this really big multi-level apartment building on Woodward. And immediately, we thought to ourselves, *score*! If only a couple of people in that place would buy some of our overpriced wares, the Wayne County Firebirds would be okay financially for another year or so. We weren't expecting much, what with the economy gone south and GM going bankrupt and all, but maybe there'd be a chance. After all, it was a pretty big place!

So we went up all the floors of the place, each of us alternating between giving the pitch and towing the pulley. Since I'm taller and stronger than Carla, she would've preferred that I did the pulley work full time, and since she's prettier and more eloquent than I am, she also would've preferred doing the pitch full time. And, if we were adults, that might've been how it worked out, but we're kids, so we know how to compromise a lot better.

Oh, yeah—the body. Well, that happened as soon as we got up to the fourteenth floor from the twelfth via the stairs—they're really superstitious at that place. I got up to the floor first, took off my beret, and wiped off the sweat that was rapidly accumulating on my lemon blonde hair. Carla came next after I helped her steady the pulley up the final steps, her mop of brown hair firmly in place as she glared penetratingly at me through her glasses.

"Are we almost done, Lenni?" she asked. "We haven't made a lot of cash here, and there's only a few hours of daylight left!"

"Just one more flight, Carla," I answered. "And then, I swear, we're done here!"

"We'd better be!" she replied, firmly. In spite of the fact that she wears glasses and everything, she's as tough as I am, so I didn't wanna risk pissing her off or anything like that. And that was how it was gonna be—until we heard the noise coming from the end of the hallway!

"What the hell is that?" asked Carla, taken somewhat aback.

"I haven't got the faintest idea," I answered, stepping forward bravely. "But I aim to find out!"

"Are you crazy, Len?" Carla said to try and talk me out of it. "That could be a serial killer or something like that!"

"Are you forgetting what we learned at orientation?" I replied. "Firebird Scouts are supposed to help people, regardless of who they are! We're supposed to be going one-on-one with danger all the time, just like the boys! They only got us doing this sewing and cookie selling stuff to put us in our 'places', whatever the hell that means! If they put us in a cage match with the boys or anyone older than us, we'd kick all of their butts, for sure! So if you want to back out and be craven and cowardly, Carla, be my guest! I'm looking danger in the face and spitting on it!"

"Go ahead and risk your ass if you want to, Len," Carla responded. "You're a braver girl than I!"

"You're just saying that!" was my answer.

I moved down the hallway to the apartment at the end of the hall, where the noise had been coming from. Finding the door unlocked, I pushed it open, since it was already leaning sideways.

And that's where I found the dead body.

It was the body of a white man in a nifty pressed blue suit and red tie. He wasn't moving at all, so obviously he had to be dead, by my guessing, and soon I was able to confirm this suspicion. When I drew closer, I saw that the man had a large gash in his throat, but I also knew that no knife could have done that. I'd seen knife cuts on dead bodies before—you see a few when you've lived in Detroit as long as I have—and this wasn't done with a knife. There were jagged cuts in the neck that looked like something long and tooth-like had made its mark on the victim. Had his dog turned on him perhaps? Or was it something worse?

I couldn't confirm this for myself, since I hadn't earned my detective badge yet, so I went out to call in Carla. She had hers.

"Carla!" I hissed sharply. "Come into the room!"

"But, Lenni," she protested, "we aren't supposed to..."

"Just get in here, damn it!" I hissed more sharply with exasperation.

She did. And when she saw the body on the floor, she knew there was a game afoot as much as I did.

"Did you do this?" she asked.

"Certainly not!" I answered with wounded feminine dignity. "He was like this when I came into the room!"

"All down on the floor like that?"

"Yeah!"

"You didn't take anything from him, did you?"

"Why the third degree, Carla? I was only in the room for a minute!"

"I'm just trying to do an objective analysis, Len. I mean, we have to establish what happened here. It is possible that you could have done it and that you're lying about it now!"

I grabbed her sash forcefully and lifted her up on the top of her toes with a sharp pull.

"You accuse me of anything like that again," I warned her, "and I'll slap you good!" I don't like being wrongfully accused of anything—especially by my friends.

"Okay, Len!" she said. "I'm sorry. I was out of line on that one. Just let go!"

I did.

"Besides," I said, pointing to the man's torn throat, "you'd have a real hard time proving that theory with that there! I haven't exactly got the chompers to do that kind of damage to a guy!"

"Well, obviously!" Carla answered. "But who could, realistically? Those aren't exactly knife marks on his..."

We were interrupted by a loud, bellowing noise from the shadows of the room. And that was when he came in and confronted us!

He was quite clearly a wolf in human form. I don't know much about the supernatural or nothin' like that, but I know monsters when I see 'em, that's for sure! This fella had this coarse gray hair all over his body, even covering his face. Where his nose shoulda been was a snout, and there was a big tail that had magically sprouted out of his back, plus big claws in his fingers that he unsheathed the moment he saw me and Carla.

Neither of us screamed—one thing you learn right away as a scout is not to get easily intimidated by anything or anybody, no matter what it happens to be. But Carla, being the emotional wimp that she is, looked like she was going to faint any second, so I had to act fast. Seeing a chair in the corner, I grabbed it and thrust myself between Carla and the beast, just as it opened its giant jaws and lunged towards her neck.

"Listen, buddy," I said sharply. "If you're gonna munch on the neck of my pal, you gotta get through me first!"

He didn't get the point—and demonstrated this by biting through the chair!

"Run!" I ordered Carla as I dropped the remnants of the chair.

I found another chair at the table where the first one had been and laid it against the door as Carla closed it on the way out, having flicked the lock on the outside as she did. Then, after panting outside for a few moments to get our breath, we decided unanimously to give up selling cookies for the day after this unceremonious spooking.

"Remember," Carla warned me, "not a word of this to anybody!"

"Yeah," I agreed. "Except one."

* * *

"Lenore Finkleman! Do you seriously expect me to believe that rigmarole you just handed me? A werewolf, here in the city of Detroit, Michigan, in the year of our lord 2010? Are you off your damn rocker?"

Carla and I had flipped a coin the day after our encounter with the werewolf over which one of us was going to tell the story to the person we felt we could most trust with our secret—the leader of the Wayne County Firebirds troop, our boss, in other words. Needless to say, I lost. And also needless to say, she didn't believe me.

Okay—a little background here. The Wayne Country Firebirds have their headquarters on West Grand Boulevard, near the Motown Museum. We bought one of those cheap houses that were going for $200 each 'cause of the economy and all, and fixed it up nice so it was worthy of the Firebird name. So now it's our hangout and everything. Everywhere else we gotta be nice and polite to the adults and all, but at the clubhouse we can be something more like our real selves, when we don't have to be doing official Scout business and whatnot. That is, rough and tumble, playful, thoughtful, and always on guard in case our boy or girl rivals try to muscle their way into our turf. Here, we're not Lenore, Carol, Valerie, Maxine, Samantha and Isabella, those sissified alter egos we have to play so we can at least put on the surface appearance of how we were 'raised'.

Inside here, and on duty as scouts, we're just Lenni, Carla, Val, Max, Sam and Izzy—and we like it like that!

Izzy is our undisputed fearless leader, symbolized by the fact that she can walk around bare headed while the rest of us still have to wear our berets all the time. She's pretty and all, with long black hair and blue eyes, and all that, and pretty short compared to me, the tallest of us, but she can pistol whip all of us, including me, any time. Her seniority is reflected not only by this aggression, and the fact that she's a year older than the rest of us, but also by the fact that she has her own room in the house. The rest of us have to carve out our own digs in the place since it's not very big otherwise. The others in the troop, aside from Izzy, Carla and me, are Val, Max, and Sam.

"I tell ya, we saw it!" I said, doing my best to do a facial impression of our lupine attacker as we continued to talk. "He was all like..." and I growled in an attempt to make it convincing. Izzy still wasn't buying it, though, and she held up her hand to silence my extremely unconvincing imitation of the supposed werewolf.

"This all true, Carla?" Izzy asked her.

"Yep," was all she could say. "It's just like Lenni said?"

"Uh-huh."

"You wanna be more specific?"

So Carla made a more precise and orderly restatement of everything I had just said, minus my hyperbole and overacting, and they took her dead seriously-like. Typical!

"Okay. So there's a werewolf running around Detroit," Izzy said when Carla finished. "But what can we possibly do about it?"

"We can kill the sucker!" That was Val's commentary on the situation. It was a bit of a non-sequitur, so we all turned around and looked at her with shocked faces.

"You got Lenni's idiot disease, Val?" Izzy snapped.

I glared at her for that one, but she glared right back at me and I stopped.

"How are we gonna kill a werewolf?" Izzy asked.

"Simple," Val replied. "We just track down the sucker and put a bullet in him! Ain't none of you seen any of them old monster movies?"

"You mean," Max interjected, "like those old black-and-white Universal flicks you made us sit through? The ones I nearly wet my pants watching during the scary parts?"

"I did," Sam added, holding her hands and her head low in embarrassment.

"Exactly," Val said. "This sucker's a werewolf, ain't he?"

We all nodded.

"And werewolves always come out when a full moon's out, don't they?"

"In the movies," I said. "But this is for real, Val!"

"It don't make no difference!" Val answered. "Where you think those movie guys got their ideas about werewolves in the first place? That whole thing about 'any man who is pure of heart' and all that. That stuff is real! But them adults won't believe us 'cause they blocked out all that stuff when they start thinking 'bout sex all the time, so we've got to handle this ourselves! So all we got to do is wait till the next full moon, track down the sucker, and end his life with a silver bullet!"

"But where are we gonna get a silver bullet?" Max asked. "Or a gun to fire it with?"

"Girl, get your head on!" Val said, knocking Max's beret off her head. "You know my daddy's got more firearms than the state militia! And I've seen him putting silver bullets in all of them guns! So we've just got to get one of them guns and fire it at that sucker werewolf's heart!"

We got ourselves all pumped about going on a werewolf hunt with chants and cheers, until Izzy whistled loudly for our attention and got out from behind her desk.

"Hang on, here!" she snapped. "I'm the troop leader, and I'm the one who decides whether or not we engage in acts of barbarism like this! I mean, taking human lives isn't exactly part of the protocol of the Firebird Scouts."

"What!" Val interrupted. "This werewolf ain't no 'human life'! And, 'sides which, ain't you always tellin' us we need to be helpin' the community instead of hangin' round here all the time?"

"Well, yeah," Izzy said, her old words now biting her in the butt. "But I didn't mean like this!"

"What did you mean?" Max asked. "Having those fluttery tea socials and all that? That stuff don't wash with us, Iz', and you know it!"

"I never said..." Izzy began.

"But you do keep reminding us about our obligations," I told her. "And isn't one of them protecting our community from harm—whatever it happens to be?"

"Here it is," Carla said, looking at her Firebirds rulebook. "By-law 26 says that we, in effect, become a military taskforce in presumed times of threat."

"Are you really serious?" Izzy sounded desperate now. "Those stupid bylaws were written over a hundred years ago! And, back then, there was no way they would have let a bunch of girls fight in a war or rebellion or something like that."

It was Sam who tipped the balance in our favor by grabbing one of Izzy's wrists with one of her hands and holding her tight.

"I want to do this!" Sam insisted with soft but powerful menace in her voice. "We all want to do this, Izzy! We're within our rights, and nobody will believe us if we go to the police or tell our parents! I believe Lenni and Carla, and you should, too! And we need to do this, Izzy. We can't have someone else getting their throat torn out 'cause we didn't stop it!"

"All right!" Izzy said, giving in. "We'll do it! But you let go of me right now if you don't want a dishonorable discharge—and a beating!"

Sam did as she was told, not wanting either.

"Now, all of you, come around here," Izzy said. "If we're going to do this, we might as well do it the right way!"

* * *

Izzy's plan was simple enough. With Carla and me leading the way, we would make our way to the apartment house on Woodward where we first found the werewolf and confront it. Most likely, as Val made it clear, we'd have to put a bullet through the beast's heart. Getting possession of said bullet was no problem for Val: she slept with one given to her by her father due to his rather paranoid—I think—speculations about a rapist breaking into their house and trying to rape her. When we slept over there, he insists we do the same thing, as crazy as that sounds.

Unfortunately, we could only accomplish our goal under the light of a full moon, and this wouldn't occur again for another three weeks. But, as Izzy noted, that was more than enough time for us to hash out and execute a structured plan for dealing with the werewolf when we found it. So, as it turned out, we were more than ready for that werewolf when it came time to confront it.

But the trouble was, he was more than ready for us, too.

* * *

After uttering some minor white lies about sleeping over at each other's houses, we were prepared on the night of the full moon to confront this threat to the safety of the city of Detroit. Well, one of them, anyway.

We soon reached the Woodward apartment house where Carla and I met the werewolf for the first time. Izzy, as usual, took charge. Sam and Max were to stand outside and provide cover for our actions, complete with the cookies Carla and I hadn't been able to sell. We weren't taking any chances, understand? Meanwhile, Carla and I, accompanied by Izzy, and Val with her gun, were going to go upstairs and confront the werewolf, if he was up there.

It was fortunate for us that very little seemed to have changed from the first time I was there. The place was still falling apart and threatening, but at least this time Carla and I had backup and didn't have to carry around our weight in cookies.

I pointed out the apartment at the end of the hallway where Carla and I had first seen the werewolf, and they followed me across the hall into a tight phalanx until we got to the door of the offending apartment.

"Cover me," I said as soon as we arrived. "I'm going in!"

"You sure about that, Len?" Izzy asked. "I mean, we could just..."

"Nah!" I said dismissively. "I'm the biggest, aren't I? Well, I just need to get in there and drag him out! Just like you said, huh, Iz'?"

"Not exactly," Izzy replied. "But if you have your heart set on being your usual idiotic, foolhardy self, then go right ahead!"

"Thank you," I said with a stony glare before proceeding with my intended goal. My idea was to kick down the closed door, confront the werewolf, and pull him outside to the cheers of my associates. I had rehearsed this in my mind repeatedly in the three weeks since I first confronted the werewolf, and it was now to the point where I knew my part exactly. Unfortunately, nobody else knew theirs!

This was made most evident when I tried kicking my way through the door, the way my favorite girl heroes in the *Science Fiction and Fantasy Magazine* were always doing. Unfortunately for me, the wood in the door was quite cheap, and my kick splintered it apart! I flew through it and landed in the room, with my colleagues following suit. We were promptly joined by the room's sole tenant, who, from my vantage point on the floor where I had landed, bore a strong resemblance to a certain lupine creature I had already encountered. He was the same height and even though there was no hair and he was human, the eyes were the same.

"What's going on here?" he shouted. "I ain't paying taxes to have some dumb scouts come and bust in my door in!"

"Sir, remain calm!" Izzy said, in her best formal tones. "We have reason to believe a werewolf is in the vicinity, and we are merely taking precautions in order to..."

The man laughed, cutting Izzy off. "Are you serious, girl?" he snapped. "What kind of crack you been doing? Who's gonna believe that load of shit? Now, you better get the hell out of here before I call the..."

"Before you what?" Val said, drawing her gun out. "Don't do nothin' you'll regret later, werewolf!"

"How do you know I'm a werewolf?" the man snapped.

"Oh, I think there are ways to know that!" I said as I went over to the window in the corner and prepared to rip the shade off.

"Don't touch that window!" he shouted. "I don't want that moonlight in here!"

"And with good reason!" I said, ripping off the shade in one stroke.

That did it! As the moonlight streamed into the room and bathed him in its pallid glow, he underwent an immediate change. He grew fur all over his body in seconds, his nose and mouth abruptly converted into a snout, and he uttered a bloodcurdling howl that had a chill running down my spine. This was definitely our man—or wolf!

A snarl emanated from his throat, and he looked at all of us as the courses in a four 'scout' meal. There was only one thing we could do, and we did it post haste.

We didn't scream, since Wayne County Firebird Scouts don't do sissy stuff like that but, if you could see our eyes, there wasn't anything in any of them except terror. We ran as quickly as we could down the stairs of the apartment building while the werewolf came bounding after us. When we finally reached the ground floor, Val, with a grunt, ordered us to the far end of the room while she prepared to shoot at the werewolf.

"Keep growling, 'cause you ain't gonna be doing that for much longer!" Val yelled in response to his baying howl echoing down from the stairwell. When the beast came down the stairs, she fired the gun and...missed.

"Shit!" Val yelled. "Jackass moved out of range before I could hit him!"

Unfortunately for Val, that moment was when the werewolf chose to rush up to her and knock the gun right out of her hand. She took the hint and told the rest of us to run—which she did as well. Fortunately, our salvation was close at hand- and in an unlikely way.

Sam and Max saw us as we ran out of the building with the werewolf in pursuit. Since Max, at least, is pretty smart, it wasn't long before they put two and two together and acted really quickly. Before we said or did anything else, each of them started throwing boxes of unsold cookies, tightly bound since they were still unsold, at our friend the werewolf while barely missing us in the process. Sure enough, a couple of those heavily packed cartons with those overcooked rocks they always stick us were finally useful to us. The werewolf was down on the ground in seconds after those cartons hit his head.

But he was only knocked down and if we hadn't acted fast, things might have gone very differently, but when he dropped to the ground, covering his face, we jumped on him and we were able to finish him off by pounding his head further with our feet and fists. Val even picked the wagon up and slammed it down on his head, causing a sickening crunch to fill the air.

Soon, the werewolf had reverted back to his human form, and seconds after that, he was dead.

"Phew!" I said by way of the relief we all felt. "That's some quick thinking you guys did! How did you know to do that so fast?"

"You needed help," Max said. "That was for sure. We didn't have anything else to throw at that thing to stop him, so we did what we could!"

"And besides," Sam added, displaying her chipped front teeth for proof. "There's nothing else around Detroit that's harder than Firebird Scout cookies!"

All we could do was laugh at that one.

THE LIGHT OF THE FULL MOON

ANTHONY GIANGREGORIO

"What have we got here?" the doctor asked as he flashed his penlight into the eyes of the man on the wheeled stretcher.

"Man in his early thirties, has been bitten multiple times by what we believe to be a dog. He's suffered blood loss and lacerations to the upper right clavicle and right arm," the paramedic said as he wheeled the unconscious man into the Emergency Room of Boston City Hospital in Dorchester, Ma.

Two nurses ran up to the stretcher and the doctor hovered over the prone man as he checked vital signs.

The doctor looked at the first nurse to arrive. "Get an IV drip going and prep O.R. 2," he said as he peeled back the pressure bandage to inspect the wound. "Jesus Christ, it looks like this guy went three rounds with a Doberman and lost."

"I know, right?" the paramedic said. "That's what I thought."

"Where did this happen? We're in downtown Boston, for Christ's sake," the doctor asked as he probed the wound. "Wild dogs don't usually roam the city streets."

"Near Boylston Street. He was barely conscious when we found him. He was babbling something about a wolf jumping out of an alleyway and attacking him, but he was delirious. It had to be a dog and a big one at that."

"Shit, every friggin' full moon all the crazies come out to play. All right, let's get him to the O.R. before he bleeds out," the doctor said.

The paramedic stepped back and let the nurses take over, pushing the stretcher through the doors labeled **Authorized Personnel Only** printed in bright yellow letters.

His partner came up behind him, carrying a clipboard with all the relevant information on the wounded man. "They take him?"

"Yeah, he's going up to the O.R. now."

"Then he's not our problem anymore. I'm gonna drop off the paperwork at the nurse's desk and I'll meet you back at the rig," he said. "The sooner we get back out there the better."

"Yeah, I know what you mean. Like the Doc just said to me, all the crazies come out at the full moon."

His name is Vincent Miller, but at the moment, he doesn't know his name or how he came to be in a hospital room.

As he lay supine in his hospital bed in recovery, he slowly began to change into something not human as the light of the full moon filtered through the window.

It had been three hours since he'd been attacked by what to him looked like a wolf, only this wolf stood on its hind legs and had shoulders as broad as a wrestler, with large claws and teeth that gleamed in the gloom.

The creature had appeared from the shadows of the alley and had pulled Vincent off the sidewalk, where he then found himself battling for his life.

He didn't remember much about what happened after the creature grabbed him, only brief visions, flashing images of teeth, claws and blinding pain as he was attacked.

Luckily, from the far end of the alley, a passerby heard the attack and had yelled out, scaring the creature. It was gone in seconds, climbing up a fire escape to disappear over the edge of the roof of the closest building.

Filled with blinding pain, Vincent had crawled out of the alley where he had collapsed onto the sidewalk, his blood seeping around him to mimic a halo.

Soon, there were flashing lights as a police car pulled up, and the last thing he remembered was a paramedic leaning over him trying to get him to state his name as more passersby gather around him, eager to see blood and carnage firsthand. He had babbled something but then the darkness had enveloped him and he slipped blissfully into unconsciousness.

Now, all he felt was more pain as the Lycan virus suffused his system, morphing his body into that of an animal.

He shook his head back and forth as his mouth and nose began to elongate, bone growing where none should exist. His teeth began to grow, becoming pointed, the razor-sharp incisors gleaming in the overhead florescent lights. Every pore on his flesh began to open and thick, matted hair burst free, a dark carpet that covered him from head to toe. His ears recessed, becoming more pointed and his eyes shifted from the brown they originally were to a yellow the color of gold.

His arms and legs began to twist and reshape as the man took on the form of a werewolf, and as he shifted and changed—he screamed, as if his very insides were on fire, or better yet, being torn out—which wasn't far from the truth.

His screams filled the hospital, and no sooner did they begin, then three nurses came running into the room, while a fourth paged the on call doctor.

When the women darted into the room, each stopped in horror and amazement to watch the man twist and jump on the bed, his body spasming as if he was being electrocuted.

One of the nurses, braver than the others, burst forward to aid the suffering man, and when she was close enough to touch him, the newly transformed werewolf lashed out with a large paw-like hand filled with razor-sharp claws.

The woman was eviscerated in the blink of an eye, her intestines spilling forth to splash over her white nurse's shoes. The redolence of offal filled the room as the woman's bowels let go in death. Before she could crumple to the floor, the werewolf reached its clawed hand into her gaping cavity and lifted her off her feet as if she weighed nothing. As the other nurses screamed, the beast threw the dead nurse at them, the body flying through the air to strike the other two nurses in the chests, all three falling to the floor. The two struggling nurses attempted to free themselves from their very dead coworker, one shrieking uncontrollably as she was covered in gore.

The nurse who had the lower half of the corpse on her was almost free when a shadow fell over her. Looking up, she gazed into the yellow eyes of the beast as it reached down and snapped at her with its open hand.

She screamed, long and loud, but it was cut short by one slash of the already bloody claws. Half her throat was torn out, the blood spurting across the room like a water fountain with its top broken off, her legs kicking as she thrashed in her death throes.

The remaining nurse was now shrieking as she was splattered in warm blood. Her eyes were closed and she shook her head back and forth, her tongue sticking out as she let loose a voice filled with terror.

The beast swiveled on its clawed toes, and with one meaty swipe, sheared her head from her shoulders. As the head rolled across the floor, more blood shot upward, the scream continued for another second. The decapitated head's eyes blinked once or twice, the woman seeing her own headless body slump to the floor. But the oxygen in her brain was fleeting, and she had just enough time to witness her demise before the eyes glazed over in death.

The werewolf saw none of this as it burst through the door and into the hallway. The nurse at the desk that had been paging the on call doctor dropped the phone and stared in astonishment at the mythical creature before her. She had time for one quick bleat of fear before the werewolf attacked, covering the distance between them in less than a second. The nurse, though panicked, turned and tried to run, but let out a gasp of shock as the werewolf split her back in two, the long vertical slice exposing her spine. As she dropped face first to the floor, her spine glistened amongst the seeping blood as she struggled to pull herself along. The beast watched her as she dragged herself across the floor, her legs now useless. It cocked its head in curiosity, much like a cat would to a mouse it was playing with.

Then the beast pounced, and using both its clawed hands, wrapped them around the woman's head before twisting. The neck began to show stress marks as the head was turned like a cork-screw, and when the head had almost reached a full revolution, weak flesh gave in to tension and split, spurting more blood out in front of the beast to bathe the floor in red.

The werewolf let the body slump to the floor and turned and roared to the ceiling, the very walls shaking from the vibration. The heavy tread of running men filled the hallway, and a moment later, three security guards rounded the bend, each with weapons drawn.

"What the fuck is that?" the first man yelled as he stopped in his tracks.

"Who cares, just fucking shoot it!" the second guard yelled as he pulled his sidearm and fired three times into the beast's chest.

The werewolf staggered back from the impact of each blast but still remained upright. It lowered its head, and before another round could be fired, it dove into the mist of the three guards.

The first man let out a high-pitched scream as he was disemboweled with one quick blow. As his insides splashed to the floor, his scream faded to be lost in a sea of gurgles as he drowned in his own blood.

Before the body had struck the floor, the second guard was feeling the wrath of the beast. With one clawed hand on the right side of the guard's torso, the left did the same on the other side, and with one squeeze of its muscular arms, the hands closed together, severing the man in twain. The upper half splattered to the floor and the guard's arms went out before him, as if he was falling after slipping on a wet floor. It was as he fell that he realized his legs weren't coming with him and he looked back to see his intestines were splayed out in front of him. As he watched, the last security guard took a faltering step and placed his boots onto the intestines, causing them to erupt like uncooked blood sausage. The bifurcated guard was screaming, which quickly changed to shrieks, and when the first guard looked down and realized he was stepping in his coworker's organs, he too, joined the cacophony of yelling, his face now pale as a ghost.

But he didn't have long to voice his terror before the werewolf reached out and lopped off his head, severing his voice box and jugular in one massive swipe. The head rolled away like an errant kickball as the body toppled to the floor to join the other two corpses, more blood geysering in all directions to paint the walls crimson.

Once more, the werewolf growled to the ceiling, the end result a low howl. Seeing nothing left to kill, it loped down the hall, until coming to a window.

With no way of knowing what lay beneath the window, it smashed through the glass and landed ten feet below. By luck or fate, the beast had been on the first floor.

Landing amid a spray of glass, it howled once more to the moon and galloped into the street.

As soon as the beast reached the street, a racing ambulance, complete with flashing lights and siren, struck the werewolf head on and sent it soaring twenty feet into the air.

The fur-covered body flew gracelessly, its arms and legs seeming to flap on their own accord until the body landed in a pile of trash next to a battered dumpster. The body was quickly lost amidst the trash as the ambulance came to a halt with screeching tires, and two paramedics jumped out, the driver's face one of terror at hitting a pedestrian. The patient in the back of the rig was stable and they had enough time to see to yet another wounded soul before leaving to deliver their charge safely to the Emergency Room.

Both men ran towards the pile of trash where they'd seen the figure end up as the driver continued to say, "Oh, man, it wasn't my fault, the guy ran right out in front of me. It wasn't my fault."

The second paramedic didn't know what to say. He had been in the back of the rig with the patient when the accident had occurred. As the two paramedics approached, they each paused at the sight of the one leg protruding from the trash.

The driver then moved forward, shoved the trash bags away, and checked for a pulse at the prone body of the naked man with bloody hands and torso before him.

"Well?" the second paramedic asked.

The first man shook his head. "He's dead." He pointed to the man's chest which had multiple lacerations, most looking like old scar tissue, but in the middle of all the scars was one, bright red hole an inch in diameter. "This guy looks like he's been in a war. If I'm right, these look like old bullet wounds."

The second man turned and looked back at the ambulance and his eyes went to the silver plated grille, which was now smashed and broken. A few of the mesh bars that made up the grate were now bent and twisted, and one of them that protruded had blood on its tip.

"Looks like the guy got stabbed by the grille when you plowed into him, Mike."

"I didn't plow into anyone, he ran out in front of me."

"Okay, okay, I believe you." He shook his head. "To bad for him huh? He never had a chance."

Mike nodded. "Yeah, you know, it's the weirdest thing. When I hit him, I couldn't see him very well, I could've sworn he was wearing a fur coat or a heavy jacket."

"I doubt that, Mike, the guy's naked." He shook his head once more and slapped his partner on the back. "Come on, we got a patient to get to the E.R. We can call this in on the way. Poor bastard ain't goin' anywhere."

Mike stood up, and with one last look at the naked, bloody man, he turned and headed back to the ambulance. "What do you think he was doing out here naked like that?"

The second man shrugged. "Who the hell knows? Shit, man, it's a goddamn full moon. All the crazies come out tonight."

THE PACK

MARK M. JOHNSON

Peering over the edge of the world, the full moon's poisoned orange glow spilled across an overgrown grass field in suburban Detroit like the waking eye of a world-devouring beast as it crept over the edge of the eastern horizon. Shimmering through the pollution stained sky, shining bright, it appeared to be stalking the earth for prey.

The pale glow cast long shadows off the three silhouetted figures making their way across the open field. Driving back the Friday night darkness, the dim light exposed three teenage boys on a nocturnal weekend adventure in the spring evening.

The three boys trekked single file along a narrow, well-worn footpath that led into the distant tree line of the Lowlands Recreational Park Forest. Their Levi's blue jeans were darkened at the knees from the moisture clinging to the knee-high winter browned grass. The forest bordered the field on three sides, and behind the advancing group, the lights of a middle-class Detroit neighborhood twinkled in the distance. The boy leading them along the trail, the shortest of the three, noticed the shadows stretching away from their feet and swung his head over his shoulder to look back at the swollen rising moon.

The moon's rising illumination fell across Jimmy's fresh young face, and he drew a sharp breath as his soft, almost feminine features lit with astonished joy.

"Wow, look at the moon!" Jimmy whispered with honest wonder. The moon's glow flashed across the Detroit Lions symbol on the back of his black windbreaker as he turned. His two older companions turned as well, and all three of them stopped walking. As the moonlight illuminated their faces, a gentle breeze flurried their shoulder length hair around their ruddy faces and broadening shoulders. Jimmy's was thick and dark brown, much like the other tall boy wearing glasses, and the shorter, slightly heavy-set boy's blond and wispy locks. In a momentary silence, three pairs of young eyes gazed eastward across the surface of their world at the magnified image of the moon.

"That's too cool," Jimmy said. "Why's it look so big when it rises?"

"I think it's an illusion," John said. "It's magnified by the earth's atmosphere or something like that." Reaching up almost absentmindedly, John adjusted the heavy lenses over his eyes and reached his fingers under them to massage the crown of his eternally aching nose where the frames pressed on the skin.

Jimmy glanced around the other boy and up at John, grinning. "Like how your glasses make your eyes bug out?"

The third boy, Jerry, chuckled slightly, but kept his eyes on the moon, concentrating as he tried to recall something from his memories.

John smirked a little and his eyes flashed brightly. Reaching around Jerry, he shoved Jimmy playfully. "Shut your hole, *pretty boy*." John growled in mock aggression, using the nickname he knew his younger friend hated. Jimmy, the best looking, and youngest of the three at fifteen, flipped both of his middle fingers up and waggled his tongue out.

"It's the harvest moon," Jerry said, smiling proudly because he'd managed to remember the name that the moon's shimmering image conjured in his mind. His pudgy round face, that could look violently scary when his mood darkened, appeared serene and passive with sparkling eyes and a wide mouthed grin, an expression that his friend John often referred to as Jerry's village idiot impression.

"No," John disagreed. "It's called the harvest moon in the fall, like for when farmers harvest their crops."

Jerry's gaze fell away from the rising moon and he eyed John with a menacing scowl. "So says the brain?" he grumbled, as his eyes greedily stared at John's old tattered leather jacket with the Led Zeppelin patch on its back. The 'Zeppelin leather', as they called it. John had discovered it in a local thrift store over the winter and had worn it with pride ever since. Although Jerry was fiercely jealous of the Zeppelin leather, he would've rather died than admit it.

John nodded. "So says the *brain*." With his eyes locked on the shimmering moon, John failed to notice that Jerry was no longer staring at the moon, but at him.

Jerry's eyes hardened into a dark, intimidating stare. John's irritating habit of correcting him, and everyone else with his above average intelligence never failed to irk Jerry.

John's extensive knowledge, and Jerry's lack of such, had led to some lengthy and passionate arguments in the past and usually, Jerry would just let it go, knowing most often that in the end his bookworm friend would be proven right. This time however, the anger of being corrected boiled up and over, and out of sight behind his back, Jerry clenched his right hand into a fist. Lashing out suddenly, he socked John in the arm just below his shoulder. Even though Jerry had pulled the punch, he could see the pain in his friend's face as John staggered sideways, though he struggled not to show it.

"Fucker," John protested, though he resisted reaching up to hold his newly aching bicep.

"You asked for it, *brain*," Jerry said. A born brawler, Jerry could take a punch as well as he could throw one. He'd taken on grown men twice his size in fisticuffs and beaten them. As his two closest friends would've said, he knew how to 'throw-down'. Over the course of their long friendship of the years, he'd become their unofficial body guard. Many times, he'd chased off or beaten down other boys that threatened his friends.

Jimmy and John greatly valued Jerry's friendship, even though he could turn his powerful fists on them when provoked, though he'd never really hurt them. Slightly taller and wider than Jimmy, but a few inches shorter than John, Jerry's body resembled that of a bulldog's, and tonight he wore a black-hooded sweatshirt to ward off the spring night's chill.

John mumbled something too low for Jerry to hear and then dropped his shoulders in resignation.

"C'mon," Jerry said and now smiling again, he reached out and patted John on his shoulder. "We're gonna be late. Let's go."

With a few mumbled agreements, Jimmy and John put their backs to the shimmering sphere in the sky, and set out once again for the tree line at the north/west end of the field with Jerry in the lead. As soon as Jerry and Jimmy turned their backs to him, John reached up and rubbed his arm where Jerry had punched him, wincing as he massaged out the sharp receding pain. Nearly a head taller than Jerry, John had the longest hair of the three.

Many who first met John immediately compared him to John Lennon, in the legendary rock star's later years, a comparison he'd tired of quickly. In the coming summer, John's sixteenth birthday awaited, a milestone his best friend Jerry had crossed over months ago.

The steady easterly breeze gusted, and the grass rustled around them, hissing and undulating under the breath of the night. High above, scattered clouds raced across the star-speckled heavens, wetting the rising moon with fleeting kisses.

"Getting chilly," Jerry said and shivered.

"Getting?" John asked, and then he clasped his leather jacket's zipper together, drawing it up. Ever the boy with the wild imagination, John loved to invent tales of the Zeppelin leather's origins, and its many badass owners. His reputed imagination broke loose and ran wild with nefariously amusing tales as they approached the dark tree line.

The trail before them seemed to vanish in a wall of inky black, the encroaching trees creating a cavernous opening into which the trail led. For anyone who had never walked the trail before, continuing at this point in the night's darkness would've spelled disaster. The impression that the trail ended in the thin air of the forest's darkness was no illusion. This was a place the local kids of years past had aptly named, Stick Shift Hill. Just beyond the opening in the forest wall, the trail dropped abruptly into an almost vertical, forty-five foot drop.

At the bottom where the trail's steep incline lessened, a natural dirt ramp worn smooth by thousands of bicycle tires awaited any brave dirt-bicyclist who dared to test the hill's formidable drop. Only the most fearless and craziest of the local kids would take the plunge over Stick Shift, to catch the massive air off the dirt ramp at the bottom. The trail was far too steep to descend on foot, and in the darkness, any who tried would find themselves at the bottom far more quickly than they'd anticipated.

The three late night adventurers crowded together at the edge of the wall of darkness, veered into the trees on the left side, and plunged fearlessly into the black of the nighttime forest. Using the trees on the edge of the trail to slow their descent, they quickly made it safely to the bottom. At the bottom of the hill, a complicated maze of interconnecting trails branched off in every direction. The three friends chose the centermost trail and hurried down it with a confidence born of many past evening adventures in the familiar forest.

Local children long since grown and gone had named this swampy part of the Lowlands Forest, Frogs Paradise, a name still used to this day. To anyone visiting this particular section of the forest during the warm months of summer, the deafening symphony of croaking frogs would make the name's reason obvious. However, the frog genesis of summer lay months ahead. Unlike the fresh air gusting across the high ground, the forest smelled damp, earthy, with a hint of rotting vegetation in the bouquet of scents floating in the cool air.

The night's breath gusted again and the trees above them whispered their reply as a leafy rain of early spring buds pattered the ground around their feet. The rising moon cast shifting shadows through the trees as they creaked under the strain of the wind, filling the woods with eerily moaning echoes.

A devilish grin stole over John's face as the trees crowded in close to the trail's edges. "It's creepy in here at night," John said. "It feels like something could just reach out from between the trees and snatch you up."

Jerry snorted. "That's why you're in the back, dumb ass. So we can take off after something grabs you."

He was trying to sound smug, but John knew the woods made Jerry nervous at night, too. John briefly toyed with the idea of dropping back a few paces, and then letting out a scream as he leapt into the thick brush along the trail, but then a better idea took hold and began to blossom in his mind.

Last weekend, they'd watched an old R-rated werewolf movie, and the film was still fresh in all of their minds. They'd been raving about it all week, and had been discussing it in Jerry's basement bedroom only a few hours ago. With this in mind, John's practical joke quickly took shape.

"What would you guys do if I turned into a werewolf right now?" John asked. He could almost *feel* the hairs rising on the back of Jerry's neck.

"You wish," Jerry said.

Almost as if he'd picked up on John's thoughts, Jimmy said, "While you were ripping Jerry up for a late-night snack, I'd be running my ass off for the Rollerdrome."

"You'd never make it, the Rollerdrome's too far away," Jerry said, referring to their destination, the roller-skating rink a half mile down the road from the gate at the far end of the park.

"I'd make it farther than you," Jimmy retorted.

Behind Jerry, John hunched over and hooked his hands into claws. A low rumbling growl gurgled out from his throat as he leapt onto Jerry's back, hooking his fingers over his friend's shoulders and wrapping his legs around Jerry's waist.

Jerry loosed a high-pitched scream and spun hard to the right, clawing at the thing on his back. Unable to sustain the sudden weight, John tumbled sideways off balance and they both fell to the ground. John rolled away, laughing hard as Jerry jumped up and stumbled backwards, gasping for breath.

"You, fucking asshole!" Jerry hollered and strode forward, angrily delivering a kick that John easily evaded. "That shit ain't funny!"

John and Jimmy disagreed, and both of them laughed raucously as Jerry caught his racing breath.

Jimmy doubled over as the laughing fit crested. "He scared-the-shit-out-of-you!" He managed to gasp out. "Oh-my-God, you screamed like a girl."

"Fuck off!" Jerry spat towards Jimmy. However, as his pounding heart slowed, his raging face gradually smoothed into a vengeful grin. "Fuck you both," he laughed as his mind raced with amusing thoughts of retribution. "Crazy bastard," he shot at John, who still lay giggling on the ground. He blew out a puff of air and ran a shaky hand through his blond hair. "Fuckin' A man, I just about shit my pants." This only rekindled the giggling, and Jerry joined in.

A ring-tone version of AC/DC's song, *Back in Black,* interrupted their hilarity.

Jerry reached into his pants pocket and retrieved his cell phone. "It's Leroy," he said and upon turning away from his chuckling friends, he raised the phone to his ear. "Yeah, what's up, dude?" he barked into the phone. "Already? Shit, we're still, uh, about fifteen, maybe twenty minutes away." Jerry paused as he listened to his older cousin's complaining voice on the phone. Behind him, John got to his feet, and he and Jimmy leaned in closer to listen.

"Hey, man, the bus schedule said eleven-ten. What is it, fifteen to?" Jerry asked.

Behind him, John pulled a cell phone out from his leather jacket's inside pocket, checked the time, and then said, "It's ten forty-three."

Jerry glanced over his shoulder and nodded. "Yeah," he said into the phone. "We're coming through Lowlands...who? You're sure he's cool?" A few minutes passed as Jerry nodded his head several times. "Uh-huh, that's cool. All right, just wait by the Rollerdrome's back door, the cops won't bother you there. We'll see you in a few...later." Jerry closed his cell phone and returned it to his pocket.

"So, what's up?" Jimmy asked.

Jerry turned to face them. "The bus was early and Leroy's already up at the Rollerdrome."

"Yeah," John quipped sarcastically, "we got that."

"Yeah, well, he brought somebody with him," Jerry smirked.

"Who?" Jimmy asked.

Jerry shrugged his shoulders. "Don't know, but the guy's name is Dennis. He's some old friend of Leroy's. He talked about him a while back; he just got kicked out of the Navy for smoking pot. Leroy says he's cool, and get this." Jerry paused for effect. "He's *twenty-one.*"

"He can buy for us!" Jimmy yelled and did a little celebratory dance. "Sweet!"

John grinned and nodded his head in agreement. "Did he say anything about the weed?"

"On the *phone*?" Jerry scowled.

"Yeah, right," John nodded.

"Well," Jerry said. "They're waiting, so let's hustle!" He motioned towards the dark trail extending out before them.

"Let's boogie." Jimmy said, then clapped his hands and rubbed them together.

"And you," Jerry growled, gesturing for John to pass him. "You ain't walkin' behind me."

John grinned wide and made a show of ambling past his friend. "What's wrong? Is your pussy scared?" he giggled.

Jerry held up his right fist and said, "You want another one, smart ass?"

Reaching up and rubbing his arm again where Jerry had punched him earlier, John shook his head back and forth. "Nope, I'm all set there."

"What's–a–matter, *bug* eyes, your pussy *hurtin'*?" Jimmy asked. John made a loose fist and took a halfhearted swing at Jimmy, who ducked, effortlessly avoiding the punch, and then Jimmy turned and quickly broke into a steady jogging pace.

"You better run," John laughed, and then he and Jerry quickly followed close behind.

The three friends knew the trails so well that they could have navigated them with their eyes closed. The trees whipped by them as they picked up speed, trunks flashing by in a dark blur of bud covered tree branches and thick brush. Running through the trails at night reminded John of their summer excursions through the woods, when they *had* to run to avoid the hordes of mosquitoes that infested the forest during those warm months.

"At least there's no bugs yet," John puffed out. His two friends grunted in agreement. The trail swung right and conjoined with another. The new trail ran along the bank of the Rouge, the river that bisected Lowlands Park. Ranging in width from ten, to nearly thirty feet wide, the Rouge River ran for miles out in the outer laying counties, all the way down to the Detroit River. Still heavy with spring run-off, the filthy dark-brown water of the Rouge River surged high against its banks, hissing wetly from down in the dark shadows to their left. Here and there, the rising moon glinted off the dark rushing water.

In the past, they would have had to take the trail all the way down to the Warren Avenue Bridge to get to the Rollerdrome on the other side. However, the year before, a massive oak tree growing in the mucky bank of the river had finally succumbed to the water's erosion and fallen across the river. When the tree fell, it created a natural bridge across the river, and the tree's four-foot wide trunk provided ample walking space for easy crossing.

"Hey, Jimmy," Jerry puffed out from behind John. "Who are the Lions losing to in the home opener this year?"

"Bullshit!" Jimmy replied breathlessly. A fanatical, Detroit Lions football fan like his father, he took the question as an insult. "They're gonna kick Minnesota's ass!" Although they would never speak it aloud, both of Jimmy's friends were envious of his family, as Jimmy was the only one of them living with both his parents.

"Dream on!" John giggled, and Jerry laughed.

"You wait," Jimmy said. "This year we're making the playoffs!" Then they arrived at the fallen oak. Jimmy leapt fearlessly through the dark roots of the tree jutting up from the bank of the river that were nearly invisible in the gloom. John and Jerry followed. Beneath their shoes, the bark of the tree had worn away in places from the constant foot traffic. Under the slick bare-wood surface of the fallen oak, the shit-stained water of the Rouge churned noisily, promising a possible death by drowning to anyone who slipped from the oak tree bridge. Once they were across the river, the trio jumped down through the branches of the fallen oak onto another well-beaten path.

"If the Lions ever win the Super Bowl," John said as they hurried up the inclining trail. "That's gotta be one of the signs of the apocalypse."

Jimmy harrumphed. "I think you getting laid is one of those signs," he hollered back over his shoulder.

Jerry burst out laughing. "I think we're safe for a while then."

John grumbled an incoherent reply as the trail angled uphill and ran for just under fifty yards before opening into another moonlight-bathed field. Huffing and puffing through their overworked lungs, the three boys staggered out into Lowlands Recreational Park. All three of them paused, breathing heavily and leaning over with their hands on their knees.

"Shit," Jerry complained. "I must be getting old."

"Naw," John said. "It's the Marlboros, man."

"Speakin' of which," Jerry said. Reaching into his hooded sweatshirt's pocket, he removed a pack of Marlboro cigarettes. He took one out and then offered the pack to his friends. Jimmy and John both took one each, and the three lit up off Jerry's lighter. Jerry took a deep drag on the smoke, puffed it out, and then stifled a light cough. The steady night breeze stole the smoke away as fast as it emerged from his mouth. "Screw Leroy," he said. "I ain't runnin' no more."

"Leroy's not going anywhere," John said.

"Yeah," Jimmy agreed. "Let em' wait."

"C'mon, let's go," Jerry said through the cigarette dangling between his grin.

The field on the west side of the Rouge differed greatly from the east side. Here, the groundskeepers kept the grass cut low. As the three young men turned their backs to the forest, John's gaze fell across the moon-shadowed park and he paused in mid-step. The present seemed to fall away as the moonlit recreational area took in all of his mind's focus. The roofed picnic pavilions, children's play areas with their climbing ropes and spiral slides, the football/soccer field, and the three baseball diamonds, all lay dark and empty of their intended inhabitants.

The park seemed abandoned to the night, as if Armageddon had come and the darkness held sway over all in a world now empty of humans. John's breath froze in his lungs. When he realized he'd stopped breathing, he gasped. His two friends stopped and glanced back, curious at the sound. The moon's corrupted orange glow, splashed across their features, darkening their eyes and mouths while silhouetting their bodies with otherworldly light. For a fleeting second, John saw his two friends as ghostly skull-faced apparitions, a portent of their final destination.

"Hey?" Jerry inquired and though he pretended nonchalance, his eyes betrayed his concern. "You all right? You look like you've seen a ghost."

John shook his head, clearing out the cobwebs as reality crashed back into focus. "Sorry, got lost in my head," he said casually, as if nothing were wrong. Inside, he trembled.

"He does that shit all the time," Jimmy said, looking at John as his friend seemed to come back from somewhere very far away.

Jerry nodded in agreement. "Yeah, it freaks me out every time."

John shrugged his shoulders as they resumed walking. "Didn't you ever get lost in thought before?"

"Not like that," Jerry said. "Fuckin' space cadet."

The numerous picnic tables that would normally cover most of the open ground of the park were absent, opening day still a few weeks away. Above the park, loomed the forty-foot high Lowlands Park sledding hill. The dirt road running along the right side of the sledding hill led to the upper portion of Lowlands Park, and the three boys headed for it, walking side by side with Jerry in the middle.

As the gravel of the dirt road crunched beneath their feet, John moved to change the subject. "Are Sherry and her friends gonna be at the party?" he asked.

"Yeah," Jerry said, forgetting about the uneasiness that had fallen over him moments before. "They'll be there, and I'm gonna tell Wendy you like her!"

John shoved Jerry lightly. He stumbled into Jimmy and both of them nearly fell over like a pair of dominos. "Hey!" Jimmy protested.

"Don't fuck around, man," John directed his anger at Jerry. "Seriously!"

Jerry righted himself and lightly shoved John back. "Well, you do."

"So," John grumbled.

Jerry smiled devilishly. "Do you want me to find out if she likes you, *or not*?"

John fell silent, and then hesitantly mumbled, "Sure, yeah."

Already planning on how to exact revenge for John's earlier prank in the woods by embarrassing him at the party, Jerry padded John on the back. "I'll hook you up, buddy," he said through his smirk. "Trust me."

"Trust me?" John said. "That's what the scorpion said to the frog just before he stung him to death."

"What?" Jerry asked. "Man, what're you talking about?"

"Old saying," John said. "The scorpion promised not to sting the frog, and then he did it anyway, because that's his nature."

Jerry grimaced and shook his head. "What's that got to do with anything?"

"You said, *trust* me," John said. "But it's in your nature to be untrustworthy."

"In my nature?" Jerry shook his head. "Where do you get this shit? I just don't get you, man. You read too much."

John sighed. "It means I know *you*, and I know you're going to screw me somehow, even though you said you wouldn't."

"Ah," Jerry grunted and then laughed. "That, I understand."

They crested the hill at the top of the road and the upper portion of Lowlands Park opened before them. The dirt road cut through the center of the park, ending at the gate attached to the seven-foot high fence that separated it from Parkland Road. The north half to the right held more picnic pavilions, areas for playing volleyball and horseshoes, and barbeque pits. The south side lay empty; nearly as large as three football fields, the wide-open field was the territory of the Detroit Model Aviators Club.

In the summer, crowds would gather to watch the club members fly their gas powered miniature airplanes in the sky over the field. At night in the early spring, the field was empty and quiet. The thick Lowlands forest surrounded the park on all sides, and even on the other side of the fence along Parkland Road, the woods lay dark and deep.

The three friends continued walking along the dirt road that led to the padlocked gates at the entrance, a good hundred and fifty yard hike from where the road dropped into the lower portion of the park.

"So, you are going tell Wendy I like her?" John growled.

"No, not me," Jerry protested through a mischievous grin.

"Ooohhh shit!" Jimmy whispered from behind them.

The two arguing boys hadn't realized that Jimmy had fallen behind, and they both stopped short and turned. Jimmy crouched several feet back, gazing wide-eyed off to his left onto the moon-washed, empty field.

"What're you trippin' on?" Jerry asked.

"Look!" Jimmy hissed, pointing off towards the south tree line that bordered the empty field. Their eyes followed Jimmy's pointing finger and they spotted them instantly. About two hundred yards away from where they stood, a group of dogs were emerging out of the darkness of the woods and into the bright glow of the full moon.

"Shit," Jerry whispered, and instinctually copied Jimmy's posture.

John crouched down as well. "It's wild dogs," he whispered. "They must be those wild dogs they were talking about on the news."

"Wild dogs?" Jerry asked, nervously twitching where he crouched. "They look more like wolves."

"Yeah, I guess," John confirmed. "Some people said they saw them over by Joy Road and Outer Drive the other day, they were running around Rouge Park at night, howlin' an' shit. They were worried the dogs might hurt some kids or something."

The pack of dog-shaped shadows moved slowly away from the edge of the forest, frolicking in the moonlight that bathed the field. There were five of them in all: one very small, two medium-sized, one large, and one impossibly massive dog that looked like a cross between a wolf, a German shepherd and a grizzly bear. The two largest dogs walked side by side, one nearly dwarfing the other while the remaining three ran around them in circles, jumping and prancing in the moonlit grass. Eerily, none of them made a sound, no yipping or barking; not even a faint growl drifted across the field.

"Jesus, that one's huge," Jerry whispered harshly, and then he fell silent.

John heard the naked fear in Jerry's voice. "Don't move," he cautioned. "It's dark, put out your smokes. They might not see us if we stay still."

All three of them hastily stabbed their glowing cigarettes to death in the dirt. Jerry's head turned slowly, his eyes shifting from the pack of wild dogs to the distant padlocked gate at the entrance to the park, and then back again. "We can make it to the gate," he whispered.

"They haven't seen us yet," Jimmy whispered back.

"Don't move," John insisted.

"Fuck this," Jerry hissed. He shifted his body towards the distant gate and tensed. "I'm runnin' for it."

"No," John insisted, and reached for Jerry's arm a second to late. Jerry sprung from his crouch and broke into an all-out dash for the safety of the other side of the locked gate. The very second Jerry's running feet crunched loudly on the gravel of the dirt road, the dogs stopped their playful frolicking and froze. Their eyes began searching and ears were twitching as they swiveled their heads around and locked onto the running boy like heat seeking guided missiles.

Even from the great distance between them, Jimmy glimpsed the moon's orange glow reflecting in the eyes of one dog that seemed to be looking directly at *him*. "They've seen us!" he cried out.

John grabbed Jimmy by his arm and sprung up, dragging the younger boy to his feet. "Go!" he yelled, thrusting Jimmy forward, and the two of them took off like race horses out of the starting gate, chasing behind Jerry as they all dashed for the gate. Out in the moon-bathed field, four of the shadow dogs broke from their paralysis and separated into a line nearly side by side, as they loped across the field in pursuit without a sound.

Behind them, the largest dog pivoted on its hind legs and vanished as it leapt into the darkness along the tree line.

Jerry shot a glance over his shoulder as he ran. "They're coming!" he screamed, and his pace quickened as terror-fueled adrenalin pumped into his system. By far the fastest runner, John quickly caught up to Jerry and began to overtake him while Jimmy faltered behind.

"Oh my God," Jimmy gasped. "Oh, God."

John glanced back and saw Jimmy clutching his side, bending over slightly and staggering. "Jimmy's got a cramp!" John shouted, and fell back to help his friend. "Help me!" he snapped at Jerry, who glanced over towards the advancing dogs before falling back to help.

"C'mon, man, help!" Jerry shrieked, the panic bubbling over in his voice apparent as he grabbed Jimmy's right arm. "They're coming fast."

John grabbed Jimmy's left. "We got you, buddy," he gasped. They nearly lifted Jimmy from his feet as they dragged him faster down the road towards the gate.

Jerry glanced over his shoulder and saw the dogs were still just loping shadows, the shade of their fur seeming blacker than the night's darkness—and the shadows were gaining. The dogs were close enough for him to see light reflecting in their hungry eyes, even though their furry faces lay in the moon's shadow. He swung his frightful, bulging eyes back to the gate.

"Too far," Jerry mumbled with breathless panic, shaking his head as he released Jimmy's arm.

Without Jerry's support, Jimmy stumbled, lurching to the right. "I can't," he wheezed, and then he staggered and fell, pulling John to the ground with him. Both of them hit the unforgiving gravel hard, knocking the breath from their lungs. Their bodies rolled and skidded in the moist gravel, scraping flesh from the palms of their hands and drawing blood. Jimmy rolled sideways and came up on his knees. "Oh, God," he blubbered tearfully, as he tried to scramble back to his feet.

John rolled head-over-heals and came to rest on his back. Unaware that Jerry had left them, he assumed he'd been caught and dragged down by the dogs.

John kicked and screamed for a second, and then he stopped and lay prone on his back, stunned and breathless. His over-stimulated brain blanked for a split second, forgetting why they'd been running. Jimmy lay somewhere close by; he could here the boy blubbering for his father.

Then, he felt the passing of two dark shapes leaping over him, blurred shadows on the Devil's errands. A terrible sense of urgency slammed into his brain as his fight or flight reflexes rebooted, flooding his veins with adrenalin. He rolled, found his feet and sprung up. He caught a brief flash of Jimmy on his knees, just a few feet away to his right, and then he heard scattering gravel and a deep rumbling growl from behind. A freight train plowed into his back, the road vanished from under his feet, and he was a rag doll tumbling through the air, arms flailing as the ground came up and knocked stars into his eyes.

A symphony of pain erupted throughout John's body, rising and falling, undulating agony from head to toe. He groaned and tried to blink away the darkness in his eyes. His sight fazed in and out and he tried to sit up.

"No," John wheezed and rolled gingerly onto his left side, struggling to sit up. He heard screaming—Jimmy's screaming. His eyes followed the scream and he caught sight of Jimmy's body dancing horizontally in the air as a massive growling shadow shook him like a lifeless chew toy.

"Oh, Jesus," he whimpered in disbelief. Turning from the macabre sight, he tried to close his ears to the trembling screams that suddenly fell silent.

"Jimmy," John whispered, and then he saw the fence. The seven-foot high chain-link fence that separated Lowlands from Parkland Road lay only a few feet away. The fence trembled and shook as if someone were climbing it hastily.

"Get off!" Jerry shrieked hoarsely. "Get the fuck off me!"

John glanced over and spotted Jerry hanging from the top bar of the fence a few yards away. A snarling dog had its jaws hooked onto Jerry's left foot, twisting and shaking its head as it tried to pull the boy down. A second dog leapt onto his back, attempting to bury its fangs into his shoulder. It missed his shoulder but latched onto the dangling hood of his sweatshirt and hung from it, viciously twisting and yanking as the dog dangled in the air. With the weight of two violent dogs pulling on him, Jerry lost his hold on the fence and fell away from it screaming. Jerry landed hard on his back as the air whooshed out of his mouth in a loud grunt. The dogs scattered back to reassess and Jerry wheezed heavily, and sat up on his hands.

"Motherfuckers," Jerry sobbed as they came for him again and he screamed like a mad man. With Jerry on his back and vulnerable, the two dogs went for his face and throat. Still screaming incoherent sobs, Jerry kicked the first dog in its snapping jaws, deterring it for a second. The second leapt up at his face and Jerry threw a right hook into its head, knocking it back to the ground. The first dog lunged again, impossibly fast, and closed its gaping jaws around Jerry's face, muffling his screams. John heard the wet snap of Jerry's neck breaking and cried softly as his friend's screams abruptly ended. Turning away, John somehow found the strength from his terribly bruised body to get his feet beneath him, took three staggering steps, and jumped onto the fence.

Only seven feet high, an easy climb for John and his friends on any other night, the fence suddenly seemed a mile high. Babbling wordless sobs of terror, John dragged his body up and over, exerting every ounce of strength he had left. He reached the top bar, limply tumbled over it, then fell and crumpled into the ground on the other side. Wheezing in agony from the impact, he dragged his eyes open and gazed heavenward. Sucking in a deep breath, he cried out to a God he'd always professed a disbelief in. Something crashed into the fence inches from his face, he rolled away and propped himself up on his elbows, staring back at the shaking fence.

The small dog leapt onto the fence again, snarling and snapping its little jaws viciously, spraying John's face with spittle. Closer, John stared at its eyes and saw an intelligence there he would never have imagined in a canine. And now that he was closer, he saw the ears were more pointed than a common dog. Now that he had a better look, the animal did resemble a wolf more than a dog.

He backpedaled, crab walking away from the fence without taking his widened eyes off the raging little dog. The small animal looked menacing with its thick black fur and large pointed ears, its eyes like twin shimmering orange moons that gazed hungrily from its dark fury face. It snarled again and shoved its snout through the fence's chain links, flicking its tongue through its teeth like a snake. Drawing back, it bared its fangs and lunged at the fence again, this time grasping the chain link and twisting it in its jaws. Incredibly, the animal managed to pull a few links apart, and then it abandoned the effort and stood back.

The beast fell silent and locked gazes with John; holding his eyes for second. Deep inside the beast's luminescent orange eyes, John glared at the monstrous intelligence at work and the realization chilled his soul.

The animal looked away from the terrified boy and gazed up and across the fence, and though crazy as it seemed, it seemed to be studying the construct of the fence. The beast dropped its hungry gaze to John again and jumped forward, resting its paws on the chain links. John's mouth dropped open in a silent scream as small, fur covered fingers grew out from the dogs paws and hooked into the chain links. He stared in shock as the face began to morph into something more human. Though the fur still remained, there was no doubt the outline of a human visage was apparent. The ears recessed and the muzzle retracted, the eyes looking clearer than before.

It took less than a minute, and no sooner had the transformation finished, then the jagged claws on the ends of the dog's horrendous furry fingers clicked and scraped on the metal of the chain links as the werewolf began to climb.

John's mind reeled at the unbelievable sight. "No!" he cried out, shaking his head violently. Nevertheless, the creature continued to defy reason as it inched closer to the top. "No fucking way," he sobbed. "It's not possible."

Struggling to his feet, John turned and focused on the distant lights of Warren Avenue a half mile down the road, so close, yet so far. Cars whipped past the view in both directions and John staggered towards them. "Help me," he tried to call out, but only managed a strangled croak. He tore his eyes from the beckoning lights and chanced a glance over his shoulder without stopping. It was too dark to see the creature climbing the fence. He wondered crazily if it was already over the top, coming for him even now, and he mumbled insanities to the darkness.

He heard a muffled thump from somewhere behind him on the dark road, and knew that the werewolf was on his side of the fence now. Despite the unbearable pain that throbbed throughout his body, John broke into a staggering run. "Please," he sobbed breathlessly. "Please, oh God please."

He could see the blinking lights on the Rollerdrome's sign high over the building drawing closer with each lurching step, and then something blocked them out.

A massive shadow rose up out of the darkness in front of him. John's head snapped up, gaping at the orange eyes and flashing white fangs towering over him. The thing stood on its hind legs, like a man, and with one of its paws raised high, the paw now resembled a human hand, the fingers tipped with long wicked looking claws.

"No," John cried softly. "Mommy." Then he drew a breath to scream one last time.

* * *

"Did you hear that?" asked Cindy, one of the pretty young girls flirting with Dennis. Warily, she looked over her shoulder into the darkness of the Lowlands forest. Everyone in the Rollerdrome's parking lot stopped and gazed out beyond the fence at the back end of the building.

"It sounded like a scream," Tammy said; she was Cindy's friend. For a few seconds no one spoke, the silence stretching out. The sound failed to repeat and they all began to doubt their ears.

"Could've been an owl or something," Leroy suggested.

"Didn't sound like any owl I ever heard," Dennis added as he shrugged his shoulders and smiled suggestively at Cindy. The four of them stood just off to the right of the Rollerdrome's parking lot entrance. Roller skaters exiting the building emerged sporadically every few minutes as it was only half an hour till closing. The two girls had been on their way out, roller skates dangling from their hands, when they'd spotted the pair of boys waiting near the back door. Their eyes had slid past the boy in the red flannel jacket with the freckled face and the large mop of curly red hair, and stopped dead on the handsome one standing next to him in blue jeans and a denim jacket. Both girls were attractive and under eighteen, *the perfect age*, Dennis had thought, just before he'd hit them with his heart stopping smile.

"So," Dennis said, refocusing their attention back to where he wanted it. "Cindy, you know about this party at Kenny Mewton's house?"

Cindy pulled her eyes away from the darkness and smiled. "Sure, Kenny Mutant, his parties' rock."

"Mutant?" Leroy asked.

The girls both tilted their heads like curious puppies. "Yeah," Cindy said. "Kenny Mutant, he has a blue/green Mohawk and a load of tattoos. He's a hardcore punker, that's why everybody calls him mutant. He's cool, though."

Dennis rocked back on his heels and grinned. "Ah, that makes sense."

Cindy sharpened her eyes and grinned wider. "You guys aren't from around here, are you?"

"Westland," Leroy confirmed. "My cousin told me about the party. We're supposed to meet him and his buddies here but they're late."

"Oh my God," Tammy squealed. "You're from wasteland?"

Dennis grinned at the nickname for their city. "Yeah," he laughed. "We're Wastelanders."

"Sweet," Cindy said as her eyes slid down Dennis' body. "You guys wanna come with us? We're on our way to Kenny's right now."

Dennis glanced over and nodded at Leroy. "Sounds good to me."

Leroy bent over towards Dennis and lowered his voice. "I still got Jerry's shit, and I need the money."

Tammy leaned in and said in a conspiratorial whisper, "You got weed?"

Both Leroy and Dennis' expressions deadpanned. "You guys, cops?" Leroy asked with a profound seriousness.

The two girls giggled. "No," Tammy said while laughing some more. "We're not *cops*."

"Then why do you want to know if we got any weed?" Leroy asked.

"Because we'll buy some off you," Tammy offered.

"Cool," Dennis urged. "Sell it to them, Leroy."

"But I brought this for Jerry, he'll be pissed."

"Come on," Tammy begged with pouting lips that quickly eroded Leroy's resolve.

"Fine, I'll sell you an eighth, half what I got. How's that?"

"Sweet," Tammy chirped. "Let's go."

The four of them started strolling toward Tammy's car, and then Leroy hesitated. "We should really wait for Jerry to get here."

Dennis stared back at Leroy, frowning at his friend, as if to say, *Are you insane*? "C'mon dude, we'll see them at the party."

"Okay, but just let me call him," Leroy said and pulled out his cell phone. He dialed the number and waited as it rang. As if in answer, a long undulating howl echoed up out of the darkness of Lowlands Park. The deep throaty howl swelled, rising to a crescendo, dwindled, and then rose again as one, then two, and then three more joined in.

All four of them, as well as everyone else in the parking lot, froze in place at the sound. The howling drifted up, rising into a symphony that sent shivers down the spines of everyone within earshot.

Dennis' eyes drifted up and landed on the full moon peeking over the treetops. "You gotta be shittin' me."

Leroy clicked his phone shut after getting Jerry's voice mail. "Uh, maybe we'll just see them at the party," he suggested.

"Yeah," Dennis agreed, nodding enthusiastically without taking his eyes from the moon's orange glow. The howls died off as an age-old instinctual fear rose up in the four of them, and everyone else in the parking lot that was leaving the building. Words failed them as they hurried to their cars like rabbits running for the safety of their burrows. Keys hastily found key holes and cars roared to life, some screeching their tires as they sped out of parking spaces.

Dennis sat next to Leroy in the backseat of Tammy's car as it pulled out onto Warren Avenue, still staring at the full moon's brilliance. "You think that was Jerry and his buddies fucking with us?" Dennis asked as his mind struggled to explain away the inexplicable fear that the howling had caused.

"Had to be," Leroy said.

"Then those guys got a weird sense of humor," Cindy said.

"Yeah, freaks," Tammy agreed.

* * *

Within the moonlit shadows of the park, the werewolves finished their howling tribute to their Goddess the moon, as they busily finished stripping the flesh from the bones of the three teenagers. When they finished, as always, nothing but scattered bits of bone and shredded, bloody clothing would remain amongst the fading blood stains covering the ground.

The alpha female tossed a severed head into the air and her oldest daughter caught it in her jaws as it fell back to the bloody earth. Already nearly crushed by her mother's powerful jaws, the head crunched wetly as it collapsed under the pressure of her clenching teeth, oozing bloody brain matter that splattered across the ground at her feet. She spit the malformed head from her mouth and grasped the shredded forearm clenched between her twin brother's teeth. The two of them growled and snarled, dancing in circles as they played tug-of-war with the bloody limb.

They were all now transformed into their human forms, only their thick coarse hair still covering their bodies. Their faces, though resembling a human, still had sharp teeth and wolf-like features.

Growling contentedly, the five-year-old and the smallest of the pack, buried her bloodied snout into the gaping chest cavity of the body sprawled in the middle of Parkland Road, seeking the juiciest of the tender organs within. Her alpha male, who'd taken down the boy with one deft swipe of his immense forepaw, returned the growl as he tore away a stripped lower limb and crunched the thicker bones between his teeth. Cracking them apart, he licked at the marrow before devouring the remaining scraps of flesh still clinging to the bone.

Habitually, his pack and most of their kind mostly hunted the unwanted of humanities masses, the homeless, the drifters, the ones who wouldn't be missed. The meat was seldom as tender and sweet as the flesh of the three young men, but it was safer. They rarely took prey that was so young as it raised the level of the danger of exposure.

Soon, the search would begin for the three teenagers and they knew they could leave no trace of their kills; they must even lick the blood clean from the dirt. The gnawed bits of bone, bloody shredded clothing and the human's electronic devices, would be cast into the dark water of the nearby river. The world was a big place that continued to grow smaller as man advanced on their habitat, but there were still wild places for them to roam and hunt beneath their Goddess the moon, and when they finished feeding, they would move on as they always did, knowing the forest was no longer safe for hunting.

Heaving a heavy growling sigh, the werewolf bent to the task of cleansing the road of blood. His young daughter began snapping off rib bones, and his mate and their twins were making short work of the other two bodies.

High above them all, the glowing eye of the moon watched, cold and indifferent, as its pale light glinted off the shattered and twisted eyeglasses lying in the grass along the edge of the road.

RUNNING WILD

KEITH LUETHKE

Running...the dreams always started with him running. He would be in the forest, devoid of clothing and uncaring. He would crash through the dense brush, scatter dead leaves in his wake, and stare at the moon.

The dreams came in flashes and would dissipate by dawn, leaving him restless and weary. Every night was the same for nearly two years now. Strangely enough, he couldn't remember his life before the dreams. Where was he from? Who were his parents? Did he have any brothers or sisters? Life was one convoluted mess day in, day out. Days, weeks and months would blur together. He'd try to remember why he was in this house. Who had put him here? He worked a day job at a factory cutting sheet metal and nobody really spoke to him. He went to a doctor for his lapse in memory but the doctor had a record of him always being who he was, but wasn't. Something was missing in his life. Some intricate puzzle piece from the past he couldn't place or had thrown away. Even his name made no sense at times. Jim Madison. It never felt like the name really belonged to him. He was a part of something once but it had left him long ago. Or had he left it? He was given pills and told to get more sleep, but sleep never came; only more dreams of running, until one night, something stirred in the basement of his house.

There was a soft patter of clawed feet below, and the faint sounds of rats gnawing on rotten wood. He left the bedroom and went to the basement door with the stealth of a cat on the prowl. His heart thumped like a jackhammer, and excited, he opened the door.

There was a sudden burst of movement in the darkness, then nothing at all.

"Hello?" Jim's voice fell flat, as if the walls of the underground shelter had soaked them in the moment he spoke. He sucked in a lungful of air and made his way down the wooden steps. His feet pounded down each creaky step. The air was damp.

"Is anyone down here?" The basement echoed his words, but made no reply: silent and cold, it waited.

When he approached the light switch, he clicked it on but nothing happened. An early winter wind seeping in through the fragmented cracks in the walls cut his throat like a jagged knife. He crossed his arms and shivered. He tried the light switch again but the light didn't even flicker. He stumbled down the stairs and bumped into the wall.

There was a crash from the far corner of the basement.

He jerked backwards and fell onto the last step.

Suddenly, there was a loud crash and the sound of glass shattering as it landed on the floor.

Staggering to his feet, Jim saw the basement door leading to the front of the house swing wide open. The streetlight from outside illuminated a dark humanoid figure running.

"Wait, come back!" he called.

Turning slightly to glance over its shoulder, it paused. The figure erupted in a horrible cry, baring a row of long, white teeth. When the wind blew, Jim could smell the scent of rotten flesh.

"Who are you?"

The beast growled and then disappeared into the night.

Gasping, Jim slowly walked outside. The basement door swung away from him in a strong gust of wind. He searched for the creature and caught a glimpse of it crawling into the neighboring woods behind his house, then it vanished from his sight. He wiped beads of sweat from his forehead and tried to close the basement door, but the wind held it open.

His mind raced with questions he couldn't answer. His hands shook and he had to squeeze them into fists to make them stop. He went to the storage closet to fetch a chain and a padlock to use on the door when, in the corner of the basement, he saw the lifeless corpse of a woman lying on the floor.

Jim covered his mouth in shock.

She was around twenty, with short brown hair, pale skin, and green eyes open in the shock of death. There was a slit across her throat that resembled a wide, laughing, bloody grin.

He made his way toward her. A trail of bright crimson led up to her corpse. The concrete would not forget the blood which had flowed through her veins; her stain would stay for years to come. He reached out and touched her flesh: it was still warm and firm.

He shivered and ran upstairs with the fear of a madman. He slammed the door and bolted it. He never felt more alive in his life.

* * *

Jim scanned through the contact list in his phone and stopped at Brenda's number. He hit 'send' and waited as the phone rang.

"Come on, honey. Pick up, pick up...pick up!"

She answered on the fourth ring. "Hello? Jim, it's really late."

"I know but there's a dead body in my basement."

"What?"

"I have a dead body in my basement."

"Is this a joke?" she asked.

"No, this isn't a joke. Come over as soon as possible. And there's something else. Something broke into my house, something large and...hairy."

She didn't answer, but he could hear her breathing into the phone.

"Brenda?"

"Did you call the police?"

"No, I didn't. I should but I won't. I can't really explain it. It seemed so familiar."

"I told him not to try this?"

"Excuse me?"

"Stay put," she said. "I'll be over soon. And don't do anything stupid."

She hung up the phone before he could protest.

He put the cell phone on the dresser and lied in his bed with both of his hands placed over his head. His mind raced. The darkness in the bedroom reminded him it was nighttime and everything that had happened could've been a dream. He took a deep breath through his mouth, exhaled out of his nose just like the doctor told him to do when stressed, and listened to the howling wind lightly tap on his window as though politely asking to be let in.

He sat up. The muscles in his back gave a slight tug. He had to go back to the basement just to make sure. Scanning the bedroom, he found his work boots and put them on.

"There's nothing down there," he said to himself. "Only shadows and a dead body. It can't hurt me."

Wiping the sweat from his brow, he forced himself to stand. Placing one foot after the other, he left the comforts of his warm bed.

The house was silent. All but the soft tapping of his boots against the hardwood floor could be heard as he walked. He turned on the hall light and stood alone before the locked basement door.

Then an awful sound shook him from his reverie. It was a wet slurp, and was soon followed by a loud *crunch*.

Jim placed a shaky hand on the cold metal doorknob and began to turn it. He swung the basement door open and peered into the darkness below. The horrible sounds came to a sudden halt. He slowly descended the wooden stairs again.

No more noises came from below.

"I'm going crazy, that's it. There's nothing down here...this is just my basement. I was just dreaming before. Yes, that's it...it was just a dream."

His last step brought him to the bottom. He flicked on the light switch but it still didn't work. There was a soft mutter in the corner, then sharp claws raking against the concrete floor. Then footsteps sounded as the figure approached, getting faster and faster, each step roaring in Jim's ears.

He turned and ran up the basement steps. He could feel the beast's rancid breath on his bare legs, its claws reaching out of the pale shadows to grab him.

And then, curved nails wrapped around his right leg and dug into his soft flesh.

He howled and kicked with his free leg into the darkness. When his work boot connected with something hard and furry, he brought it down again and again. The thing holding him let go and he scrambled up the stairs screaming. When his hands had found the metal lock, he bolted the basement door shut and leaned against its wooden frame, trying to catch his breath.

There was a loud thump against the door.

Jim held firm, using his grip with the work boots to hold him in place. Despite his reluctance, the beast in the basement wouldn't let up. It continued to claw and smash into the door relentlessly in an attempt to get him. With every thump against the door, his mind raced with visions of stalking dark alleyways for potential prey. He was naked and alone, but free and hungry, always so hungry. In one of his dreams, he had stalked by the moonlight, and crept about the shadows in search of prey.

He heard laughter and drew closer to the sounds of a gleeful couple holding hands in a park. In the dream, he killed them. Their blood was sweet, their meat tender and juicy. He ripped into the bodies until all that remained were a few bloody scraps of clothing and a few leftover bone fragments. But that was just a dream.

The thumps grew more intense, the door shaking in its frame. The smell seeping under the door was odd, yet he couldn't recall it.

He covered his ears and clenched his fists. "Go away damn you. I don't want to go back home!"

The beast only pounded harder.

He held his breath and then slowly exhaled. "What am I saying? Who am I?"

The basement door cracked and splintered.

Jim placed both of his hands upon it and pushed. The flimsy hinges made a metallic clank as they popped off and rattled on the polished floor.

A low growl seeped through the door, setting his nerves on fire.

He couldn't hold the door any longer.

Sharp claws tore and broke through the wood.

Jim toppled over and landed on his backside.

At the threshold of the stairs was a creature like none he'd ever seen before. But if that were true, then why did the creature look familiar?

Yellow eyes narrowed as the hairy beast reached for Jim's exposed leg. Yelling and kicking were of no use as the beast's claws dug into his flesh, causing a surge of blinding pain to arc up his thigh. The beast hunched over and gave another growl.

Jim gazed into its maw, staring at the sharp, stained red teeth. "What do you want from me?"

The beast growled louder and dragged him down into the basement.

Jim's limbs went numb, much like his mind. He could feel the pain in his leg as he was yanked but didn't seem to register it. The back of his head smacked the stairs as he was dragged down into the darkness.

When he reached the last step, the beast grabbed both of his legs and tossed his body near the dead woman. There was a soft, wet smack when he hit the concrete floor.

Drooling and growling, the beast came for him.

"Get away from me!" Jim yelled.

The beast diverted its path and went for the woman. It tore an arm off the corpse with one quick, jagged pull from its teeth. The beast seemed to groan in delight as marrow seeped out from the bone and fell in a gooey clump on the floor.

Jim stared in wonder and horror, blood splattering his face. It was still warm. He wanted to shout, to scream, but his lips wouldn't issue a sound. Red crimson ran in gushes down his face; the sweet smell of copper filled his nostrils. His heart thumped like a war drum, racing in his chest. He could remember the city at night, the wind, and the chase.

Blood soon filled his mouth as the beast grabbed him by the nape of his neck and force fed him the severed limb. The blood was nourishing, giving him back old memories and forgotten pleasures in a sea of red. He could recall the blood of man, running on all fours, and howling at the full moon on hot summer nights. Soon the growls from the beast didn't seem so strange—they seemed very familiar.

The beast bent down, placed its claw upon Jim's shaggy head and spoke in a low guttural voice. "*Return to us.*"

He shot up at the beast's words and bumped his head against an adjacent shelf.

The beast shoved him away. It ran to the open door leading outside, and stood in the doorway, waiting.

Somewhere in the night came a group of howls coming from the forest. From the different tones, Jim assumed there must've been somewhere in the range of six to eight of the creatures outside, each of them salivating and waiting.

Jim smelled the night: it smelled of excitement, pleasure, and freedom.

"*Return to us*," the beast beckoned once more.

Jim stood up. Through the dark blood on his hands, he felt a change. At first, tiny, dark hairs penetrated through his skin, and then his nails grew long and sharp.

"It has been a long time since you left, Kelmare. We need you to lead once again. The pack awaits," the beast growled.

Just as his jaw began to elongate and his teeth sharpened, there was a sudden flash of movement from behind the beast.

It was Brenda.

She appeared from the darkness and moved into the basement. She wore a pink see-thru nightgown and matching slippers. She was stealthy and he never heard her when she descended the stairs.

"Is this what you really want, Jim?" she asked.

"I...I don't understand," Jim said.

"You told me you wanted another life. A life away from the pack, and I gave it to you. You knew I was the only one who could."

Jim could still taste the blood on his lips, it was a tantalizing pleasure. His stomach growled. He craved more.

"I don't belong here. Why did I ever leave this behind?"

Brenda got down on all fours and she quickly changed before his eyes. Bones snapped, reddish fur appeared, her mouth elongated into a wolfish snout, and her eyes turned a vibrant yellow. Once transformed, she stalked over to the corpse of the woman in his basement.

"She was innocent. Her name was Samantha and she had just broken up with her boyfriend. She was walking home from his house when she was hunted down and slain. She didn't put up much of a fight. Few of them ever do. It's as though they want their lives to end and we're the catalyst." Brenda stared at him. "Do you still want this curse? Or would you rather have a normal life with me?"

"But we don't belong here," he said.

He went to the corpse of Samantha and pressed his newly formed teeth into her flesh. He tore out a large chunk of her thigh and began to feed. The meat was tender in his mouth, soft, and life giving. His old life was coming back to him in a red flood. He was a part of the night, he belonged to a pack that he'd forgotten, and was now fully reborn to lead, hunt, and kill.

"You won't get a second chance," Brenda said. "You're only allowed to leave once." She looked around the basement in distaste. "If you decide to go back to this life, they'll destroy you."

"You can stay if you want," he said. "Keep your day job and all the mundane pleasures of a human life. I need more, I know that now. I've known it for a long time."

"I'll go with you no matter what your choice, Kelmare. I don't belong to either world. I belong to you," she said.

He wasn't Jim anymore, now he knew who he was. He was Kelmare.

He raised himself on his clawed feet and looked past her into the welcoming night. He raced for the open door, crashed past the beast he'd feared only an hour ago, and drowned himself in a new darkness.

Brenda took off after him, her long loping strides covering the distance easily.

Mournful howls echoed down the suburban neighborhood and festered in the dark city streets.

A few half-eaten corpses would be found in the morning, but Kelmare—formerly Jim Madison—wouldn't be among them.

He finally knew who he was and where he belonged.

He had finally tossed his everyday life aside to run wild and free.

UPON A MOONLIT NIGHT

K.M. ROCKWOOD

Sandra Jennings' cell phone rang just as she pulled into the driveway of her parents' house.

Her house, now, she supposed. Her eyes filled with tears as she stopped the car and reached for the phone. It must be Peter, her fiancé, calling to say he would be coming right over.

"Miss Jennings?" Not Peter but an indifferent female voice. "This is Moira, Peter Regens' secretary. I'm calling to tell you that Mr. Regens has been unavoidably delayed and will contact you later in the evening, or tomorrow if his meeting runs too late."

"Tell him to call whenever he can." Sandra tried to keep her voice steady. "I need to talk to him."

"I'll relay the message." Moira hung up, leaving Sandra clutching the small bit of plastic to her ear.

How could Peter leave her alone at a time like this? Sandra put down her phone and stared out the windshield, tears swelling in her eyes and blurring her vision. Evening shadows gathered around the garage—the garage where her parents and Julia, her sister, had been found slashed to death. Torn to pieces, the police had told her. She hadn't seen the bodies herself; they had been removed before she had returned from Charlottesville, where she was finishing her education to become a teacher.

Not something anyone should have to see, the funeral director had assured her, his professional comforting presence at its best under the circumstances. They had closed coffins at the service.

Julia's estranged husband, Monte, had been found in the hills behind the house—dead of self-inflicted wounds.

She shivered as she looked up at the half moon rising over the hills.

In the back seat, her tiny niece, Wendy, stirred in her car seat, whimpering. She was Julia's child and the only survivor of the massacre.

"Just you and me now, kid," Sandra murmured through clenched teeth. She wasn't prepared to take care of a baby. She wasn't prepared for any of this. How could anyone be?

Sandra opened the car door and hesitated. She couldn't possibly carry Wendy and everything else into the house at once. She'd never been one of those women who thought there was nothing to taking care of a baby, or that the skills would come naturally when she needed them. But she hadn't realized there would be so many details to master.

Wendy shouldn't be left in the car so she decided to take her into the house and feed her first. Actually, feed both of them. Sandra hadn't eaten all day and felt a little light-headed. Then, after Wendy was asleep, she could come out and get the other things out of the back of her car.

The other things were the four urns she had just picked up from the crematorium—one for each members of her family.

Angrily, she wiped her eyes as she leaned into the car to lift Wendy out of her car seat, but the tears kept coming, making it hard to see the buckles on the straps.

A vague yet familiar scent reached her nostrils; a subtle masculine scent of musk, leather and soap. Where had she smelled that before?

Monte! Julia's husband. But Monte was dead; she had an urn with his ashes in the back of her car to prove it.

She should have eaten something today; her senses were playing tricks on her.

"Excuse me," a deep male voice said from behind her.

Sandra hadn't heard anyone approach. Startled, she straightened up, slamming her head into the doorframe. The world exploded into swirling colors.

She felt herself collapsing and grabbed frantically to keep the baby from falling. As her vision faded, she saw a large bearded man with startling golden eyes.

Definitely Monte.

Sandra had always heard that hearing was the first sense to awaken upon a return to consciousness and it was true now. Her head pounded and she felt an overwhelming desire to go back to sleep, to worry about everything later.

She could hear someone moving around and knew she couldn't go back to sleep; there was something she needed to take care of. Wendy.

The baby couldn't wait; Sandra didn't have the luxury of lying here. She should get up and make sure Wendy was all right—as soon as she could move. Her arms felt trapped against her sides and her legs wouldn't move.

She heard a deep voice crooning nearby and concentrated on understanding the words. "Such a beautiful girl," the voice said. "We should think about getting these clothes off."

Sandra tried to sit up but couldn't. She felt very weak, but as she struggled, she realized something was wrapped tightly around her, keeping her from moving. She opened her mouth to scream, but only managed a choking cough.

"Ah, are you waking up?" the same voice asked a little louder. "Don't try to get up. I'll be right over. Just let me finish changing the baby and get some dry clothes on her."

Sandra forced her eyes open. The light seared into her head but she was determined to see where she was and what was happening.

She was lying on the couch in the family room of her parents' house. Combined with the kitchen and dining area, it was what her mother called the 'soul' of the house. Her sister Julia had set up all the baby equipment for Wendy in here when she'd moved it.

Since returning from school to deal with the mountain of problems and details wrought by the violent deaths of her family, Sandra had been living almost exclusively in this room, putting Wendy to bed in the playpen in the corner and sleeping on the couch. Not that she slept much. The rest of the house felt too unfriendly, almost threatening.

She pushed against her restraints and realized a light blanket had been tucked tightly around her and that she could easily free her arms by pulling the edge of the blanket out from under herself.

The large man busied himself at the changing table in the corner. A few minutes later, he lifted a fully dressed Wendy and cradled her comfortably in his huge arm.

"Monte?" Sandra asked uncertainly.

The man gave a dry laugh. "No. I'm afraid not. Although I wish it could be! I'm Craig Vilkson, Monte's brother."

She didn't remember Julia mentioning Monte's brothers. "Not much family," was the way she had put it.

"Older or younger?" she asked, although she didn't know why that would be important.

"Monte was older than me by about ten minutes," Craig said, picking up a full baby bottle from the table and carrying Wendy to an armchair next to the couch.

"So you were twins?"

"Twins? Yes. We are—were—twins." He tested the temperature of the formula on the inside of his wrist. "I'm afraid babies don't much care what else is going on. They still need to be changed and fed."

He settled into the chair and held the bottle so the nipple touched the baby's lips. Wendy opened her hungry mouth and her little hands grabbed onto Craig's massive fingers. "Such a beautiful girl," he crooned. "So, let's have supper."

She closed her eyes. "You look so much like Monte. Although I really didn't know him. I live in Charlottesville. I go—I was going—to the University for a Masters Degree in education. Until..." Her voice trailed off.

The big man nodded. "Such a tragedy for everyone. But especially for young Wendy here. She lost both her parents and two of her grandparents."

"But how could it have happened?" She felt tears gathering in her eyes again. "The police said Monte must have had a big dog with him—they were just torn to pieces!"

Craig reached up and brushed an eye with the sleeve of his rough linen shirt. How must he feel, knowing that his twin brother was responsible for this?

"*Why* did he kill them?" she asked. Despite the warm evening, Sandra felt chilled. "How could he do that to his own family?"

"I don't know," Craig said, shaking his shaggy dark head. "I know they were having problems —Julia had taken Wendy and come back to live with your parents—but the Monte I knew would never have done that."

"It's a miracle he didn't kill the baby, too." Sandra said, drawing the blanket closer around herself.

"Wendy was his *child*," he said. "He would have done anything to save her; even if it cost him his life."

"But he must have gone berserk and after, when he'd calmed down, he must have realized he couldn't live with himself and what he'd done."

"He must have." Craig looked down at the baby in his lap. "Do you know how he killed himself?"

"He stabbed himself in the throat with a silver letter opener my mother kept on her desk. He used some of her stationery to write his suicide note." Sandra shivered again.

"What did he say in the note?" he asked.

"That he was sorry, and to please make sure his body was cremated."

"Did someone see to that?"

She felt her clenched jaw muscles relax. Talking was a relief. She hadn't realized how tense she had been lately.

Peter should be here, she thought angrily. I need to talk about this, and he's the one I should be talking to. Not someone I don't know. Especially not the twin brother of the murderer!

Craig waited patiently and asked again, "Have Monte's remains been cremated?"

"I had all of them cremated. I just picked up the urns from the crematorium today. They're in the back of my car. I wonder if he killed the dog, too? They never found it."

"Probably." Craig looked at her, his golden eyes filled with anguish. "I'm so sorry you had to go through this, Sandra. That we *all* have. My family is totally devastated." He covered his shoulder with the diaper and held Wendy against it, gently rubbing her back.

"I never heard Monte talk much about his family," she said.

Craig shook his head. "My father didn't approve of the marriage. He felt Julia was too...*different*, I guess is the best word. From our family, I mean. So they eloped. Papa was furious! He said he was going to totally disown Monte."

"But he must have changed his mind. Monte and Julia went to live with your family, even before Wendy was born."

"When Papa heard that a baby was on the way, he changed his mind and tried to welcome Julia into the family. I don't know how she felt about that."

"Too little too late, I'd imagine," she said.

"I'd think so," he agreed.

"Julia told me she was trying to get Monte to move away with her," Sandra said. "She said he was afraid he wouldn't be able to get a decent job. He'd never worked anywhere but on the family property. He didn't think he'd be able to get a decent job anywhere else."

Craig looked thoughtful. "Perhaps that's why she decided to take Wendy and move back in with your parents. Maybe she hoped Monte would follow."

"Monte could have gotten a job. My dad would have helped him get a job at the mill. I don't see why they wanted to move in with your family in the first place. Don't they live way back in the hills?"

"Yes. The family owns several thousand acres, most of it mountain and forest land. Wendy will eventually inherit a share of it. I guess Monte wanted her to grow up in the midst of her inheritance, like we did."

"Do you have any more brothers and sisters?" she asked. "What about your parents?"

"Two more brothers, both younger. Wargo and Forrest. Wargo was born crippled; we all look out for him. My mother left when we were all young. We haven't heard from her in years. My father and his brother, my Uncle Farkas, raised us."

Wendy let out a surprisingly loud burp. Craig smiled and wiped her mouth.

"You're very good with her," Sandra said, a trifle enviously. He handled the baby's care with such ease.

"Everyone helped care for Wendy," he said and shifted the baby's position and began to rock her gently. "Monte hoped Julia would become pregnant again soon. We all did. We didn't want her to be overwhelmed and tired, taking care of a baby. I usually took the night shift, so Julia could get some uninterrupted sleep."

Another baby so soon! Sandra wondered what Julia thought about that, but there was no way to check now, unless it was on the autopsy report which she couldn't bring herself to read. She sup-

UPON A MOONLIT LIGHT

posed it didn't really make any real difference. It would just make an unspeakable tragedy even worse. She laid her head back against the back cushions of the couch.

"How are you feeling?" Craig asked. "That was a nasty bump on the head. Fortunately, I did manage to catch both of you before you hit the ground."

Her skin felt warm at the thought of his strong arms around her. She blushed. "How did I get in here?"

"I carried you, of course. You're not very heavy." He peered fondly into Wendy's face. "She's falling asleep. I'll put her down in a minute."

Momentarily, Sandra wished she could be back in Craig's strong arms. She'd feel safe and protected there, she thought. She imagined burying her face in his chest, inhaling his musky fragrance.

Get a grip, she thought. *It's just your overwrought emotions.* She opened her eyes and sat up straight.

Craig laid Wendy in her playpen then turned to Sandra. "Now, when did you last have something to eat?"

"I haven't eaten all day. But my head really hurts," she said. "I don't think I could eat anything at all right now."

"Let me fix you a milkshake," he said as he went to the refrigerator and began rummaging through it. "Chocolate or vanilla?"

"Chocolate. But I'm not kidding about not feeling like eating. I might throw up all over myself."

He looked at her and raised a bushy eyebrow. "Then I'll just have to clean you up. You should at least try to eat."

She felt her face grow red again at the idea of Craig's strong, capable fingers moving over her clothes, unbuttoning her blouse...

She shook her head, trying to clear it but that only made her feel dizzy. The blow to her head must be what made her thoughts go in such an odd direction.

When Craig brought the cool chocolate milkshake and sat down beside her, she could hardly keep herself from collapsing into his side. Her fingers burned where they touched his as he handed her the glass. Under his intense gaze, she lifted the glass to her lips. His lips parted in a small smile, and as she started to drink, the tip of his tongue licked his top lip approvingly.

What would that lip taste like if *she* were to lick it with her own tongue?

When she was finished, he took the glass from her hand and reached over to pull the blanket around her. He ran his hand lightly over the sore spot on her head. "Maybe you should get some more sleep," he said. "I think you'll feel better in the morning, although you may still have a headache."

"Maybe I should go to the emergency room and get this checked out," she said, reaching her hand up to gently feel her head. "Sometimes there's brain swelling from head injuries, like in a concussion. Aren't you supposed to wake up people with head injuries a few times at night to make sure they're not unconscious?"

"I don't think it was that serious a blow," he said. "But if you want to go to the emergency room, I'll take you. If not, I can wake you up every two hours or so. Although you won't have a restful night if I do that."

"You're going to *stay* all night?" she asked.

"You shouldn't be left by yourself. And you shouldn't be responsible for taking care of Wendy until you feel better. I'll stay here and keep watch over both of you tonight. We can discuss the things I came to talk about in the morning, when you feel better."

"You're going to stay awake all night?"

"I do my best thinking at night." He smiled, stroking his beard. "I see a whole shelf of books. If you don't mind, I'll explore them. Now you go upstairs and get yourself to bed. Leave the door open; I'll be up in two hours to make sure I can wake you."

"I've been sleeping here, on the couch," she said, a trifle embarrassed. "I just haven't been able to fall asleep upstairs in my old bed. I grew up in this house. I used to feel so safe here. But now..."

"I understand," he assured her. "Certainly, sleep on the couch if you're more comfortable there. I can turn out the light if it'll bother you."

"I've been sleeping with the light on," Sandra admitted.

She thought about changing into her pj's, but the idea of Craig seeing her in them stopped her. They were a long sleeved affair, bright red with little black kittens all over them. If she'd had a sexy negligee, she might have been tempted to put it on, but maybe not.

She was puzzled by her feelings and she felt like she was entering dangerous territory.

Craig exuded some kind of animal magnetism which she couldn't explain. Monte had the same effect—she could remember thinking she understood why Julia had been so in love with him. Now, despite everything going on in her life, despite her exhaustion and grief and, yes, her engagement to Peter, she felt an undeniable attraction.

Of course she couldn't act on such irrational feelings.

She lay back on the couch and he smoothed the blanket over her.

"Just let me make sure you're not running a fever," he said, brushing her forehead and cheeks with his rugged fingers.

Sandra sighed involuntarily at his soft touch.

"Sleep well." He smiled at her, his hand momentarily cupping her cheek. It had to be her imagination that she could feel his intense gold eyes burning into her brown ones.

She smiled back. With an effort, she stopped herself from flinging her arms around his neck and pulling him down on top of her. She hardly knew him, she reminded herself firmly.

Why didn't she ever remember feeling like that with Peter? After all, Peter was her fiancé. She loved him. She'd loved him every since her first year at the University of Virginia where he was a senior preparing for law school. Everything fell in to place so easily, like it was meant to be. She had accepted the engagement ring happily. She would study to become a teacher; he would complete law school, pass the bar and open a law office here. They would get married as soon as they had both finished their education and his practice was established. Peter was a 'good catch.' Her parents approved. Right now, she should be back at the university, finishing her MA in education, and looking forward to working with her mother to plan a wedding.

Instead, she had no mother. She was here, taking care of Wendy, trying to sort out what had happened and figure out how to go on with her life.

She and Peter had been planning for so long that she supposed they took each other for granted by now. Maybe she should think about how to re-ignite the spark they used to feel. They *had* felt a spark once, hadn't they?

Come to think of it, where *was* Peter? Shouldn't he have called by now? He had to know how distressed she was. When he had called to say he couldn't accompany her to the crematorium to pick up the urns, she'd almost cried, but he had promised to come pick her up and take her to dinner. Then she had received the phone call from Moira, his secretary.

But she *needed* him.

She drifted off to sleep, comforted by the knowledge that Craig was sitting across the room with one of her father's books spread out across his lap.

When she awoke in the morning, Sandra dimly recalled being awakened several times during the night. Each time, Craig smoothed her hair and caressed her cheek, then tucked the blanket around her and whispered for her to go back to sleep. Once, she thought his lips had brushed against her forehead, but that might have been wishful thinking.

Sunlight flooded through the French doors that led to the deck as the aroma of fresh coffee filled the air. In the kitchen area, she could see Craig opening the refrigerator door. Wendy was cradled in one arm.

He glanced over at her. "Awake, are we?"

"Yes," she said as she struggled to sit up. She now only had a mild headache and she was ravenous.

"Would you like to hold Wendy while I fix us some breakfast?" he asked. "She's been fed and changed."

"First let me run to the bathroom," she said, standing up.

Why should she be embarrassed about that? Of course she had to use the bathroom when she first woke up. Who didn't?

"Of course," he smiled while cradling the baby closer to his chest.

In the bathroom, she stared at herself in the mirror. Her makeup was long gone, and her long curly hair was in disarray, but even she had to admit she still looked pretty good. A lot better than she had since she got word about her parents and sister. This morning her face had a healthy glow. She brushed her teeth and then reached for the mouthwash to banish her morning breath. How silly. She didn't expect to be kissing anyone, did she?

Back in the family room, she sat on the couch and Craig handed Wendy to her. "Such a pretty girl," he crooned to the baby, who smiled up at him.

Sandra took the baby and looked at her closely. Of course she was cute; all babies are cute. And now she was going to be a mother to this poor child. But she couldn't bring herself to call her 'pretty.' Her ears seemed to be set too low on the sides of her head. She had a full head of dark hair, not surprising since both Monte and Julia had sported thick dark locks. Her eyebrows while wispy, met over her nose, just like Craig's. And her eyes, dark blue at birth, were changing to the same vivid gold as Craig's. The color was startling enough in a grown man, but in a baby, Sandra found the color downright disconcerting.

"How about omelets?" Craig busied himself in the kitchen. "I found some eggs and veggies."

When breakfast was ready, Craig lifted the sleeping baby from Sandra's arms and laid her in the playpen. He had set the dining table, complete with embroidered placemats and folded napkins.

The omelets were excellent, perfectly formed and fluffy. Sandra ate two of them, washed down with several cups of remarkably good coffee. She was surprised at her appetite. While she knew she was still grieving, this morning she felt like there might be a life ahead for her—and for Wendy, of course.

"I'll do the dishes," she said, pushing back her chair and standing.

"No. You rest. I'll take care of them." He took her by the elbow and steered her back to the couch. "I'm sure your headache isn't completely gone."

Her skin quivered at his touch. She had to fight an urge to turn around and throw herself into his arms.

When he had finished cleaning up, he came and sat next to her. She could feel the muscles rippling in his thick thigh when it touched hers. He took her delicate hand in his powerful one, the diamond on her engagement ring winking at them in the morning sunlight.

"I'm so sorry I startled you and you were hurt," he said. "I feel responsible. Is there anything I can do to make up for it?"

Pick me up and carry me upstairs, she thought. *Make passionate love to me.*

She was more than a little shocked at herself. How close had she come to saying that out loud? Certainly closer than she was comfortable admitting. The shock, compounded by what she perceived as Peter's desertion—just when she needed him most— must be playing havoc with her logical thought process, not to mention her self-control.

"No, thank you," she managed to answer, staring at her hand engulfed by his. She'd never before seen so much hair on the back of anyone's hand. And his nails—well manicured, but strong and curved. They looked like he could use them as tools.

"Then I hope you won't mind if I get to why I came here to talk to you in the first place," he said. "I hate to bring you any more pain but..."

Sandra steeled herself for what might be coming. "Go 'head and talk. If we don't deal with this, we won't be able to move on."

"Yes. And we *do* need to move on," he said. "What are you planning to do with the ashes?"

"I'm not sure. I had them put in nice brass urns. For the time being, I thought I'd put them on the mantel. I can always decide to do something else with them later."

"Monte's, too?" Craig asked.

Sandra tensed. "I'm not sure I want to put Monte's with the others," she admitted. "After all, he's responsible for their deaths, isn't he? Do you think he killed the dog, too, before he killed himself? Suppose it's roaming up in the hills somewhere? It might kill someone else."

"I don't think you need to worry about it," he assured her. "The dog must be dead, too. I'm sure of it."

"Did you know about the dog? The police said it must have been *huge*. Something like a wolfhound or a mastiff."

"I was familiar with it." Craig patted her hand. "If you don't mind, I'd like to have Monte's ashes. I want to bring them back to the family homestead. Perhaps bury them in the graveyard."

"Certainly you can have them," she said. "It would be a relief to me, not to have to wonder what to do with them."

"How about Julia's? After all, she was married into the family."

"No. I want Julia's ashes and my parents' together, at least for now."

"I understand." He dropped her hand and slipped his muscular arm around her shoulders. She found herself relaxing, sinking back against his protective arm.

"Now," he said, "about Wendy..."

She sat up straight. "What about Wendy?"

"Well, Wendy is part of our family, too. I know Monte and Julia planned to raise her on the family lands."

"Julia may have said that at first, but she moved back here."

"I think she probably would have eventually returned to the Vilkson homestead. Or at least let Wendy return there."

"Julia would never have allowed someone else to raise her daughter."

Craig sighed and shook his head. "You may very well be right. That's why I think she would have moved back."

"Well, she's dead, so we can't ask her, can we?" She pulled away from his embracing arm. "And the reason she's dead is because of Monte Vilkson." She felt tears gathering in her eyes. "My parents are dead, too, because of Monte."

Craig looked down at the floor. "Yes. I'm painfully aware of that. It would never have happened had Julia stayed with us."

Sandra glared at him in rising fury. "You're saying it's Julia's fault she's dead? Because she took her baby and left? Look what Monte did to them. He was a monster."

Craig spread his hands before him, palms down, and shook his head. "I'm saying this poorly. Not her fault. Never."

"She left a man who was capable of killing her when she wouldn't come back to him. It was the right choice. She just didn't survive it." She clutched her fists angrily.

"I don't think it happened like that."

"No? Then how *did* it happen?"

Craig shook his head again. "I don't know. Monte should never have married Julia. Papa was right; we're too different to marry most women. We should seek only women who...have been *raised* the same way we have."

"And how is that? To kill people who don't do what you think they should?"

"No. Away from other people, back on our own lands."

"And you want to take a perfectly normal baby girl and raise her that way, isolated from everyone else but your family? Which consists solely of adult men?" Sandra wiped her eyes angrily.

"She's not...she's going to inherit a share in the land. Perhaps all of it, if none of the rest of us find wives and have children; which looks even less likely than before this fiasco. Wendy should be raised learning how to care for her legacy."

"Were *you* raised that way?"

Craig nodded. "Yes. Forester and gamekeeper. We care for the land, protect the wildlife habitat. We contract for selective logging, never clear-cut. That pays the taxes and provides for our modest needs. And we have never permitted mining."

"Has *everyone* in your family stayed on the land? Nobody ever wanted to be a doctor or a teacher, or even just live somewhere else?"

"No. Even in the old country, generations ago, we lived in the forests and worked as foresters and gamekeepers. It's a strong family tradition."

Julia could believe in strong family traditions, but not that no one ever left. "What would happen if someone did want to leave?"

Craig looked thoughtful. "They never did."

"Maybe because someone would have *killed* them if they had tried?" She spit out the words.

Craig sat up straight and sighed. "I can see I'm upsetting you. That's the last thing I want to do. But I'm serious about Wendy. Our family has a real interest in her, too. She would want for nothing. We all love her and would give our lives before we would let anything happen to her."

"It seems to me that her mother already has given her life for her child. So did her grandparents."

Craig stood. "Just think about it. For now, at least let us arrange to have her visit, once a month or so."

Sandra relaxed a bit. "I'll think about it, but probably not until she's older. And now I think you'd better leave."

"Are you sure you feel well enough? I can stay for as long as you want, take care of Wendy. And you." He gave her a sad smile.

"I don't need anyone to take care of me, thank you." She got to her feet. "I appreciate what you did for me last night and this morning, but..."

"But it was my fault in the first place, wasn't it? Startling you like that." He turned toward the door. "May I take Monte's ashes with me? He belongs back on the family lands."

"Definitely. Let me get them out of the car for you." She led the way.

A minute later they were at the car. The four heavy brass urns were identical, and they had to turn them upside down to read the labels on the bottom.

Sandra frowned. "I should have had the names engraved on them," she said.

"You can always have that done later, if you want," he said, hefting the urn with Monte's remains. He turned toward his truck, parked further up the driveway.

Sandra was surprised she hadn't noticed the white box truck when she'd pulled into the driveway last night. She'd been distracted, she remembered, and her tears had blurred her vision. Probably just not paying enough attention, she figured. That was why she hadn't notice his approach. She'd have to work on that.

Craig opened the back door of the truck to put the urn inside. Inside the sturdy rear door was a metal grate, which he unlocked and swung open.

She looked more closely at the vehicle. It was a heavy-duty four-wheel drive box truck, with a small high window on the rear door and on each side of the body. She could see thick bars behind the windows.

"Why is the truck outfitted like that?" she asked. "Bars and everything?"

Craig closed the doors. "Remember, I'm a gamekeeper. Sometimes I have to restrain or transport an animal. The truck has to be strong enough so the animal can't escape. Or another break in."

"Like bears?" she asked.

163

"Bears, yes. Things like that." He pulled on the door to make sure it was latched. Then he turned to Sandra. "Please think about what will be best for Wendy. I'll come back in a week or so and we can discuss it again."

"I'll think about it. But don't expect me to change my mind," she said.

He looked at her for a minute. Then he walked back to her, reached out, and gathered her in his strong arms, crushing her to his broad chest. The scent of musk and leather overpowered her senses and she closed her eyes. She felt herself go limp as he lifted her from her feet. His beard brushed her face as his lips sought hers and pressed against them.

Locked in the embrace, he kissed her for what seemed like an eternity—an eternity from which she never wanted to escape.

Finally, he drew back, placed her gently back on her feet, and let her go. His hand caressed her cheek. "Ah, if only you were my kind. How I would love you. I'd prove to you that life in the forest could be good. But I can't do that to you—to us. One tragedy in the family is more than enough."

Sandra thought she saw tears in his eyes.

He turned abruptly, climbed into the cab of the truck, and backed out of the driveway.

Her entire body throbbed with awakening desire.

How could he make her feel like this? she wondered. If he'd persisted, she knew she would have yielded to him—willingly.

Seeing Craig again was probably not a very good idea. She should have told him to contact her lawyer about visitation arrangements with Wendy.

Her lawyer—Peter, her fiancé.

Peter never made her feel like this.

And where *was* he?

Wendy was fussy as Sandra lugged her carrier and diaper bag into Peter's law office on the second floor of an office building downtown.

Why had Wendy seemed so content when Craig cared for her? Sandra remembered that he hadn't used a carrier; he had cradled the baby in his arms—or one arm. Wendy had fit so comfortably in the crux of his elbow.

Sandra decided she would try that—later. Now, she urgently needed to see Peter.

Moira sat at her desk, her blond hair in an elegant twist, her make-up perfect. Sandra was sure that under her desk, her feet were enclosed in fashionable shoes with three inch heels.

Sandra became suddenly conscious of her worn jeans, loose blouse and comfortable sandals. She should have dressed up before coming here. Oh, well, too late now.

"I need to see Peter," she said, resting Wendy's carrier on the edge of Moira's sleek black desk. Wendy screwed her eyes shut and let out a wail.

Moira smiled a tight, professional smile. "I'm afraid he can't be disturbed right now. He's with a client."

"I'll wait," Sandra said, crossed the room, and plopped herself down in one of the luxurious leather armchairs in the waiting room. Wendy continued to cry.

Moira's smile faded. "He's booked solidly all morning, until lunch," she said.

"Then he can take me out to lunch." Although, she thought, if Wendy continued to cry, they might be limited to fast food in the car.

"He may have a lunch meeting..."

"He can tell me that himself." Sandra pulled a bottle from the diaper bag and offered it to Wendy. The baby accepted it and began to drink noisily.

Moira's lips pursed.

"I thought Peter was going to call me last night," Sandra said. "That's the message you were going to give him."

Moira's smile returned. "I *did* give him your message. But he was very busy working on a case until late last night."

Sandra bit her tongue. Who Peter hired to be his secretary was not her business. He hadn't had time to build up a clientele yet, so he might not be able to afford an experienced legal secretary. Maybe he valued the undeniable touch of class Moira gave to the office. And perhaps she did have decent secretarial skills. No good would come from Sandra antagonizing her.

"At my apartment," Moira said, a sly smile playing on her lips. Sandra looked up sharply. "What?"

"I said he was at my apartment, working on a *very* complicated case."

Sandra choked back her response, deciding Peter could explain for himself.

A well-dressed couple entered the office and Moira admitted them immediately to Peter's inner sanctum. Since no one had left since Sandra had arrived, she wondered about the truth of Moira's statement that Peter was with a client. She supposed it was always possible that this couple was meeting with someone already in the office.

When they left a half hour later, the woman crying into an embroidered handkerchief and the man looking stern, Sandra decided Moira was being less than truthful. Especially when a man in blue jeans and a union jacket arrived and was admitted immediately.

Sandra was didn't remember another exit from the office, unless someone climbed out a window and down the fire escape.

But Peter *had* to come out sooner or later. She would wait.

When the union man left, Sandra considered whether to confront Moira, or just to continue waiting. Before she made up her mind, Peter opened the door to his office and stepped out. "Is my eleven o'clock appointment here yet, Moira?" he asked.

"No, he cancelled," she said. Moira hadn't taken any phone calls since Sandra had been there; Peter must have had this time slot free when Sandra had first shown up.

Peter caught sight of her in the waiting room. "Sandra!" he said in surprise. "What are you doing here?"

"I need to talk to you, Peter," she said, keeping her voice even.

"Why didn't you call?"

"I can't seem to get through to you," she said, gritting her teeth.

"You can't expect me to take a call when I'm with a client," he said reasonably. "But you could have left a message."

"I have, and you don't seem to return my phone calls." She glanced at Moira, who busied herself with some files on her desk. "Perhaps you don't always get the messages."

"Well, come in and tell me what's on your mind," he said, stepping back so Sandra could enter his office.

Picking up Wendy in her carrier and the diaper bag, she walked in and settled herself in one of the chairs used for clients.

She hoped he would sit in the chair next to her and take her hand, but he went around his desk and plunked himself down. "Now, tell me what's so important," he said.

Tears pricked at her eyes. Angrily, she blinked them away. "Where were you yesterday?" "You said you'd come with me to pick up the urns."

He looked surprised. "I'm sorry I wasn't able to go to the crematorium with you, but I had a last minute development in a case I'm working on. It needed immediate attention."

"And last night?"

"Moira and I went over the transcripts of a hearing on the case. I may have to move quickly on this." He leaned back in his chair, a smug smile on his face. "If I'm successful, this may be the case that makes my reputation."

"And you had to work at Moira's apartment?"

"Well, yes. As she pointed out, we were working well into the evening so we might as well have been comfortable. So we stopped for dinner and went to her place."

"I thought you were going to call me."

"I asked Moira to call you when it became apparent that I'd have to work all evening," he said, running a hand over his dark blond buzz cut. "She said you sounded like you were doing well and were going to get some rest. She didn't say anything about you wanting me to call."

Sandra closed her eyes and took a deep breath. "My parents and sister were killed—slaughtered is a better word—I've taken over the care of my niece, and you were supposed to come with me to pick up urns with their ashes but then you didn't come. And you thought I might be *doing* well?" She could hear her voice rising shrilly.

"Now, don't get emotional," Peter said uneasily.

"Don't 'get emotional?' I think I have every right to 'get emotional.' And I think any reasonable fiancé would understand that he needed to *be there* for his wife-to-be!" To her dismay, she felt tears streaming down her face.

Wendy stirred and began crying.

"Now, look, you don't want to get the baby all upset now, do you?" he said, reaching over his desk to hand her a box of tissues.

Sandra took one and dabbed at her eyes.

"I'm sorry," Peter said. "Of course you're not 'doing well.' That's not really what I meant. I thought you might like some time to yourself, to sort out your thoughts." He swiveled around in his chair so he was looking out the window. All Sandra could see was the back of his chair. "You have to understand that this is a big case for me. It could mean a lot for our future if I win it. I might start making decent money and then we could get married this summer."

Sandra didn't understand why he needed to be making a 'decent income' before they could get married; they'd manage. But she decided it was not a good time to add another layer to their disagreements.

"I would think everyone around here has heard about my family," she said, forcing her voice to remain even in tone. "And I'd think they would understand if you told them you needed to spend some time with me. I am your fiancée." She glanced at the ring on her finger.

"Not everybody knows we're engaged," he said. "After all, we haven't set a date and made a formal announcement yet, have we? We'll take care of that as soon as this whole thing blows over."

"It will never 'blow over'," she said, feeling a sharp pain in her chest.

"You know what I mean," Peter said. "Look, I have some work to do and a few appointments this afternoon. Suppose I pick you up about five and we can go out to dinner? Think you can find a babysitter for the baby?"

"I don't want to find a babysitter for her. She's been through a lot, too. Let's eat in. You could pick up some Chinese food or something."

Peter looked aghast. "Eat in the same house where they found the bodies?"

She glared at him. "Where do you think *I've* been eating? And sleeping? Besides, they were found in the *garage*." She didn't add that she hadn't been able to go into the garage yet herself.

He recovered quickly. "I just meant it might do you good to get out for a little while—away from the baby."

As if she understood, Wendy squalled. Sandra lifted the carrier to her lap and began to rock it.

"Since you're already here," he said, "how about signing some of the paperwork for your parents' estate? We don't want that to drag on any longer than we can help."

"Should you be handling the estate?" Sandra asked. "Isn't that like a doctor treating his own family?"

"Not the same," he assured her. "After all, your parents came here to make a new will as soon as I set up my practice. They said they *wanted* me to handle it, be one of my first clients. They knew we were planning to get married. You know, they had a surprisingly substantial estate...and life insurance. I had no idea."

"What does the will say?"

"It leaves all their assets evenly to their two daughters. In the event of the death of one, the other inherits all of it."

"So Wendy gets Julia's share?" she asked.

"Not exactly. The will was written before Julia eloped and became pregnant. There's no provision for grandchildren inheriting from your parents."

"But wouldn't she automatically get Julia's share?"

"She would if your parents predeceased her. But all the evidence is that Julia died first and your parents afterward. The police think they were responding to her screams; coming to help. But Julia died before they got there."

Sandra shivered. "So Wendy gets nothing?" She shook her head, that didn't seem fair.

"She'll get social security payments until she's eighteen. And she may inherit from her father. I don't know if he had anything to leave."

Sandra thought of Craig. He had indicated that Wendy would have an inheritance from that side of the family.

"That reminds me," she said. "Monte's brother Craig showed up. He wanted to discuss plans for Wendy."

"Oh? What did he want to do?"

"He wanted his family to take custody of her."

"What did you tell him?"

"I said definitely not. Then he asked for monthly visits. I said I'd think about it."

"I'm sure the court would view their request favorably," he said as his arms flexed above his head as he stretched. "The child has no parents and no grandparents on the maternal side. Paternal grandparents could be considered next of kin."

"This is the family of the man who *killed* her mother! And her grandparents. Besides, it's only a grandfather, and uncles," she said.

"They might be Monte's family, but they didn't kill anyone," Peter pointed out. "They might be in a better position than you to raise a child."

"Peter! I can't believe you'd take their side against me." She felt lightheaded again. She was glad Craig had made her eat breakfast.

He swung his chair around to face her again. "It's not a matter of taking their side. It's a matter of who can do a better job of raising the child. Sandra, raising a child is expensive. Social security won't begin to cover it. You may have to put your education on hold for a while. And you're a single woman with no family. The courts like to see children in a family setting."

"I thought we were getting *married*?" Sandra burst out. "Then I wouldn't be single. And don't we plan to have children? Then Wendy would be in a family. She'd be the oldest child!"

"Of course we're getting married. And we'll have children. I'm just thinking about Wendy's well being. Would she ever really feel a part of our family? After all, our children will be, well, *ours*. I wouldn't want her to feel like a step-child or something. Which she would be."

Sandra stood up, holding Wendy's carrier between herself and Peter. An unnecessary move, since Peter didn't get out of his seat.

"I think I'd better leave before I say something I may regret." She picked up the diaper bag.

"What would you like me to get you from the Chinese place for dinner?" he asked, reaching for a memo pad and a pen.

"Don't bother," she said.

"I thought you wanted me to come over?" He looked perplexed.

"I think you may have been right about me needing time to sort out my thoughts. I'll call you. Just make sure Moira knows to tell you I called."

"Don't forget to sign the paperwork before you go?" He reached for the phone. "It's all ready. I'll ask Moira to get it."

"What is it?"

"A power of attorney, so I can handle everything. Then you don't need to be bothered with any details."

"Thanks, I'll look at it another time." She opened the door and strode into the waiting room.

Moira reached over quickly and pushed a button on her phone. Had she been listening on the intercom? Sandra wouldn't put it past her.

Sandra waited a few days, hoping Peter would call her, but he didn't.

Well, she *had* told him she'd call.

She tried calling his cell phone, but got his voice mail, where a charming female voice invited her to leave a message. She thought she recognized Moira's voice and decided Moira was probably screening the calls. She called his office.

"I'm sorry, Miss Jennings," Moira purred. "But Mr. Regens is on another call. May I take a message?"

"Will he get the message this time?" Sandra asked.

"Why, Miss Jennings. *Of course* he'll get the message." Sandra could just picture the snide look on that beautifully made up face. "Shall I tell him you've finally cooled off enough so he can talk to you without all that *yelling*?"

Sandra felt the muscles in her neck tighten up. "Just ask him to call, please."

"Certainly, and would you like to stop by to sign the paperwork you didn't get a chance to sign when you were here last? Later this morning would be convenient."

A suspicion snuck into Sandra's mind. "Doesn't Peter have to be in court later this morning?" she asked.

"Why, yes, I do believe you're right. But I have the paperwork right here. You wouldn't have to wait or anything."

"Is it the power of attorney paperwork?" Sandra asked.

"Yes. Mr. Regens was very disappointed you left without signing it last time."

"I just bet he was," Sandra said. "I need to talk to him, though, before I sign anything."

Moira made an odd noise that she may have started out as a snicker, but turned into a cough.

When Moira cleared her throat so she could talk again, she said, "Would you like me to set up an appointment? I think I can squeeze you in early next week."

"Just ask Peter to call me." Sandra faced her growing suspicion that Moira was working hard to prevent her from interacting with Peter. As a lawyer or as a fiancé.

She snapped her phone closed and slammed it down on the counter. Then she took off her engagement ring and put it in a drawer. No point in making a permanent decision when she was so upset.

Wendy was starting to whimper.

It was bath time.

She steeled herself for the ordeal. She'd read books about it, and asked the nurse at the pediatrician's office, but she still couldn't manage to bathe her without Wendy crying nonstop and Sandra coming near to tears because of it. It shouldn't be that difficult. What was the matter with her?

As Sandra lifted the sobbing baby from the bathwater, the doorbell rang. She wrapped Wendy in a large fluffy towel and went to answer the door. Craig stood there with his hat in his hand. Sandra hadn't fully remembered the way his scent—the leather and musk—threatened to overwhelm her senses. She felt weak-kneed as soon as she got a good whiff of him.

What she remembered was how rugged and capable he looked. He still did. He smiled and reached for the still-sobbing Wendy, cradling her in his powerful arms and rocking her. The baby calmed down immediately.

She would have to get him to tell her how he did that.

"I hope you're feeling better," he said, his golden eyes mellow beneath his bushy brows.

Sandra felt her heart beat faster. She blushed, confused and said, "Yes, thank you. The headaches are gone."

Craig frowned, patting Wendy's little bottom through the towel. "You look thin. Have you been eating?"

"Of course I've been eating." But as she said it she realized she'd had nothing since some canned soup the previous night.

"And Wendy has been well?"

"Yes, I was just finishing up her bath."

"So I see. Would you like me to dress her? You could probably use a break. Babies can be quite demanding," he said.

She opened the door open wider for him to enter.

"Thank you." He stepped inside. He took Wendy over to the changing table in the corner.

Sandra watched in fascination as Craig took the tiny sleeves of the baby suit and scrunched them up so he could slip them quickly over the tiny hands, all the while smiling at the baby and assuring her that she was the most beautiful child in the world. No tugging and pulling, Wendy smiled back at him instead of fussing the way she did when Sandra tried to dress her.

"Would you like to feed her?" Sandra asked. "I could fix us a quick bite to eat."

"Thank you," he said, taking the bottle she offered. "But I was hoping to take you out to lunch."

"What about the baby?" Sandra hadn't found a babysitter.

"She would come with us, of course."

"Suppose she cried? We'd disturb everyone else in the place."

"Then I would take her outside, where she wouldn't bother anyone," Craig assured her. "Just let me finish feeding her and we can go. If she's just been fed, she may very well sleep the entire time."

Sandra packed the diaper bag. She'd never really thought about the huge bags young mothers toted around with them; she'd always supposed it was a choice, like carrying a large purse instead of just sticking keys and a wallet in a pocket. As she stuffed in several extra diapers, a blanket, two bottles, and cans of premixed formula, she realized it wasn't a choice, it was a necessity.

Craig held Wendy comfortably in one large arm while he rinsed out the now-empty bottle in the sink. He turned to Sandra and smiled. "Ready?" he asked.

"I'd better get a sweater," she said.

"Good idea. It's likely to get chilly." He took a blanket from the playpen and wrapped it around Wendy. "Where would you like to eat?"

"How 'bout that little Italian place on Main Street?" she suggested. "It's casual, and I'm sure they get a lot of families for lunch, so Wendy would fit right in." Later at night, she knew, they would get couples sitting at the small tables with red-checkered table clothes and candles. Peter had taken her there the night he'd proposed to her.

Craig headed toward his truck, which was parked in the driveway next to her car.

"My car has the car seat," she said, realizing that she hadn't grabbed the carrier that strapped into place in the car.

"The truck has a crew cab, with a car seat in the back," he assured her. "Remember, Monte and Julia lived with us. We have everything we need to care for a baby."

"Oh, okay."

Three minutes later, they were out of the driveway and on their way to the restaurant.

At the restaurant, Sandra let Craig order for both of them: calamari, veal marsala, fresh salad, and a bottle of wine. Sitting across the table from hi, she inhaled the wonderful scent of the food and felt her hunger sharpen. They were too busy eating to talk and when she was finished, she sat back and stared at her empty plate in disbelief.

"I've *never* eaten that much before." She wiped her mouth with her napkin. "Especially at lunch."

"You were just hungry," Craig said, smiling as he poured the last of the wine into her glass. "Finish this."

"You finish it. I can't drink any more."

"I'm driving and it would be a shame to waste such good wine." He smiled again, those yellow eyes warming her.

She smiled back and accepted the wine.

"I've come to plead my case again," he said as he placed money, including a generous tip, on the table for the meal. "Have you considered letting us have custody of Wendy?"

Sandra stiffened. "I *have* thought about it and I'm afraid I still would never agree to that."

"I understand." He lifted a sleeping Wendy into his arms. "How about visitations?"

"I suppose we could work something out," she replied reluctantly. "But I'm afraid overnights are out of the question."

Craig shook his shaggy head sadly. "Overnight is the only thing that would work. The drive here takes over three hours. My father and uncle are getting too old to make a trip that long, and we want Wendy to grow up knowing the land she'll inherit and live on as an adult."

Sandra gathered the baby's things and they left the restaurant, stepping out into the afternoon sun, and heading back to his truck.

"Suppose she doesn't *want* to live there as an adult?" she asked.

Craig just looked at her. "We'll worry about that then. But I'd be very surprised it she didn't want to live there."

She shook her head. "Maybe when she's older..."

"This puts me in a difficult situation," he said. "You see, I promised I'd bring her to visit my family. They'll be devastated if I return without her."

"You shouldn't have promised them something so uncertain," she told him, tightening her seatbelt once they were in his truck.

Craig finished strapping Wendy into the car seat and climbed into the driver's seat. He started the engine and drove toward the highway.

"My house is the other way. Where are you going?" she asked, alarmed.

"Just to the look out, so we can talk." He drove up the winding road and pulled into the parking lot overlooking the town. Sandra had been there—once—with Peter. On summer evenings, young people with nowhere else to be alone would park and make out. She remembered she had been relieved when Peter had stopped in the middle a sloppy kiss and said he wanted to wait until they were married.

Craig put his arm around her, drawing her close to him. Her skin tingled at his touch. When his lips touched hers, she returned his kiss hungrily—nothing sloppy about the way he kissed.

He took her hand and his fingers caressed hers. "No ring?" he asked.

"I took it off," she replied.

"It was an engagement ring, wasn't it?" Craig's hand stroked the back of hers.

"Yes, but so much has happened. I can't be sure of my feelings for Peter anymore." She closed her eyes and concentrated on the touch of his fingers on her hand, her wrist, her arm.

"Why don't you come up with Wendy to see the family?" he asked. "You can stay overnight, or as long as you like."

Sandra was leaning on Craig's arm. She felt herself melting into him and she laid her head on his shoulder. "I shouldn't," she said.

"Why not? You could see for yourself that we're quite capable of caring for her."

"I don't doubt that. I've *seen* how good you are with her. That's not the issue," she sighed.

"So what is?" His lips sought hers as his hands ran lightly over her arms, her shoulders, and her neck. "Come, please."

She would probably regret it, she thought, but she said, "I guess I could come for just one night. If you have an extra room for me..." She didn't plan to spend the night in his bed, and didn't want him to assume it.

"It's a big old house," he said, starting the engine. "Plenty of room."

They drove in silence and soon, Sandra dozed off, more relaxed than she had been in weeks.

Sandra woke up gradually. They had stopped.

The truck was parked on a gravel driveway in front of a solid stone garage with a heavy barred door. The forest closed in on all sides, the evening falling quickly under the shadow of the trees.

Sandra sat up and looked around in wonder.

The house, towering four stories at the end of the driveway, was also made of stone. She shivered—up here the temperature noticeably lower.

Craig was nowhere to be seen.

Footsteps approached and it was more than one person. She pulled her sweater closer around her and pretended to be asleep.

"Did you bring the cub?" a voice asked; a wavering old man's voice.

"That I did, Papa," Craig's voice answered.

"So the sister let you take her?"

"In a manner of speaking," Craig replied.

"What do you mean? You didn't *do* anything to her, did you?" The old man's voice rose in alarm.

"Of course not." Craig sounded shocked. "Sandra cares about Wendy just like we do. She didn't want me to bring the baby up here overnight unless she came."

"So you brought the sister, too?"

"Yes, she's asleep in the truck." They were now standing right outside the truck.

"What do you plan to do with her?"

"Handle it just like we did with Julia. That worked," Craig said.

"Until the last time," the old man said and coughed.

"If Monte had handled the last time the way we planned, it would have worked then, too." Craig sounded angry. "I have no intention of letting anything happen to Sandra."

"You sound like you care about this woman."

"I do, Papa." Tenderness crept into Craig's voice. "I'm going to ask her to marry me."

"Never. Look at what happened to Monte. We can't have that kind of tragedy again. If you marry, it must be one of our own kind."

"I love this woman," Craig said firmly. "Even if we were to find a female of our kind—and we haven't had much luck so far, look at how long Uncle Farkas has tried to find someone—I don't know if I could ever love anyone else."

The old man snorted. "You just haven't met many females. You'd fall in love with any you met."

"I don't think so," Craig insisted. "This one's special."

"You'll probably end up like Monte. Killing her, then killing yourself when you realize what you had done." The old man sighed. "We can't have a repeat of that."

"Julia didn't know what she was getting into, Papa. I intend to tell Sandra everything ahead of time."

"And you think that'll work? Monte thought Julia would never have married him if she'd known the truth," the old man said.

"I'm not Monte. I won't trick Sandra. I respect her too much. I'll tell her so she can make up her own mind. If she doesn't want me because of what I am, then I won't marry her." Craig sounded stricken.

The old man sighed again. "One of these months, I'm not going to come back. I'm getting too old. I'm not as strong as I once was. The same goes for Uncle Farkas. I know that and so do you. So someone—you, now that Monte's gone—will have to be responsible for *everything*."

"Yes, I know all that."

"What did she say when you talked about marriage with her?"

"We haven't discussed it yet," Craig admitted.

The old man laughed. "Then what makes you think she wants to marry you? Women don't fall in love with you just because you want them to, you know."

Craig sounded less certain. "She melts into my arms when I kiss her. I can't get enough of being with her. Isn't that *love*?"

"You're so naïve, boy," the old man said. "It's almost dark. Now that you've got her up here, you'll have to make sure she's safe. She may not take kindly to being locked up—Julia didn't. But you'll have to do it, there's no choice."

"I'll explain it to her," Craig said unhappily.

"Monte tried to explain, and Julia didn't believe him. Until she had Wendy. *Then* she believed and left."

One set of footsteps retreated and the truck door next to Sandra opened.

"Sandra." Craig laid a strong hand on her arm. "Wake up. I need to talk to you."

Sandra sat up and opened her eyes to see Craig's golden eyes were clouded with concern. "I owe you an apology. There's something I should have told you. I don't even know how to go about saying this," he said.

"Just say it then," she said. "I'm an adult. I can handle it."

"I hope so." He avoided her eyes. "What I'm about to tell you defines my entire life and the lives of all my family members. It'll define Wendy's life, too. That's why it was so important to bring Wendy up here tonight."

"Does it have anything to do with why your father didn't want Monte to marry Julia?" she asked.

"Most definitely." He paused and looked up at the sky through the trees, to the full moon just beginning to appear over the horizon.

"And why everyone had to die?" Tears blurred her eyes.

"I don't think they had to die," he said, his face twisted. "But it is why they died."

"Tell me," she insisted.

Craig lowered his eyes and examined his right hand, turning it over so the palm was facing downward. "Have you ever heard of a werewolf?" he asked.

"You mean those mythical creatures who are men most of the time, but every full moon, they turn into a wolf and ravish the countryside?" she asked in disbelief.

"Yes. Only they're not as mythical as you might think."

Sandra's eyes followed Craig's to his hand where the hair now seemed thicker, the nails longer and more curved.

"Are you trying to tell me...?" Sandra couldn't bring herself to finish the question.

"Yes. And tonight is a full moon." His voice now sounded deeper, rougher.

"So you're going to...?" She still couldn't put her thoughts into words.

"Turn into a werewolf, yes. And I need to make sure you're safe."

"How're you going to do that?" She looked around in growing concern.

"Put you in the back of the truck and then put the truck in there." He gestured toward the garage. "I'll bar the doors, lock the truck, and give you the key so you can get out when you want to. But don't, not until dawn."

"How do you know I'll be safe in there?" She fought down the panic rising in her chest.

"Julia was safe in there for months...until she took Wendy and left."

"What about Wendy?" Sandra turned toward the back seat. "Will she...?"

"Look at her." Craig gestured toward the baby.

Sandra turned and peered into the back seat and her eyes opened in horror.

Hair was beginning to cover Wendy's hands as she sat in her car seat, and her ears were growing pointed and poking through the thickening layer of dark hair.

"Wendy's a werewolf, too?" she gasped.

"Yes. That's why I couldn't just leave her with you. Not tonight."

"What'll happen to her?"

"She's a werewolf cub. A baby, still, but a werewolf." Craig was no longer standing up straight; his shoulders were hunched over. He stripped off his leather vest and shirt, flinging them onto the seat of the truck. His chest and back were now covered with thick fur.

"What will you do with her?" she asked.

"I can put her in the house. Werewolves are very solicitous of their cubs. No harm will come to her," he said.

"Who'll take care of her?"

"Cubs are perfectly fine left in their beds for a few hours."

"You can't leave her alone!" she said, her concern for Wendy overriding her fear.

"She could stay with you. She's tiny, like any baby animal. She won't hurt you." Craig's teeth were beginning to protrude beyond his lips. "We need to hurry, Sandra."

"Leave her with me, then," she said.

"Get in the back of the truck," he said. "Quickly. I'll get Wendy. I thought you might decide to keep her with you. I put everything in there you'll need for the night; the both of you."

Sandra scrambled out of her seat. She went around to the back of the truck to see the door and the steel grate were both open.

180

Inside, was a bed with blankets, a cooler, a flashlight and dog toys. She climbed inside.

Craig came around with Wendy, but now he walked on all fours and carried the baby firmly grasped by the scruff of her neck in his teeth. He lifted his front paws onto the floor and gently dropped his furry burden.

Wendy's little suit had ripped apart and was hanging from her body. Her body, too, was now completely covered with dark fur.

"I'll lock the back," Craig said, his voice so gravelly Sandra could barely make out his words. "Then I'll pull the truck into the garage and bolt the door."

"What will keep someone—the werewolves—from unbolting the door and coming in?" Sandra asked. She couldn't tear her eyes away from Craig's face. His nose was becoming a muzzle.

"When the transition is complete, werewolves don't think like humans. They're animals. They can't figure out mechanical things like unbolting doors. And when they hear other werewolves in the distance, they—we—won't be able to resist joining them.

"So you won't recognize me?"

"No! If Monte had recognized Julia, do you think he would have killed her, or your parents?" Craig slammed the grate and the door shut, slipped the keys through the window in the back door, and threw open the garage door. He climbed into the cab of the truck. The truck lurched forward and rolled into the garage.

Sandra heard the driver's door slam. When she peered out the back window, the huge dog-like creature paused by the door and looked at her.

"Wait until the sun is up," Craig said, his growling words almost indistinguishable. "Then you can unlock the truck. There's a metal rod in the corner of the garage. You can slip it through the crack in the door and lift the bar when you want to leave."

"Where will you be?"

"I'll be exhausted in the morning. All of us, and we'll have to make our way back here, from wherever we are when the moon goes down." Craig's words were now guttural.

"But you'll come back?" Sandra asked.

"Yes. I'll come as soon as I can. I have a question I need to ask you—when I return."

181

Sandra thought she knew what the question would be.

Craig licked his lips and made a visible effort to make his words understandable. "It will not surprise me if the answer is 'no', and I'll blame only myself if it is."

On all fours, he trotted out of the garage. The heavy door slammed shut and Sandra heard the bar fall into place.

She reached out and touched the squirming furry ball that lay on the floor. Wendy rolled over on her back, her long tongue lolling over her sharp baby teeth. Her paws waved in the air, inviting Sandra to rub her tummy. Her golden eyes sparkled in the fading light. She looked like a playful puppy.

Sandra gathered the little creature in her arms.

A mournful howl sounded in the distance and a chorus responded from right outside the garage, making her jump. Sandra listened as they headed off toward the distant sound, answering once more as they loped through the forest.

The full moon rose until its light streamed through a high window in the wall of the garage.

Holding Wendy, Sandra settled down on the bunk. She knew she wouldn't sleep tonight, and she could do nothing but wait for dawn.

The howls traveled further back into the hills, leaving her in silence.

She knew what her answer to Craig's question would be. She would have to learn a new way of life, but she didn't feel like she would be leaving behind anything of value. It would be best for Wendy. And she knew she would always love Craig, whatever he was.

LEADER OF THE PACK

TOMMY RYAN VII W/ MARK RIVETT

Jim ran through the snow, feeling its cold softness against his paws. To any casual observer, he would have appeared to be an ordinary wolf, running across the Alaskan tundra. Perhaps the fact that he was a lone wolf—not traveling in a pack—might have tipped someone off to him being unusual, but not to his true nature. His reddish-brown fur may also have seemed out of place in such a starkly white place, but no one would suspect what he truly was.

Jim was a werewolf: he was part man and part beast, and he was able to change between five different forms. There was the man form and the wolf form, which are just what they sound like, but there were also three hybrid forms in between. There was the manwolf form, an extremely large and hairy brute that's usually mistaken for an exceptionally muscular man by the casual observer. There was also the great wolf form, a wolf-like monster out of the darkest depths of human nightmares. It was the huge and hulking legend upon which literature and video games were based. Finally, there was the true werewolf form, which was a giant clawed and furry beast with a muscle bound man-shaped body that has the head of a wolf.

Jim was once a man, until he was bitten by a werewolf. He discovered soon after that the legends were true: he became a werewolf himself.

Unlike most werewolves, however, Jim didn't give himself over to the fury and the bloodlust of being both man and beast. He made it his duty—a duty he had carried over from his life as a human—to hunt down other werewolves. His mentor, Grif, taught him about controlling the bloodthirsty urges of his kind. It wasn't always easy, but he had a reason—a someone—worth fighting for.

Jim was in Alaska because he had followed recent tales of entire wolf packs being slaughtered there. According to the reports, signs pointed largely to other wolves having done the killing. It looked to the untrained human eye that there was some sort of territory war between wolf packs, but he knew better. He recognized the scenes of carnage: wolves ripped in half, claw marks across their faces, one wolf with a hole punched clear through its torso...and Jim knew there was a werewolf at work in Alaska.

Finding and killing this werewolf was now his mission.

* * *

Jim's true wolf form helped him to stay warm and also to keep a low profile. He could move much faster in his great wolf form, but it would be obvious to anyone who saw him that he was more than just a wolf. Over four and a half feet at the shoulder, and considerably longer than any wolf on record, he would immediately attract unwanted attention. Even in the nearly deserted wilderness of northern Alaska, it was unwise to take chances.

Despite his best efforts, however, he had attracted the attention of someone...or rather, something—something that had no trouble noticing the signs and smells of something so unorthodox. Some of the remaining packs of wolves had come across their slaughtered brethren, and had noticed an odd scent. Though Jim's scent in wolf form was different than it was in any other form, it was still not the same as a regular wolf. Though he was trying to help the wolf packs, the ones that scented him now didn't know that. They only knew that he smelled like the creature that had been killing wolves, and that he was a threat to their survival. Jim didn't know it yet, but he was under attack.

As he passed by a large snowdrift, he saw motion in the corner of his eye. Before he could react, he felt the bulk of a full grown male wolf slam into his side. An instant later, there was a shock of pain as teeth bit into his leg. He quickly swung his body around and knocked the other wolf to the ice-covered ground. Almost immediately, his jaws were at the throat of his attacker, as he offered his opponent a chance to submit. The wolf didn't move, but Jim's mercy would not be repaid with kindness. He felt another bite to his hind legs as a second wolf joined the fray and he moved just in time to avoid a third wolf that was leaping for his throat.

Realizing that he was quickly becoming outnumbered and outmatched, he realized he had no choice but to risk changing forms.

Going on the defensive while his attackers looked for an opportunity to strike, he shifted into his great wolf form. His body lengthened, and he grew taller at the shoulder, his jaw became wider and his chest more massive. The other wolves seemed frightened as this change came over him, and temporarily stopped their attack.

He was now nearly twice the size of any of them now, and his supernatural werewolf constitution was already closing his wounds. He snarled at them, a deep and guttural sound, hoping that he might scare off these wolves without having to hurt them. But their survival instincts regarded him as a threat and they came at him again, answering his challenge.

The center wolf leapt at him, while the other two rushed around to flank him. Jim didn't want to hurt them, but he knew that if he bit them and they survived, he would make more like himself. He didn't want to make more werewolves. He stepped to his right, tripping one of the charging wolves, and clamped his massive jaws down on the neck of the airborne wolf.

The power of the great wolf's bite was tremendous. Jim felt his teeth drive through fur, muscle, and bone as the severed head of the wolf he was fighting fell to the ground. The snow was stained red as a river of blood gushed from the headless body.

He turned to face the wolf he had tripped, feeling a new shock of pain as the wolf he had been forced to ignore clamped down on his hind leg. With a powerful shake, he felt the jaws loosen on his leg. He then bounded on top of the other wolf that was now rising to its feet again. He landed on top of it as it was getting up and pushed its body down into the snow. Its legs were completely submerged in the soft powder of a drift and he knew it would take a moment to climb out. It was the moment he needed and he turned to face the wolf that had bitten his hind leg.

Fearless, the wolf charged him, teeth bared in a growl. It was getting ready to leap at him, but Jim was faster. He quickly moved forward and caught the wolf as it was bending to leap. He clamped his giant maw down around the nose and head of the animal. He felt his right canine tooth smash through the left eye as his powerful jaws crushed part of the skull of his attacker. With half its head mangled, the lifeless wolf fell to the ground, oozing blood. Jim heard the howls of the wolf that was stuck in the deep snow, and he turned to give it as merciful death as possible.

He stopped short when he saw six more wolves coming to join the howling one. The rest of the pack had been nearby, and they had heard the cries of their pack mate. Jim knew that even with the increased size and strength of his great wolf form, he would quickly be overwhelmed by so many attackers. He began to change into his true werewolf form. His body lengthened more and great paws became large clawed hands. His hind legs became bipedal and he stood erect as a giant beast of nightmares and legend. The true werewolf form was half man and half wolf, and it was all killing machine.

As he readied for the assault of the wolf pack, he felt a twinge of remorse for what he was about to do. He had come to Alaska to prevent wolves from being ripped apart by one of his kind, and now he would have to do the very same thing to avoid his own death. But he knew this wasn't his fault.

These wolves would have left him alone if there wasn't another werewolf hunting and slaughtering them.

As the first of the wolves grew closer, Jim was glad of not only his immense strength, but also the speed and reflexes granted by his werewolf form. He reached out and grabbed two wolves by the heads, something no normal man would be quick enough to do. He felt the claws of his left hand tearing through the ears of the one it gripped, while the middle claw of his right had gone right through the animal's left eye. He picked them up and crushed their skulls together with his supernatural musculature. The skulls crunched and cracked against one another, and now only five wolves remained. He threw the bodies aside and a spout of blood sprayed from the eye of the wolf on his right as his middle claw slid free of the socket.

Another wolf leapt at him, and he brought the claws of his left hand together into a point. He used the momentum of the animal's leap coupled with the speed of his arm to drive his claws right through the wolf's chest, impaling it. He buried his arm deep into the chest, nearly to the elbow, and then ripped his arm back out of the hole he had made. Blood and entrails spilled out of the gaping cavity in the animal's midsection, and it fell to the ground, staining the snow an even darker red.

The four remaining wolves, which included the once buried but now freed wolf that had howled for its mates, seemed to realize that trying to engage him one or even two at a time was a lost cause. They began to circle him, starting far away but moving closer with every step. Jim knew he could probably jump and grab one of them, but that would leave him open to the other three. Even with his great strength and fast healing, he would be taking a risk by leaving an opening for them.

Jim crouched down low and twisted his torso as much as possible. He extended his claws as far as he could, and prepared for the attack. As he suspected, all four wolves pounced at once, thinking that he was cowering from them and that their time to strike was now.

He stood up and spun with his arms extended and his claws flayed out in front of him. His claws caught all four wolves at different points during his rotation as he spun in place. One wolf was hit below the jaw and yelped with pain. Another was raked across the eyes and blinded. A third took a good gash to the chest, and the last was probably luckiest—receiving a slash to the throat that sprayed crimson across the white of the Alaskan tundra. The wolves with the injuries to their chest and jaw ran off. He let them go for only a bite would cause them to turn into werewolves.

Only the blinded wolf remained. It was stumbling and sniffing, trying to figure out where to go. All Jim could do was give it a quick death. Filled with rage that he was forced to kill so many of the animals he had come to protect, he picked up the animal by its torso and held it tight against his body with his arm. He then reached his free hand behind its head, dug his claws into the base of its skull, and tore the head off—ripping the beast in two. It would feel no more pain, and Jim's violent outburst was somewhat cathartic for him. All the same, he felt hot tears forming on the edge of his eyes. He would rather kill men.

He continued on his way in great wolf form and decided it was time for speed. Trying to blend in as a wolf hadn't done him much good, so he decided to go as fast as possible to cover as much ground as he could in the shortest amount of time.

He knew he was getting closer to the area where most of the wolves had been killed. His enhanced wolf senses allowed him to scent blood in the air, and he began to follow the scent. Then he felt a sting in his neck, and everything went black.

* * *

When Jim awoke, he found himself in a cage inside a cave, and his head was killing him. He despised cages, and he became enraged upon the realization that he was trapped in one. How had he gotten there? He was still in great wolf form, and the cage he was in was a bit small for him.

Artificial lighting illuminated his surroundings. The cave, like everything else in this part of Alaska, was stark and white. There was some computer equipment in front of him. On the other side of it, he heard voices.

"I'm telling you, that's no ordinary wolf! It's much too large. It could be a werewolf in some in-between form," a man's voice sounded insistent.

"Don't be a fool, Jacques." A woman was speaking now. "There are large wolves everywhere in Alaska. Besides, when we killed that werewolf in Quebec, it turned into a man after it died. This one didn't change its form. We may have just killed the largest wolf on record! It's a shame you wasted a poison-tipped silver dart to kill such a specimen. They aren't easy to manufacture, you know."

"It would've been worth it if this was our prey, Elena. Alas, you may be right. We could be famous for a find like this, but we can't explain how and why we killed it or what we were doing here. We'll have to burn the body. Where is that information on the cave? Perhaps we should continue our search there."

Jim had heard enough. On the one hand, these two were apparently after the same thing he was. On the other, they had shot him with poison and put him in a cage. The poison explained the headache. Fortunately, they thought they had killed him. He had the advantage of surprise. He was already healing away the effects of the poison, and his head was clearing. He began to change form into the true werewolf. As his size expanded, his bulk began to push against the edges of the cage.

"Jacques," the woman's voice inquired, "are you quite certain it's dead? I thought I just heard something."

"Of course it's dead! There was easily enough poison in that dart to kill a werewolf, how could this wolf not be..." Jacques paused. He heard the rattle of the cage that held Jim as it strained to hold his expanding bulk. "That cage...is only good for transport. If that thing wasn't killed...if it was only near to death..."

"What if it stays in its form while only unconscious? What if we've just brought the werewolf into our base..?" Elena asked.

"You'd better grab your..." Jacques next thought was cut off by the sound of tearing metal. The thin cage was rent apart by the size and fury of Jim in his true werewolf form. A flash of reddish brown fur came into view as he leapt over the computer equipment. He saw a slender woman and a man about his size scrambling to grab weaponry.

Jim landed next to the man, who was trying to pull a silver blade from a scabbard on his hip. Jim plunged both of his clawed hands into the man's flesh. One went into Jacques' chest, the other through his throat. Jacques' grip on the hilt of his blade, still in its sheath, went limp. Blood came streaming out of the holes where Jim's claws had been as he pulled them free and then turned to face the woman.

Her hands shook with terror as she struggled to aim a gun at the ferocious beast towering in front of her. Jim recognized it as a dart-firing gun...probably the same gun that had knocked him out and nearly killed him.

"Don't m...make me h...h...hurt you," she said, the shake in her hands spreading to her voice.

"What you said," Jim retorted in a bestial voice that was gravelly and as deep as the bottom of the ocean. It was not a human voice, but the words were understandable. In case she didn't understand what he meant, he explained, "Don't make *me* hurt *you.*"

She kept the dart gun trained on him as she shook with fear. Jim got the impression that she was trying to find the courage to pull the trigger. With preternatural speed, he swung a clawed fist forward and knocked the gun out of her hand; she fell to her knees, sobbing.

"I'm not the werewolf you're looking for," Jim told her. "I seek what you seek, but you're not ready to fight it." As he spoke, he began to transform into the manwolf. He was soon very hairy and large, but his face was more flat and human, and his voice was gruff, but not so otherworldly.

"I heard you speak of a cave. Tell me where to find this cave, and I'll let you leave with your life." His change in appearance and voice seemed to have a bit of a calming effect on her.

"You really don't know? Then maybe you're not really the one...there's a cave about three kilometers north of here. We found traces of blood outside it. We weren't able to get a sample because this massive polar bear came and chased us off before we could investigate further. But we noticed that the polar bear had a claw mark on its face. We thought maybe there had been a fight between the polar bear and the werewolf. Maybe the werewolf was surprised by the strength and ferocity of the bear. But you werewolves heal fast, don't you? I bet he'll come back and with a plan this time. Here, I can show you where it is..." She went to one of the computers and keyed up a map of the area.

He studied it quickly and said, "I'll find this cave and I'll handle the werewolf. You can go, but leave your equipment." He saw her glance to the mouth of the cave where there were two snowmobiles parked. "You can take one of the snowmobiles, but I'll need the other one."

"Can I come with you?" she asked.

"No."

"But..."

Jim let out a fierce growl, tapping into the wolf nature of his manwolf form. She didn't have to be told twice. Elena ran to the snowmobile and drove off into the cold.

* * *

Jim hadn't planned to be in human form for very much on his trip. He had wanted to keep a low profile, and he couldn't bring his silver weapons with him on the plane without arousing suspicion. Plus, he was able to travel light and his senses were heightened in wolf form. Elena and Jacques, on the other hand, were pretty well equipped despite their apparent ineptitude. And now that he knew where he was going, he didn't really need to be in wolf form for tracking purposes.

He was able to fit into Jacques' tundra clothing in his human form, and he took the silver blade that Jacques had failed to use against him. It was a straight blade, about a foot in length with a short hilt. He also found a revolver with six silver bullets and some rations. He tore into the rations—he was starving—and stuffed the rest in a backpack with a few bottles of water. They had a small refrigerator hooked to a generator that in this place was actually being used to keep things warm...or at least warmer than 'room' temperature which was below freezing. He slung the backpack over his shoulders and climbed onto the remaining snowmobile.

He hadn't been on many snowmobiles in his life, and he enjoyed the feeling of gliding over the snow, the bitter cold wind whipping his face. He headed north, thinking of what he would do next. If this werewolf was in fact headed back to the polar bear, he hoped he could catch it while in battle with the bear, or sneak in and wait for it. The polar bear might have something to say about that, though, and Jim didn't like the idea of harming such a creature. Still, if he didn't stop the werewolf, it would continue killing.

After a quick trip through the Alaskan wilderness, he saw the cave up ahead that he was confident was the one on the map. He cut the engine of the snowmobile, hid it below the low-hanging branches of a snow-covered tree, and proceeded on foot.

The mouth of the cave faced south and he approached it from the western flank. Like Jacques and Elena's cave, it was pure white, making it hard to tell if it was rock or just cut out of snow. In the Alaskan winter—as it was now—it stayed cold enough that nothing would melt, so snow and ice could be used for habitation. As he approached the cave, he thought he heard the sound of snoring coming from its depths. The polar bear was asleep.

Jim decided to use the whiteness of everything to his advantage. The clothing he wore was a little loose in human form, but it was stretchy enough to be just extremely tight in manwolf form, and shouldn't tear. He could sustain the cold temperature better in manwolf form, so he changed forms, found a good place to hide, and covered himself in the snow. Then he waited.

A few hours passed quietly, until he heard the soft crunch of an animal walking on the frozen snow. The form of a large, white wolf drew near. Jim's vision was somewhat obscured by the snow covering him, but he could still tell it was no ordinary wolf...it was a werewolf in its great wolf form. As it came nearer, his nose confirmed his suspicion: this was the prey he was seeking.

As the white wolf approached the cave, he saw its paws begin to lengthen and form into legs and arms as it lifted itself upright into its true werewolf form. He had left the revolver found in the cave in his backpack, lest the snow get it wet and cause it to misfire. He had no choice but get up close and personal. As soon as the white wolf was past him, Jim edged the silver blade out of its sheath. It was about halfway out when the enormous white werewolf stopped in its tracks and began scenting the air. Jim's presence had been discovered, but his location wasn't compromised yet. He threw caution to the wind and dove forward out of the snow with the blade before him.

The white werewolf stepped back, but Jim still caught it in the left thigh with the silver blade. Blood began to seep out of the laceration in the werewolf's leg. It howled and swung a left back-hand at Jim, catching him on the chin and sending him sprawling. The blade flew from his hand and landed out of reach.

Jim, still in manwolf form, reached out for the blade, but the werewolf was too quick for him: it leapt on top of the flat edge of the silver blade and let out a roar. Jim realized it was time to pit strength against strength. Jacques' white snow suit ripped as he transformed to his true werewolf form and swung his left claw into the face of the white werewolf.

The werewolf's coat of fur was stained for the second time with its own blood and it howled in fury.

Jim used the werewolf's temporary disorientation caused by the blood in its face to regain his feet. He then drove a shoulder into it and knocked it back. Another swipe of Jim's claws caused blood to seep from the right shoulder of his opponent. Jim stepped forward to close in for the kill...and howled in pain as he pierced his right foot on the silver blade that lay in the snow. He fell to the ground in agony.

Within moments, the white werewolf was on him, kicking and punching and clawing. The claw strikes tore vicious red slashes through his flesh and fur, and they didn't heal right away. The claws and teeth of other werewolves were the only thing other than silver that a werewolf could not fully regenerate from and would leave scars. The wounds were also slower to heal.

With his right foot still throbbing with pain, Jim couldn't regain his balance to fight back. The white werewolf brought its claws to a point to impale him and finish him off. As the white werewolf swung its claws forward, it was knocked away from Jim by an enormous flash of white. The polar bear had been aroused by the battle and had charged the enemy that had scarred its face.

What Jim saw next was an awesome sight. The massive white werewolf and the giant polar bear traded powerful blows, drawing blood from each other at an alarming pace. Red stained the snowy ground as well as the white fur of the two combatants. There was no strategy, only savagery. Jim quickly realized, however, that the polar bear was losing. The werewolf could heal from the bear's claw slashes, and the bear was losing too much blood. Its wounds from the previous fight weren't fully healed and blood oozed in red streams down its muzzle.

Jim tried to get to his feet, only to realize that his foot wasn't ready to support his weight. He fumbled in the snow for the blade, but he realized he had been kicked too far by the white werewolf's attack on him and the blade was still buried somewhere in the snow. Jim roared in despair and raised his arms above his head...where he felt something soft. He grasped a hold of the softness and found himself holding the backpack he had brought with him, the gun inside it!

Not wanting to draw attention to himself by changing form, he concentrated on only changing his hands to human form. It was hard to focus with the pain, but he managed to do it. He got the pack open and drew out the revolver. It was already loaded. He cocked the hammer, aimed, and pulled the trigger two times in rapid succession.

Two shots rang out and the white werewolf fell to the snow. Blood was now streaming from a hole in the side of its head. Jim and the polar bear both stared as the white werewolf uttered two words in a gravelly ethereal voice that was much like Jim's in true werewolf form.

"Alpha wolf," was all it said.

Jim now watched as the werewolf changed not into a human as he might have expected, but into *canis lupus*, a true wolf. Apparently, this had been a normal wolf before it was bitten. Jim realized that it was just trying to establish its dominance against other wolf packs. It had learned how to use its new abilities, but didn't truly understand that it wasn't a wolf anymore.

The polar bear now turned its attention to Jim and roared at him. He just stared back at it. The bear lumbered to within an inch of Jim's face and growled again. He looked it right in the eye, trying to tell the bear without words that he meant it no harm. It seemed to have a moment of recognition and was turning away, when suddenly it reached its left front paw to its neck before falling over onto its side. The polar bear's blue eyes were still open as it lay dead in the snow.

"I thought it was…going to attack you," Elena said. She stood at the mouth of the cave, holding the dart gun. Jim realized she must've returned to her base after he left to retrieve the weapon, then she must have followed him.

"I came back to…help you."

"That bear saved my life," Jim said in his werewolf voice. "And now you've just killed it in cold blood."

"But…but…"

"You shouldn't have come here." Jim realized his foot was feeling good enough for a good leap. In a flash of speed, he dove at Elena. All his anger at the slaughter of the wolves, the polar bear's death, and being captured and trapped in a cage, erupted as he landed on her. He gave into the fury and the bloodlust filling him, and began clawing and tearing at her flesh, spraying blood in all directions. He kept clawing through her skin and organs until there was nothing but a bloody mess staining the ice.

Jim stood up and brushed himself off. It was a long way back to the nearest city, where he had left his belongings in the cabin he had rented. His foot was still too injured to run all that way, and Jacques clothes were now hanging off him in a tattered mess. He once again focused on making his hands human, then went to

Elena's severed hands, picked them up, peeled off her gloves, and dropped the hands to the snow.

He went back to his hidden snowmobile and started the engine.

A gloved werewolf named Jim howled at the moon and sped off into the night.

DEATH IS WALKING

TERRY ALEXANDER

The heavy rain fell in sheets, driven by a fierce westerly wind. Four drenched men huddled around a struggling fire on the wind free side of a huge oak. Water streamed from the cloaks they wore to protect them from the downpour and the night's chill. Lightning arched across the sky, briefly illuminating the hillside as a sharp clap of thunder spooked the horses tied to the picket line.

"Do you think the beast will pass this way?" Connor asked, shivering despite his heavy garb. A short balding man, he owned a popular mead house in the nearby village.

"Perhaps, it's as likely to come by this path as any other." Ivan replied, a tall heavy muscled man from the wild northlands. He had wandered into the village three days ago, intent on drinking and whoring away all his coins. Bitter conflicts and boundary disputes had given him a chance to prosper, selling his sword to the highest bidder.

He wiped the rain from his brow. His long dark hair lay limp upon his head, several drops of moisture trapped within his thick black beard. A bitter gust of wind forced him to wrap his bear skin cloak around him.

Otto, the village blacksmith, a short squatty man with bulging arms, threw another rain-soaked log on the weak flames. He rarely spoke, preferring the company of horses to people.

Luther was the son of a village elder, and the final member of their group. He leaned against the tree, his arms wrapped around his torso for warmth. His fine clothes and lightweight cloak did little to protect him from the elements, being better suited for evenings at the local tavern and bargaining with whores.

"It will come this way." Otto's voice was coarse and heavy. "I know it." He placed a hand over his heart. "Death is walking."

"You brainless lout!" Luther snapped as he jumped to his feet. "You're the village blacksmith, a common laborer. What do you know of worldly things? You're here for the promise of gold from my father's purse if we kill that thing."

"Aye, that's my reason." Ivan moved closer to the fire and glanced at Luther. "And why are you here, young sir? Did your father force you to accompany us?"

Luther stared at the black-haired giant, his right eye twitching nervously. "I should kill you for that mercenary." His hand dropped to the short dagger at his waist.

"Mayhap, you will reconsider this brass act." Ivan's hand closed on his sword hilt. "And live to see the sunrise."

"Stop this," Connor said and pushed between the two men. "We must not fight among ourselves."

Ivan stared at Connor, his eyes, emotionless. "Well said, merchant. You are correct." His hand came away empty. "You're a wise man, perhaps you could tell me more about this animal we seek to kill."

A pained expression swept over Connor's face as he stared into the weak flames. "The attacks began months ago. Shepherd's found dead sheep in the grasslands. They stayed to guard the flock and the attacks stopped for a short time, but then the attacks began again and the shepherd's were slaughtered as well." His words faltered. He squeezed his eyes together and swallowed. "Several of the smaller children were devoured whole, leaving only scattered bits of skin and gnawed bones. One...one was my daughter."

"I'm sorry, I didn't mean to bring up such painful memories," Ivan said as he grasped Connor's shoulder.

"You didn't know. This thing has a pattern in its attacks, an intelligence of where and when to strike, attacking only when it has the advantage. The villagers are all afraid. They hide in their hovels when the beast roams, praying for the returning sun."

"That sound's like good judgment," Ivan agreed. "It's always best to fort up when facing an attack."

"Has it worked? Has it accomplished anything?" Luther asked and moved closer to the fire.

Connor's downcast eyes focused on the drops of rain splashing the soaked ground. "The last victim was snatched from his bed while he slept. The elders have men guarding every trail into the village. It was an effort to force the villagers out this night. Each of them is fearful of becoming the next victim." He paused to draw in a deep breath. "The last one, a small boy, was the worst of all. All that was found of him were a few scraps of bone and his severed head."

"A bear did it?" Ivan held up his bear cloak. "A bear such as this?"

"We thought so at first, but we've never seen tracks such as these before." Connor shook his head. "It is no bear. Several warriors have been hired to aid us in killing this animal."

"Some are warriors, some are merely braggarts." Ivan tilted his head to watch the lightning cross the cloud laden sky. "I assure you, sir, should the man-eater use this trail, it will die by my sword. It will not enter the village this night."

Connor sat on a log near the fire, holding his hands near the flames. He stared into the darkness, his face lined with pain and loss.

"It will be here at the gray time," Otto added as he tossed a small stick into the fire. "Before first light it will come. Death is walking."

"Curse you for an imbecile and a damned fool," Luther snapped and hopped to his feet. "Are you completely ignorant? It enters the village at night and leaves in the early morning hours."

Otto turned his head toward Luther. He remained silent, his huge paw like hand clutching his large sledge hammer. "Death is walking," he repeated.

"Tell me, smith, how do you know these things?" Ivan asked as he squatted on his haunches to meet Otto's eyes.

"I feel it." His dark eyes locked with the mercenaries. "Keep your sword at hand; we will have need of it by morning."

The night passed slowly, conversation having ended hours ago. Each man took his turn at watch, lost in their thoughts, pondering their future, and counting the gold coins they would receive once the job was finished.

Gradually, the rain turned to a weak drizzle and a pale full moon glowed through the thin clouds. The horizon grew lighter in the eastern sky, a pink glow heralding the coming of the sun.

Connor woke; he slowly gained his feet, glancing toward Ivan. "It didn't come," he muttered barely above a whisper, a hint of disappointment coloring his voice. "It didn't come this way. I hope the others had better luck." He stepped around the snoring Luther.

"So it appears." Ivan nodded. He glanced at Connor who was scurrying down the hillside. "Where are you going?"

"There are some things a man prefers to do in private," Connor replied as his hands worked at the drawstring on his pants.

"Is it wise to wander off on your own? Better to go nearer the fire," Ivan said.

"And risk waking Luther?" Connor laughed. "Don't worry. I'll return shortly." He ducked into a stand of blighted trees near the path.

Ivan glanced down at the slumbering man. "Small help he will be should the creature come this way."

"It comes. Even now it draws near." Otto grasped the smooth handle of his large hammer, swinging the weight to his shoulder.

"Connor!" The flesh prickled between Ivan's shoulders as he called out. "Hurry up and get back here!" A stray gust of wind carried a foul loathsome odor through the clearing.

The small trees began to shake violently as a blood-chilling scream echoed through the forest.

"No, it can't be. Not here." Connor ran to the path, his hands holding his pants around his waist.

A blood-splattered nightmare burst from the foliage. It stood on two legs and thick coarse black hair covered the muscular body from head to toe. The large, wolf-shaped head tilted to sniff the air. Its claw-tipped hand wrapped around the ankle of its latest victim, dragging the bloodless cadaver over the rocky, uneven ground.

"A wereling," Ivan mumbled. He remembered the tales of the creatures from his homeland. "Run, Connor, run now!"

The clawed hand released the foot, and it thudded to the ground. The beast squatted. The thick thigh and calf muscles knotted, and it leapt forward. Ivan stood transfixed; a legend from his childhood stood before him in the flesh. Fear began to burn in the pit of his stomach.

The monster landed behind Connor. Its claws slashed at the merchant's back. They punctured the flesh along the backbone at the shoulder and a crimson mist filled the air. The talons tore through flesh and muscle with a quick movement that cut the length of the spine.

An unearthly scream tore from Connor's lips, and his face drained dead white. His hands became fists in the grass as he struggled to endure the agony. "Help me!" he screamed, "Please help me!"

Ivan stood in shocked silence. The unearthly image and sheer brutality of the creature's attack stunned him to immobility.

Its huge open mouth displayed two rows of huge sharp canines and when the jaws clenched on Connor's head, blood flowed around the huge teeth, dripping to the earth. The merchant's skull crushed audibly under the pressure, as the body jerked and quivered briefly before becoming still. A shiver of dread raced down Ivan's spine.

The ruckus woke the sleeping Luther. He rose slowly and stretched, oblivious to the turmoil down below the hillside. "What are you staring at?" he asked and turned leisurely. But then his eyes widened, his face turning ashen. A panicked breath entered his lungs. "What is that?" he shouted. "It's a devil!" He jumped to his feet ready to run for his life.

Luther's feet tangled in his cloak and he fell to the uneven ground, rolling down the hillside. He came to rest beside Connor's body; the merchant's blood had drenched his tunic and cloak. "Save me," Luther screamed. "Save me, mercenary."

The aberration squatted near Connor, a long lolling tongue lapping at the bright scarlet pooling in the open wounds. At his shout, the yellow feral eyes fastened on Luther. Its nostrils flared, as the new scent washed over the elongated snout.

"Please, don't kill me," Luther begged. "Don't kill me. No!"

The creature rose, standing on two legs. A thick line of saliva trailed from the large open mouth to drip on Luther's face. Sharp claws tore into the pompous man's shoulder.

Luther's scream broke the trance holding Ivan and he lifted his bow from the ground, notching an arrow. The smith, standing at his side, let loose a wild shout and charged the beast with a berserker's fury.

Otto's speed contradicted his squatty muscular build. In seconds, he attacked as well. His thick back muscles corded, he swung the huge hammer with all his strength. A sickening thud rewarded his efforts as the massive iron head smashed into the broad hairy forehead, the beast collapsing in a heap.

"It's over," Otto said and turned away. "It's finished." The hillside grew silent and a lone cricket chirped in the undergrowth.

The sound of crunching and grinding bones broke the silence. Otto stopped walking and his head swiveled slowly. He watched awestruck, as the face of the beast knitted and healed, leaving only a few stray drops of blood clinging to the fur. The corruption of human and animal slowly gained its feet. Large canines gritted together and a low growl died in the creature's throat as two arrows thudded into its blood-splattered chest.

"Otto, move, run!" Ivan shouted, notching another arrow. "Get away from it!"

The beast's wolf-like head lifted toward the heavens and loosed a primal roar of pain and agony that echoed from the forest. The clawed hands raked the arrows from its body, leaving bloody holes that scabbed over and healed.

"Run, Otto," Ivan shouted, loosing a third arrow.

Luther's hands grasped at the smith's legs as the hammer dropped from the smith's hand. His arms wrapped around the injured man, dragging Luther from the slaughter.

"Otto, forget him. He's done for!" Ivan yelled and notched his last arrow. "Just run, get out of there!"

Despite his severe wounds, Luther tore away from Otto's grip, and forced himself to his feet as a maniacal laugh burst from his lips. He stood on stiff legs and his arms reached out to embrace the beast like an old friend. The creature showed a moment's bafflement when Luther's arms wrapped around it, but it quickly overcame its hesitation and the large teeth ripped into the dandy's throat in a spray of blood.

Otto ran to Ivan's side. They stared down at the bizarre embrace between killer and victim. Luther's laughter gradually dwindled to a chuckle and died with his last breath. Fear gnawed at Ivan and he looked to the far horizon, watching the first rays of sunlight break through the gloom.

Yellow eyes locked on the pair and a low growl came from its throat. The muscles bunched together, and the released energy carried it up the hill in three quick bounds. Muscled arms knocked the pair to the ground like straw in a whirlwind. The claws ripped into the fleshy portion of Otto's neck, catching on the bones. Gritting his teeth, the smith struck the beast's elongated jaw three tremendous blows as the beast's teeth tore the skin along the back of his right hand. While the blows would have broken the jaw and neck of a normal man, they only served to further enrage the creature.

Razor sharp claw's shredded Otto's tunic, cutting into the corded flesh along his ribs and stomach. His intestines slipped through the wounds and dangled from his belly. The clawed feet raked at his legs, tearing through the animal hide pants and shredding the muscles and tendons beneath.

"May the gods help me!" Blood frothed Otto's lips as he screamed.

Ivan gained his feet, a wave of dizziness leaving him dazed and confused. He blinked several times, and after he yanked his sword from his side scabbard, he attacked. The blade sank into the fur-covered back, the metal tip protruding from the thick chest.

"Die, damn you. Why won't you die?" Ivan drove the sword through thick hide, muscle and bone over and over, each wound scabbing over and healing in moments.

The beast threw Otto to the ground and a low moan came from the smith's lips. The creature whirled to face Ivan just as the mercenary drove his sword forward, intent on skewering the monster. Malformed hands closed on the weapon's edge, slicing the flesh to the bone. Hot fetid breath fanned Ivan's face as he stared at the particles of meat lodged in the large teeth. Bile burned his throat and nose.

Otto wrapped his arms around a fur-covered leg as the claws slashed at his exposed scalp, flaying the skin away from the skull. The smith squeezed the leg tighter.

Ivan renewed his attack, hacking at the hairy arms and legs. The tactic worked, and for a few seconds, the injured limb hung useless, allowing Ivan to slash a separate area before the injury healed.

Otto screamed in agony as the claws sank into his back. The beast yanked him high over its head and threw him as though he were weightless, striking Ivan in the chest. The pair landed in a heap near the small campfire.

As they fought, the first rays of the new sun touched the edge of the hillside, burning away the remainder of the night. Ivan rolled Otto's heavy body from him and slowly gained his feet, gasping for air. The sword felt heavy in his hands, his muscles quivered under the strain of its weight. He braced his feet to meet the next attack.

A pale shaft of light struck a malformed foot—to immediate effect. The beast's movements became sluggish and deliberate as the wounds on its arms and legs remained open. Ivan swung his sword once more and the blade sank into a fur-covered shoulder, cleaving through muscle and bone.

The sunlight grew brighter and the gentle rays washed over the thick shoulders and neck of the creature, highlighting the grotesque head. The wereling stumbled as an agonized howl broke from its blood-splattered jaws. Ivan drove the sword into its chest, withdrawing the blade only to strike again.

The beast fell to the ground, its disproportioned hands covering its head. Slowly, the bones reformed, and crunching and grinding, they shifted, becoming more human. The body began to shrink, the long, wolf-like hair receding into the smooth skin. The face of death and evil slowly changed into one of innocence. A blood-splattered young woman lay sprawled on the grass, replacing the beast.

"How many have I killed this time?" She made no attempt to hide her nakedness.

Ivan glanced at Otto; the smith wouldn't last much longer. "Four," Ivan answered.

Tears ran down her cheeks, her shoulders quivering with sorrow. Her eyes met Ivan's. "Kill me! Kill me now," she cried, wiping her cheek, smearing the blood on her face. "Don't let me endure this torment any longer. End my suffering and save untold lives."

Ivan lifted the blade high above his head but hesitated as he looked down on the young woman.

"Kill me now!" she pleaded. "Do it in the sunlight; strike off my head and burn my body. Never let me be whole again or I will return."

"How?" Ivan asked. "How did you become this...abomination?"

"I am Rowena. A man who practiced black magic wished me to share his bed. When I refused, he placed a curse upon me. I fled my homeland, but I couldn't outdistance his magic."

"Who is this man?"

"He is evil incarnate and lives in the mountains to the west. Now kill me. Anyone wounded must be killed and burned with me." She closed her eyes, bowing her head low to the ground. "Strike now."

Ivan drove the blade in a downward arc, all of his weight and strength behind the blow. The sword tip thudded into the ground and Rowena's severed head rolled in a lopsided circle to lay still, her sightless eyes staring at the sun. Blood gushed from the jagged neck stump, the warm spray covering Ivan's legs.

"Ivan, my friend," Otto whispered. "You must kill me also. I've no wish to become a soulless fiend."

Ivan nodded. He lacked any words, his mind focused solely on the job at hand. The sword fell heavily on the smith's exposed throat, cleaving the head from his body.

"I have much to finish here," he said, then turned slowly, surveying the scene of carnage. "Then I must seek out the man who caused all this bloodshed. He will pay for what he's done."

RIP AND TEAR

MICHAEL W. GARZA

Alexander leaned out over the edge of the building, the night air cold on his exposed skin. Lights dotted the landscape below like a mural of the stars in the sky. His eyes were keen and focused on the alleyway between his and the next building.

From five stories up, he saw the movements of the creature. Moving with reflexes too quick for mortal men, he saw the beast run at its prey, the screams of the two would-be victims echoing off the walls of the surroundings buildings.

He had spent the better part of his life hunting the things of myth and legend and he'd spent the last two months tracking this particular beast. It would be on top of the two young men in a matter of seconds, so Alexander took aim and fixed the cross hairs of his scope on his target.

The instant it leapt into the air, he pulled the trigger.

The impact of the round sent the werewolf slamming into the closest alley wall. Alexander jumped from the edge of the building landing softly on the closest rooftop, rolling to absorb his body's impact. Grabbing hold of the fire escape, he flipped over the side, and a moment later his boots hit the ground.

The two young men that had been only seconds away from death stood behind him as he kept his eyes on the werewolf. He could hear the men talking to each other, both scared out of their minds.

"You'd better get out of here," he said without turning around.

The two young men were able to shake off the terror enough to run.

"I will rip your head from your neck and tear the muscle off your bones." the deep voice boomed through the alleyway as the werewolf got to its feet.

"Oh," Alexander replied with a smile. "We'll see about that."

The first bullet wasn't intended to kill the beast. Contrary to popular beliefs, silver rounds couldn't kill a werewolf though it would make quite a wound and cause the creature pain. The curse of the werewolf was a blood born virus, Alexander knowing this from experience.

"Your kind isn't welcome here..." Alexander's boast faded as he heard the sound of laughter. He realized it was all to perfect, that it had been a set up; the two men had been a decoy.

"I believe..." The beast stepped into the light as it spoke. "You are the one no longer welcome."

It towered over Alexander by several feet. Impossibly wide shoulders capped the figure of a giant. Its fur was a dark brown with slight streaks of gray along its neck and head. Claws reflected the overhead lights like steel daggers.

Alexander sensed movement behind him, somewhere on the lowest rooftop above him. Cursing under his breath, he knew the trap was about to close.

The creatures came at him at once, the elder from the front and another from behind. He waited for the last possible moment before diving out of the way, and brought his rifle up just as his back hit the ground.

Firing two shots, he hit one of them and the impact of the gunshot sent it flying backwards. The wall across the alleyway nearly caved in as the creature slammed into it.

With little time to react, he dropped his rife and pulled both his pistols. The other werewolf was quick to recover from the gunshot. Alexander ducked under a paw almost as big as his head but was struck in the chest by the other one. His body lifted from the ground and slammed into the wall behind him with the force of a car wreck.

Alexander brought a pistol up and fired, the bullet piercing the werewolf's neck. It roared in pain and stumbled backward, clutching at the wound. Alexander fell to the ground with a resounding thud, and as he rolled to his feet, a searing pain in his side told him he'd cracked a rib.

Desperate to get out of the confined space, he ran towards the closest end of the alley. A long shadow moved with him as the third werewolf followed from up above. Just as he reached the entrance to the side street, the shadow disappeared and Alexander turned his attention skyward.

The beast fell from the darkness above like a crashing airplane. He dove out of the way as a set of claws missed his face by a hairsbreadth. The werewolf landed on its feet and spun around to meet him. Alexander brought one of his pistols up enough to fire from the hip. He sent three rounds into its chest before he could even get a good look at it.

It was one of the young ones, he knew. The werewolf was smaller than the other two and had been kept back at the start of the fight for just this reason. With reckless abandonment, the massive creature stepped into Alexander's line of fire as if the rounds were bouncing off its thick, furry hide.

Alexander caught the light in the werewolf's eyes as it continued forward blindly. He raised his aim when it was only a few feet away and sent a round right into its eye. The pain was more than it could handle and it reached out for him as it fell forward, striking the ground heavily.

He wasted little time in admiring his handiwork, for he could hear the pounding feet of the other two racing to join the fight. From underneath his long, leather coat, he found the handle to the 'death nail'. The foot long silver tipped stake had brought down many foul things in its time but Alexander didn't have time to reminisce. He plunged the death nail down through the werewolf's back and with the heel of his palm he forced it into its heart.

The beast slumped dead and he only had time to pull the weapon free and spin around before the other two werewolves would be on him. He backed away toward the far wall and watched as the young werewolf's body began to snap and contort on the ground. A second later, the naked and bloody body of a teenage boy was all that remained of the beast.

Alexander put his back against the cold brick wall and took a deep breath. He had to keep his head about him or he'd be a goner for sure. The elder werewolf and the other one bound toward him, leaping the length of a car with little effort. He could see their gleaming, white fangs and his hands felt behind him, searching for an escape. When his hand felt the small crack in the door to his right, he smiled widely.

Quickly, he pulled at the emergency exit and dove into the dark interior. The door closed behind him and he heard the vicious growl of the elder werewolf as it missed its mark, bouncing off the metal door instead. Alexander got to his feet as the werewolves began to pound on the door. It had no handle from the exterior and locked when it was closed.

Still holding a pistol in each hand, he reached out and leaned against the wall. His heart was racing and the cold air had little effect on him. Sweat covered his face, droplets dripping from the end of his chin. He'd faced off against much worse in the past but an elder werewolf was nothing to take lightly.

The pounding on the door grew louder as the rage in the beasts increased. They'd seen the body of the teenage boy and were more determined than ever to make him pay for what he'd done.

Turning around, he ran as fast as his legs would carry him. He knew from his starting position on the rooftop that this was a vast industrial area. There were numerous manufacturing facilities in both directions and from the echo of his boots and the pounding at the door, he guessed the building he now found himself in was vacant.

By the time he reached the other end of the wide open space, Alexander caught sight of movement off to his left. A pale light cascaded down from a row of windows high above, the metal mesh covering the windows painting an eerie pattern on the concrete floor. He thought he'd misjudged his enemy but the continuing pounding told him different. It wasn't until he heard the slight sound of a gun's safety being let off that he fully understood.

The gunshots rang out one after another. The flashes and length between the shots told him there were at least two shooters and he had a good idea who he was dealing with. The initial trap was set for him, which implied the two young men he'd initially saved were in on it.

Alexander rolled forward as bullets ricocheted near his feet. He popped back up with his pistols blazing, grinding his teeth as a wave of anger washed over him. There was nothing he hated more than werewolf wannabe's.

He fired until he reached the last round in each pistol, and then continued his run to the far side of the building. The two werewolf-wannabe's had hid behind a stack of crates when he'd returned fire and it gave him time to get away. The sound of the emergency door bursting inward across the empty factory sent an alarm ringing through his brain. He had to do something...and fast.

Guessing the two young men from the alleyway were guarding the only viable escape route, Alexander pulled the coil of rope hanging from his belt and holstered his pistols. With a keen eye and a good arm, he swung the clawed end of the rope and tossed it up high. The small metal claw on the end broke through the glass with ease, and a second later he was climbing up the wall hand over hand.

With little time to waste, he reached the window ledge and flung himself through the broken glass. The two men fired at him the moment his body became silhouetted by the outside lights. The drop back down to the street outside was twenty feet, and when he landed he rolled out of the fall, though the impact sent a shock up his spine.

It took him several precious seconds to regain the feeling in his legs. By the time he started to run, the main entrance door to the factory swung open and gun fire ensued once more. Alexander ducked behind a dumpster and crouched down low. Pressing the release, he dropped the spent clips to the ground and with one quick motion, he reloaded them. Then he readied himself to move again.

The street was clear to the west and from his vantage point, Alexander could see a tall, chain-link fence surrounding a warehouse. He came to his feet and took aim when one of the men exited the factory door. He let his trigger fingers do the talking and the man shook from the impact as three rounds lodged in his chest, spraying blood out his back to cover the wall of the building in crimson.

The second man was just stepping over his departed partner when Alexander started to run for the chain-link fence. Out of the corner of his eye, he caught site of one of the werewolves shooting through the open door in its haste to reach him. The beast slammed into the man, the force sending him into the doorframe.

Alexander laughed all the way down the street. "That's what you get for rushing!" he yelled over his shoulder.

He reached the fence and heard the werewolf rushing up behind him. Spinning, Alexander fired twice but the werewolf leapt up on the wall to its left and bounced up into the air. Alexander continued to fire but the beast's movements were too quick.

By the time he decided to get over the fence, it was too late. The werewolf's massive body slammed into Alexander's back, pushing both of them into the fence. The links on the fence where it connected to one of the posts was weak and their combined weight pushed a portion of the fence to the ground as the mass of werewolf and man rolled over it. Alexander felt the razor edges of the barbed wire located on the top of the fence dig into his forearms, to then rip away pieces of his flesh.

The werewolf was back up in an instant and Alexander went to his knees, one pistol at the ready, the other one lost in the tumble. The beast began to pace back and forth and he could see it clearly under the adjacent building's ballpark security lights. Smaller than the elder, this one was big enough that it could kill him with ease. The blood-soaked wound in its neck told Alexander that they'd met before.

"How's that feeling for you?" Alexander asked with a smile. "Hurts like hell I've been told. Too bad I was such a lousy shot last time."

The werewolf growled like a rabid dog.

"The silver won't kill you but it won't let the wound heal." Alexander took a quick glance around for his other pistol. "Sucks, huh?"

He knew it was coming for him before it jumped. He'd pissed off enough werewolves in the past to know when they couldn't take it any longer. This one had a particularly bad temper. Alexander knew the beast was just trying to stall until the elder werewolf could work its way around to a better position of attack but Alexander knew not to give it enough time.

As the werewolf jumped forward, Alexander countered, doing the same thing but staying low. Close to the ground, the beast went directly over him. Alexander spun around to face the werewolf while lying prone on the ground and he put two bullets into the creature's back. It threw its arms out to the side and howled up at the sky in agony.

When the beast turned around, Alexander was gone. He had jumped to his feet the second he fired his pistol and had dashed into the nearby warehouse. This building had stacks upon stacks of crates and machines covering the floor. The small space between the crates made for a maze of passageways.

He was halfway across the large area before he turned around to see if he was being followed. Climbing up on a stack of crates, he watched as the elder werewolf led the other one inside, the two splitting up to begin a game of hide and slaughter. As the elder werewolf went off to the right, Alexander focused his attention on the other one, hoping to keep his meeting with the elder to a one on one event.

He had everything ready. He scanned the high ceilings and in the dark he could still see the marks he'd made. His plan was still salvageable. The werewolves were about to discover they were never the ones laying the trap.

He jumped down to the floor and worked his way through the maze, and when he found the spot he wanted, he waited. Even with death looming over him, he found himself craving a smoke. He was pissed at himself and swore under his breath for wanting a cigarette so badly, especially after everything he'd accomplished in his life. He'd slain vampires, taken down packs of werewolves, and had even rid the world of a few cults bent on world domination, but no matter what, he just couldn't stop smoking.

The sound of footsteps caught his attention and he knew the time was near to close his trap. He pressed his free hand against the outside of his jacket to feel the outline of the pack of cigarettes hidden underneath. The small box felt like it had been through a washing machine on high.

"Uncrushable box my ass," he mumbled.

It was only after he realized that he was honestly considering lighting up while he had a free second that he was able to shake the notion off.

I really have a problem, he laughed at himself then swore under his breath. He looked up to discover that at least one of the werewolves knew where he was. To his left, the crates were spread further apart. There was a circular space of illumination a few feet away from a low hanging light. Alexander watched and waited. His patience was rewarded after a few minutes when the werewolf stepped into the wide path on all fours.

The beast's jaws hung open, revealing long flesh-ripping teeth. Its eyes pierced the darkness, focusing in on its prey and Alexander knew the creature hoped he'd run for it. He guessed the beast would try and herd him into the waiting arms of the elder werewolf; only he had no intention of moving a muscle.

With a ferocious roar, the beast ran towards him. Its speed was far beyond human and the rippling muscles flexed with every stride, its dark brown fur helping it blend into the shadows.

Alexander held his ground, not even raising his lone pistol. The creature's mind was consumed by the need to kill and it was that all consuming quality which he was depending on. Experience had shown him that a werewolf would leap toward his head when it was a single stride away. It would try and bring him down with its jaws and the weight of its body, then use its claws and teeth to rend.

He had known what the werewolf would do when he came to the warehouse hours ago when he'd been preparing his trap. He'd broken the bulbs in the closest lights in the ceiling and had then positioned a forklift so that it would be nearly invisible when the sun went down. And after raising the horizontal forks to the height of his shoulders, he'd draped it with a tarp to ensure it was thoroughly hidden from view.

Now he waited until he could smell the foul odor of the werewolf before he moved. He pushed himself backward, landing on his butt just before the first claw touched his jacket, the forks now above his head. The weight of the beast carried it forward before it realized its mistake. The death shriek poured from its mouth as the long, metal forks pierced its chest and tore through its body.

Blood poured from the twin wounds as the werewolf convulsed. Alexander had to silence it quickly and he sprang to his feet. The beast lashed about in pain, recognizing its own demise. Alexander pulled the death nail from his jacket and he stabbed up and under its rib cage with a single jab. The silver tip pierced the creature's heart in one blow and the convulsing stopped almost immediately.

He pulled the death nail free and stepped back into the darkness. He couldn't allow the elder werewolf to get behind him. When he looked back, the beast had reverted back into a naked man, the body hanging from the forklift now covered in blood. The man moved one last time and the metal forks ripped through his torso, severing the upper from the lower part of him. What fell to the ground, was in two pieces, and could only be described as a bloody mess.

The warehouse erupted in a horrifying snarl and Alexander knew he didn't have much time. The elder werewolf was on the move and could track him easily. He reached the rear door of the warehouse and kicked it open.

He stepped out into the cold night and found himself at gunpoint. In his planning, he hadn't counted on the werewolf-wannabe sticking around, not after being knocked against the wall by one of the beasts. The sound of the gun going off was deafening and Alexander was already dodging and spinning to the side when the trigger was pulled. The bullet struck him on the shoulder and increased the force of his spin, sending him to the ground.

The wannabe stood over him and placed the barrel against the back of his head and with little chance at getting a shot off, Alexander did the only thing he could. The death nail was still in his hand and with a backwards swing, he plunged it into the man's meaty thigh. As the man fell back, yelling in pain Alexander pushed off the ground with his other hand and came to his knees.

He had little time to spare and he pulled his pistol and sent a round into the wannabe's forehead.

"I hope it was worth it," he said to the dying man.

He cleared his head and tried to remain focused. Pushing into the long walkway behind the warehouse, he stepped behind the second of three dumpsters and hid in the darkness.

"Come out, come out where ever you are," the elder werewolf growled.

Alexander didn't move.

"I can smell your vile flesh, human."

He took a deep breath and then poked his head up to see the elder werewolf standing near the open door of the building, just under the light over the door.

"Where are all your friends?" Alexander asked. He was trying to be a smart ass but the pain in his shoulder was killing the act.

"I guess you expect me to come down there after you," the elder werewolf snarled.

"Nope," he replied. He stepped out from behind the dumpster, his pistol back in its holster on his hip. He was holding something else in his hand, something small and from the look of it, harmless. "I knew you'd be too smart for that."

The werewolf's eyes opened wide and it roared, showing its teeth as it decided what to do next. Before it could react, Alexander pushed the button on the device in his hand. The sound of the explosion could be heard for over a mile away and the sheer force of it knocked him on his back.

The walkway was covered in dust when he managed to get up. He coughed and hacked as he tried to breathe and no matter what he did, he couldn't get the ringing out of his head. He could barely see his hand in front of his face from the dust and the sound of police sirens told him he only had minutes to spare, but he had to be sure.

After stumbling blindly back down the walkway in the swirling dust and smoke, he found the rear door to the warehouse. Most of the surrounding wall had been blown in. Fragments of concrete and brick were strewn across the ground, and as he continued to search the debris, he saw a lone furry foot and then a furry severed arm. In between the piles of cement and mortar, there were chunks of hairy skin, muscle, blood and bone.

It wasn't until he found the remains of the head that Alexander knew the death nail wasn't needed. To his surprise, most of the elder werewolf's face was still intact. He looked down into its dead eyes and smiled.

"You didn't see that coming, did you?" He kicked a large stone and watched it roll onto the face. "Don't mess with a claymore mine."

He ignored the growing pain in his shoulder and climbed onto one of the dumpsters, then using his good arm, he swung up onto the one-story machine shop across from the warehouse. The sirens were getting closer and he knew he had to be gone when the police arrived.

This fight was over, but there were plenty more to come.

THE HOMECOMING

C.H. POTTER

"Holy shit, is that what I think it is?" James asked with wide eyes.

Eric looked up from the object in his hands. James was sitting across the room, his hand suspended above the box it was about to delve into.

"Yeah," Eric said softly, his gaze returning to the item he had brought down from the attic. "Barry's old .22."

Eric turned the ancient rifle over in his hands, inspecting it up and down. His fingers traced the length of the rust-tinged barrel, as if they didn't entirely believe it was truly *there*, like it might suddenly disappear as unexpectedly as the gun's owner once had.

"Wow," James said, his voice equally reverential. "I thought Dad tossed that thing in the trash when he took it away."

Eric's finger slipped into the trigger guard, tickling the cold steel. His mind traveled back to the last time the trigger had been pulled, how the final bullet to issue forth from that long barrel had marked the end of the Roberson's days as a typical American household, even if they hadn't fully grasped it at the time.

He pulled the trigger. The hollow *clack* of the dry-fire was enough to snap his mind back into focus. He lowered the .22 and leaned it against one of the dozens of boxes littering the living room.

"You know," James said, "we've been through about half of this stuff, and that's the first thing of Barry's I've seen."

"They must have gotten rid of his things after both of us had moved out for good," Eric said. "Which would have been at some point in the last five years."

"Oh, fuck off," James said jokingly, flinging an old Johnny Cash cassette tape in Eric's direction. "I only lived here for a couple years after high school, and I'm a member of the legendary Class of 2000, remember?"

"Hey, if you want to associate yourself with a motley crew that produced more felons than college graduates, that's your prerogative."

"Yeah, yeah," James said, his hand reaching into the nearest box. "What are you going to do with that?" he added.

"The rifle?" Eric asked, picking the .22 up once again. "I don't know. I guess I'll put it in the gun case with all of the others until we figure out who's taking what."

"That one's all you," James said.

"I figured you'd say that," Eric muttered as he crisscrossed through the maze of the living room.

He entered the kitchen to see Beth was sitting at the table, leafing through one of the magazines that sought to deify the lives of the rich and famous. She gave Eric a disinterested glance as he walked by with the .22. Her lazy gaze returned to the smiling face of some celebrity.

As far as his brother's long list of flames went, Eric ranked Beth at the bottom of the heap; just above the blond that vomited all over him at his cousin's wedding reception.

James sure did know how to pick 'em.

Happy to leave Beth to her magazine without being forced to muster any small talk, Eric walked down the hall for what seemed like the millionth time. He passed James' bedroom first, then his own on the left. The guestroom—*Barry's room*—loomed on the right, and just beyond it, at the end of the hall, was the door to his parent's room.

He hesitated on the threshold, his hand frozen on the door handle. He had only been in the bedroom twice since his father's death. On neither occasion had he been alone. Now that he was here, standing on the precipice with Barry's gun in his hand—of all things—Eric found that he didn't want to open the door. Walking into the room would be an admission that everything *had* changed, that both of his parents were now gone, and he had been left alone to try to find his way in a world that seemed to thoroughly enjoy kicking Eric Roberson squarely in the balls. No more family dinners, no more calling his dad to forecast the Yankees pennant chances, no more mom nagging him with the, *When are you going to find a nice girl and give me some grandkids?* spiel.

No more, no more, no more.

He forced himself to push the door open before his resolve could falter. The room looked just as it had for five decades of marriage. The pictures changed, the quality of the furniture improved, but the room maintained the basic essence of its inhabitants. Eric didn't have to look on the bottom shelf of the nightstand to know that a book of crossword puzzles sat there, probably next to a dog-eared romance novel. His father hadn't had the heart to throw it out in the past few months. God, she loved those things.

Eric sat down on the edge of the bed, fully feeling the weight of the job before him and James for the first time. All of this stuff would have to be packed up and hauled out, piece by painful piece. The attic, loaded mostly with random items that hadn't seen the light of day in years, would be a cakewalk compared to the rest of the house. Everything in the room still packed an emotional punch, right down to the collection of Hawaiian shirts in the closet his father wore on every vacation.

This stuff is still theirs, dammit, Eric thought as he surveyed the top of the dresser where there was a prescription bottle and his father's reading glasses. The thought of these items sitting in a dumpster felt somehow blasphemous, like pissing on a grave.

The doorbell rang, shoving the mental image away. Eric stood up and walked to the gun cabinet in the far corner of the room. The door creaked and the hinges creaked a bit as he pulled it open. The cabinet contained seven slots for weapons, six of which were filled. Eric placed the .22 in the open space. He pulled out each weapon—a mixture of shotguns and rifles—and gave them a quick examination. Like the .22, they could use a cleaning but were in otherwise good condition.

The flecks of dust dotting the barrels were evidence of the long dormancy of the arsenal. His father hadn't gotten much use out of the guns in recent years.

Eric lived halfway across the country, briefly returning for holidays when his work schedule allowed. James, meanwhile, was far too interested in hunting women in the local taverns to spend a significant amount of time stalking animals in the woods.

On a whim, Eric bent down and opened the drawer that pulled out of the bottom of the cabinet. It was filled with boxes of ammu-

nition, a hunting knife that had been in the family for three generations, and a few turkey calls. *Dad was ready to roll whenever his
sons displayed an interest,* Eric thought as he stood back up. He
closed the cabinet door, catching a glimpse of a figure standing in
the doorway through the reflection of the glass.

He whirled around.

"Hey, you," said the woman—an attractive blonde whose face
was just beginning to show the first worry-wrinkles of middle age.

"Hi...Cassie?"

"Do I really look that different?"

"I'm sorry," Eric said, thoroughly flustered. "It's just that it's
been...a while."

"Years," Cassie clarified. "Probably four or five?"

"That sounds about right. How's my favorite girl next door doing?" he asked as they exchanged a hug that wasn't quite as awk-
ward as it might have been under the circumstances.

"Better than the last time you saw me."

Eric looked at her blankly for a moment before realization
dawned on his face. "Ah, yes, I remember now. What was his
name? It was something very distinguished, if memory serves."

"Pompous is more like it. His name is McKenzie."

Eric laughed. "You always did like to date guys who had that
college professor quality to them."

"Yes, well, I was silly enough to marry this one. Big mistake."

"Yeah, been there, done that," he replied, nodding.

"How are you doing?" Cassie asked, abruptly changing the subject.

Eric considered for a moment. "It's tough, tougher than I
thought it was going to be. With Mom, we sort of saw it coming,
but I had just talked to Dad a week ago."

"How did he sound?"

"Kind of distracted, like there was something he knew he
should tell me but didn't want to. He sounded like that when Mom
got sick, but he was completely fine as far as his own health was
concerned. The doctors said it was just one of those things. Old
age, it was his time and all that."

"I'll miss them both," Cassie said. "When we were growing up,
I think I spent almost as much time in this house as I did my own."

"Oh, over the years you have no idea how many times I've heard, *If you had just married Cassie...*It's strange to think that I'll never hear that again," Eric's voice trailed off, choking up on the last word. Cassie took his hand and her comforting touch dammed up the flood of emotion, but he knew it would overflow his ramparts before long.

"How are your parents doing?" he asked, eager to get the conversation on more secure footing.

"They miss it out here in the sticks sometimes, but I think living in town better suits them at this point in their lives. Makes getting to Bingo on Wednesday night's a lot easier."

As she often did during their childhood years, Cassie successfully brought a smile to Eric's face. "Do they really do that?" he asked.

"Every Wednesday," she answered with a straight face. "Come on, make me a cup of coffee."

On their way out of the room, Eric's foot stepped on something protruding from under the edge of the bed. He froze in mid-stride, puzzled. He turned around and got on his knees, bending over the mattress.

"What's wrong?" she asked from the doorway.

He didn't answer. Although it was jutting out just a few inches from under the bed—his eyes quickly telling him what the object was—his mind simply refused to believe it. Or, more to the point, to understand what it was doing there.

"Eric?"

He grabbed the end of the barrel and pulled out a .10 gauge shotgun.

"Did your dad always keep a gun under the bed?" Cassie asked.

"No. I've never seen this gun before. It's a .10 gauge, more powerful than anything else in the gun case," he said as he looked the Remington up and down. Unlike the weapons in the gun case, this one was well oiled and lacked the nicks and scratches that came with years of use. "I'd say it's new," he said, getting to his feet.

"Maybe James will know something about it," she suggested.

"Maybe," he said as he looked from one end of the room to the other, wondering what other secrets waited to be discovered. He gave the gun a pump and an extracted shell flew out of the chamber, landing on the carpet with a soft *thump*.

"It's loaded," Eric said. "That was Dad's side of the bed. Why would he feel the need to keep a loaded gun within arm's distance?"

"Burglars?"

"No, Dad never did worry about that sort of thing. It wasn't his style."

"That case is full. Maybe he just didn't have space for it."

"It wasn't full until five minutes ago, when I put Barry's old .22 in there."

"Barry? What..."

Cassie didn't have a chance to finish the question before Eric was past her and heading back through the hall. He found James and Beth canoodling in front of the refrigerator, his hand running up and down her backside.

"Are you becoming a gun nut or something?" James asked as Eric strode into the room.

"What the hell is this?" Eric shoved the shotgun between James and Beth, ignoring the annoyed look that Beth shot his way.

"Is that a trick question?"

"Did Dad ever say anything about buying a new gun?" Eric asked.

"No, he didn't. What's your deal?"

"The gun is loaded, James. I found it hidden under his bed. Now why would Dad have felt the need to purchase an elephant gun like this, then stash it as if he thought somebody was going to come bursting into his room at night?"

James dropped his hand from Beth's backside. His gaze focused on the gun for the first time. His brow furrowed ever so slightly, something Eric knew was an indication that his brother's mind was working overtime.

"I think..."

A loud pounding filled the house.

BANG-BANG-BANG.

All eyes in the room suddenly went to the kitchen door that led to the backyard. A wreath that had hung on the back of the wooden frame for years teetered and fell off its hook, bouncing to Eric's feet.

BANG-BANG-BANG.

The door rattled once again, as if a host of medieval soldiers were smashing a great log against it in an attempt to storm the Roberson residence. A pile of dirty dishes in the sink collapsed upon one another, sending a shrill cacophony through the room. The noise was enough to snap Eric out of the spell of rapt silence that had taken hold of the kitchen.

"Weren't you supposed to wash those?" he snapped at Beth as he moved towards the door. Her blank expression—all of their blank expressions—only further fueled his aggravation. He put his eye up to the peep-hole of the door. Blackness greeted him. He muttered a curse and impatiently flipped the light switch to the porch up and down, but nothing happened. He cursed again, this time not bothering to keep the expletive under his breath.

"Eric..." Cassie said.

He shoved his eye against the peep-hole this time, trying to *will* whoever was pounding on the door into his line of vision.

BANG-BANG-BANG.

Eric jumped back halfway to the kitchen table, his face flushing red with embarrassment, but no one noticed the tint to his cheeks. This time, the bangs on the door were accompanied by a voice. "Open the door!" a cracked voice hollered through the oak. "*Please*! It's coming!"

Eric recovered some dignity and quickly pulled the door open. A small man in his early twenties burst into the house a split second later, shoving the door shut behind him with enough force to rattle the entire wall.

The man grabbed Eric by the collar of his shirt, pulling him within inches of his crazed eyes—eyes that looked like they had caught a glimpse of a terrible image and were utterly broken by the view.

"*It's coming! It's coming!*" the man shouted hysterically.

Eric brought the shotgun up to his chest, using it as a bar to push the man back to a more comfortable distance. The man's eyes seized on the sight of the weapon, drinking it in like it was the very elixir of life. Eric wouldn't have thought it possible for the man's eyes to bulge out of his head any further, but the gun seemed to be pulling them away from his skull, as if the pupils were magnets.

"You've got a gun!" the man exclaimed, his voice bursting with gratitude. "Oh, thank God, thank God!"

Eric glanced around the room. Each face reflected exactly how dumbfounded he felt.

"Wait, wait, wait," the man babbled. "You answered the door with a gun. Do you know about it? Have you seen it? It *tears*." The man cut the air in a Freddy Krueger slashing motion before his words devolved into an incomprehensible babble. Eric couldn't tell if his voice was streaked with sorrow or an insanity-tinged cackle.

Eric handed the gun to James, who accepted it without taking his eyes off their unexpected guest. Eric gently guided the man to one of the kitchen chairs. He sat down without protest, his talk tapering off into silence.

"Everything's going to be all right, son," Eric found himself saying, even though he had never referred to anyone as 'son' before in his life. *Is that what my life's come to? On the wrong side of thirty and I'm calling some whacked-out stranger son? If Mom and Dad could see me now.*

Despite the turmoil transpiring in his mind, Eric saw why he had made the association and called the man 'son'. Now that he had a moment to actually process the man's appearance, he realized that 'the man' was barely more than a kid. With the shock of the kid's bizarre arrival beginning to subside, Eric now placed his age anywhere between seventeen and twenty-three. His shaggy black hair was tousled every which way under his Red Sox ball cap. The colorful pyramid on his Pink Floyd t-shirt had been caked in mud and...what was that? Was that blood?

"What happened to you?" Eric asked the kid.

The kid looked up at him, eyes wider than ever. "He's dead," he stated calmly, but the words were a bomb whose explosion sent him back into a fit of tears. Eric tried to put his arms around him, but the kid shook him off and buried his head in his hands.

Eric looked to Cassie for help, only to find that she was already walking over. She knelt down in front of the kid and took his hands in hers, gently pulling them away from his face. "What's your name?" she asked.

"B...Bobby Summers," he said between sobs.

"Bobby, where do you live?"

"Over in Barlow, across from the pharmacy."

"With your parents?

"No, I got my own little apartment last year."

"Bobby, what were you doing before you got here?"

"I was spotlighting with Jared. Driving around on the back roads, working on polishing off a thirty pack of Bud. Just shooting the shit really, talking about old times back in school. Who we fucked, who we always *wanted* to date."

"Okay, and how did you end up here?" she asked.

"We turned on McHenry Road," Bobby said, speaking in a near monotone. "We were going to cut over the hill to get back home, avoid the main roads. McHenry connects with Winston Hill Road. No cops up there. Nothing up there but deer and trees or so we thought. We were on the way down the hill when Jared stopped the truck to take a leak." He trailed off. His eyes were unblinking orbs, seeing something that was far from the mundane surroundings of the kitchen.

"Bobby? What happened next?" Cassie prodded.

"Jared pissed in the middle of the road. Why not, no one was around? He tossed an empty can of beer into the woods and started to turn back towards the truck. He paused halfway. 'Did you hear that?' he asked me. I tell him I didn't hear anything but Zeppelin playin' on the radio, but he starts to walk over to the other side of the road. 'You don't hear that? It sounds like a wounded animal.' I turned down the radio, and when I look back, I see something *spring* out of the woods. It's on top of Jared before he can even raise his hands. Its fingers were claws. I saw them shimmer in the moonlight.

"Jared was screaming. The thing threw its head to the sky and it let loose a howl that made my heart freeze in my chest. It shut Jared up with one swipe. His head flopped to the side, barely still attached to his body. It tore through his chest and ripped it open in great streaks of red. His shirt, his *skin*, was gone. He was nothing but a pool of blood from neck to waist. I realized I was screaming and it looked towards me. Its eyes had that animal shine to them, like when you catch them in your headlights. Slowly, deliberately, it plucked Jared's head from his body, raised it up, and tossed it right at me. I recoiled, but not fast enough. Jared's head plopped against my stomach. I swear its mouth curled back into a smile, laughing at me. For an encore, it reached into Jared's simmering remains and pulled an organ out—his heart, a kidney, I don't fucking know. It dropped it into a mouthful of teeth that looked like they could chew glass. It made a show of licking its lips as it pointed a murderous claw at me. I shoved Jared's head to the floor and jumped into the driver's seat. I threw the truck in gear and took off down the road. I saw it in the rearview mirror, coming for me. It was bigger than a linebacker but nimble as a cat. It bounded after me, jumping impossible distances, but it couldn't keep up with the truck. Not as fast as I was driving. I didn't slow down until I began to see a few houses scattered along the side of the road. I stopped at the first one that had lights on. I pounded on the door and...and well, you know the rest."

The room fell silent, the only noise in the house the faint *tick-tick-tick* of the clock mounted on the kitchen wall.

"Jesus," Bobby said, again putting his head in his hands. "Jared's head is still in the truck. I gotta..."

"Don't worry about it," Eric said. "We'll take care of everything."

"Bobby, who attacked you?" Cassie asked. "What did he look like?"

"It wasn't a *he*, or a *who*. I told you. It was an *it*. Something...I don't know. It was covered in hair from head to toe, and its head was...was like a wolf's."

James snorted. "You do any drugs tonight, kid? Maybe try out some hallucinogens for the first time?"

"James!" Cassie protested.

"Somebody had to ask before we call the police."

"Look at the blood on his shirt, for God's sake."

"I don't do heavy stuff," Bobby said softly. "A lotta beer and a little weed, but nothing heavy."

Eric picked up the house phone from the table and dialed 9-1-1. He put the phone up to his ear, only to find that there was no dial tone. "Did you have the phone shut off already? It isn't working?"

"Yeah," James answered. "I figured why wait any longer."

"I have a cell in my purse," Beth said.

"People will be living on Mars before we get cell phone service up on this hill," James said.

"We'll just have to drive into town. Is that okay with everyone?" Eric asked. Nobody spoke up in disapproval. Bobby had regressed back into a glazed expression, while the others seemed content to follow Eric's lead.

"Good job with the kid; getting him calmed down like that," Eric said quietly to Cassie as they walked out the door.

"That's just one of the skills that teaching ninth grade in the inner city will get you," Cassie replied. "We need to get him to...Eric? Eric, what's wrong?"

Eric stopped suddenly on the edge of the porch, his eyes fixated on the driveway directly ahead. James' Mustang, normally unblemished by the slightest speckle of mud, was caked in red, the hood of the car covered. The full moon above cast just enough glow to illuminate the graffiti.

Three names were spelled out, each trickling into each other as the bloody ink ran down the slight slope of the hood. Barry's name was listed on the top, with a great **X** mark slashed through the letters. Eric was next, then James.

"What the hell! My car!" James hollered when he reached the edge of the porch. "Somebody is about to get their ass beat. Come on out, you bastard!" he jumped off the porch and ran to his car, searching the lawn for the perpetrator. "Where are you?"

"James, calm down," Beth said as she went after him.

James only let loose another profanity-laced challenge to whoever had defiled his vintage car. As if in response, a loud howl suddenly pierced the night, lasting a solid thirty seconds before it faded. Eric was vaguely aware of the sound of footsteps pounding on the porch as Bobby fled back into the house, but all of his focus was on the driveway. Both James and Beth had fallen silent, gazing up at the roof of the house.

"What is it?" Eric asked.

"There's something moving around up there," James said. "Yeah, it's coming towards the front of the house. It's...holy shit."

Eric was on the verge of descending the porch and getting a look for himself when a low, gravelly voice, barely more than a growl, issued forth from somewhere above them.

"This ends tonight."

What happened next unfolded in less than a minute, but to Eric it was like watching an epic Hollywood film in slow motion. And just like in a movie theater, he was helpless to sway the course of events.

Something leaped off the roof, a blur of dark fur that landed right in front of James and Beth. It quickly knocked James aside with a backhand blow and grabbed Beth by the throat, lifting her off the ground with one arm, as if she was weightless. Eric could hear gurgling noises coming from her throat as she tried to cry out.

The creature sniffed her up and down, its snout rapidly moving from her mouth to her belly. It then gave a loud cough and held her at arm's length. James got back to his feet just in time to see the creature tear into Beth's chest with the claws of its free hand. Blood sprayed forth, peppering the paint of the Mustang.

James let out a guttural scream of his own and charged at the creature. It towered over him by at least two feet. James lowered his head and crashed into its furry midsection. It dropped Beth's limp body to the ground and nearly fell over before regaining its balance. James was pummeling it with blow after blow, but the beast hardly seemed to notice. It seized James' neck in its mouth and swung him about like a dog playing with a chew toy, blood staining its teeth.

The wolf-creature tossed James onto the hood of the Mustang with one final flick of its neck, and James' body smeared his name on the hood into an unintelligible blur, and the seeping puncture wounds finished the job.

The werewolf turned towards the porch, its shimmering eyes fixed on Eric.

"Cassie, get inside!" Eric yelled without looking back.

"Eric..."

"*Go!*" he cried urgently.

Her footsteps padded away, and the door slammed closed. Eric doubted he had enough time to flee into the house himself, not after witnessing how fast this creature had jumped off the roof. He stood his ground, trying not to show fear.

"What are you?" he asked, stalling.

"Family," the werewolf growled, and took a step forward.

It walked toward him slowly, seeming to savor the impending completion of its checklist. Eric's mind raced with a thousand different scenarios, the countless courses of action he could take before the werewolf closed the gap between them. Nothing he came up with gave him the slightest hope of escape.

"Don't hurt the others," Eric pleaded. "Do whatever you're gonna do to me, but leave them alone. Bobby and...and Cassie."

The werewolf only seemed to smile at his plea, baring its teeth in a vicious smile. The gleam of the beast's incisors seemed unnaturally magnified in the light of the moon.

"Please," Eric begged.

The werewolf was at the base of the front steps. Now that it was this close, Eric saw that the kid had been right; the creature really did look like a two-legged wolf, although its face was cruelly twisted in a way that nature would never intend. The veneer was made even more terrifying by the intelligence that ran just under the surface—malevolent intelligence.

The werewolf mounted the first step.

"What do you want?" Eric shouted, his voice quaking a bit as his inevitable end approached.

To his surprise, the werewolf paused its advance.

"Life," it growled. The voice came from the bottom of its throat, a rough sound that Eric found puzzlingly familiar. "There can only be one Nightwalker in every clan. If another is born, I will fade and perish like the human race I left behind long ago. This is a possibility I cannot allow any longer."

The werewolf suddenly reached out and grabbed Eric's crotch and his entire body stiffened instantly, as muscles tensed. His testicles, already curled up from fear, receded further as the werewolf's claws brushed against the all-too-thin barrier of the material of his jeans.

"You hold in your loins my doom," the werewolf growled. "Unlucky for you, whippersnapper."

The werewolf took another step.

Something suddenly clicked within the deepest recesses of
Eric's mind as the beast's voice jogged his memory and at the use
of the odd colloquialism. And though it sounded crazy even to him,
he took a chance and said, "Uncle Harry?"

The werewolf's ears perked up and then somehow seemed to
fold in half, as if trying to keep the words from entering.

"Don't call me that," the beast growled.

"But it's really you, Uncle Harry," Eric said. "You always had
somewhat of a deep voice, and you were always calling us whipper-
snappers. That's about all I remember of you, other than that, well,
you were quite *hairy*."

"Silence," the werewolf snarled.

"I haven't seen you since I was five years old. I remember nobody would really say anything when we asked about you when you
disappeared, how you just kind of faded from memory."

"I embraced my true destiny, a destiny that will forever be mine
when I'm finished with you."

In an instant, the beast grabbed Eric by the throat and lifted
him off the ground, just as it had done to Beth. Eric clutched at the
hairy hands before he quickly realized how futile the effort was.
The hands squeezed tighter.

"Say hello to the family for me," the werewolf said, seemingly
content to watch Eric's life fade as he struggled for one last breath.

Eric tried to poke the beast in the eyes, but his reach fell short.
He flailed his arms about wildly and they hit one of the support
beams of the porch. He grabbed it and simultaneously curled his
legs up into his waist. He gave the werewolf a dropkick to the chest
with all the strength he could summon.

The blow took the creature by surprise and it dropped Eric to
the hard surface of the porch floor and stumbled back a step. Eric
felt the wind go out of him as he landed.

"Come here, whippersnapper," the beast said, the murderous
intent oozing from its voice. "I'll kill you slowly for that." It stepped
forward, looming over Eric's prostrate form like the Grim Reaper
himself. It clicked its claws together with both hands, considering
how best to rend his flesh. "Hmm, where to start?" the beast
growled.

Suddenly, the front door to the house swung open.

"Start with this, asshole," Bobby said as he fired off a round of the .10 gauge, then another. The first blow knocked the beast back several feet, while the second sent it falling off the porch.

Bobby strode past Eric to the edge of the porch and was shocked to find that the werewolf was already back on its feet. Eric stood up and took the shotgun from Bobby's hands, snapping it in two over his knee. The werewolf let out a hacking cough that might have been laughter. It was about to pounce at Bobby when more gunfire erupted from the porch, the report quieter than the .10 gauge.

Bobby looked over his shoulder to see that Cassie was standing behind him, pumping shot after shot into the creature's hide with the .22. The beast let out several high-pitched yelps before bounding off into the woods, leaking dark blood behind it.

"You think it's gone for good?" Bobby asked.

"Let's not wait around to find out," Eric said, as he turned to look at Cassie.

"Are you okay?" Cassie asked.

"Yeah. You used Barry's .22," he remarked, taking the gun from Cassie.

"It was the only thing I knew how to use," she said. "But why did that gun have such an impact on that thing? The bullets are small compared to that .10 gauge."

"Maybe it's the difference between buckshot and bullets?" Bobby ventured.

"I don't know," Eric said. "There's always been something special about this gun. Barry shot out his window with it one night a long time ago. He said there was a monster trying to get into his room. He was just eight at the time, and of course no one believed him. Dad took the gun away from him, and two days later Barry had disappeared. The cops said he probably ran away from home, and God only knows what happened to him after that. He's been missing for almost thirty years, but now I think I know what happened to him. I think Dad knew, too, in the end."

"Family secrets die hard," Cassie said.

"Yeah, you could say that."

ABOUT THE WRITERS

Terry Alexander lives on a small farm near Porum, Oklahoma with his wife Phyllis. Together they have three children and nine grandchildren. They both enjoy sitting back with a good book on a rainy afternoon. Terry has won writing awards at in Oklahoma, Arkansas, Kansas, Texas and Missouri.. His work has been published in Memories and Make Believe, Writing on Walls III, Echoes of the Ozarks V and Frontier tales.com. Contact him at terryale@crosstel.net.

John Atkinson is an avid reader of both horror and fantasy. The only thing he enjoys more than staying up late to read a story is staying up late to write one. Influenced mainly by the works of Stephen King and H. P. Lovecraft, he seeks to create an atmosphere of dread and intrigue in his stories.

David Bernstein writes short stories for a number of magazines and anthologies. The first four chapters of his novel Amongst the Dead are available online at Tales of the Zombie War with more to come. Check out davidbernsteinauthor.blogspot.com. You can reach him at dbern77@hotmail.com. He lives in the NYC area with his girlfriend of eight years and hates car horns.

Rebecca Besser lives in Ohio. She writes fiction, nonfiction, and poetry for various age groups and genres. Check out her website at ww.rebeccabesser.com

David H. Donaghe lives and works in the high desert of southern California. In his spare time, David writes short stories and novels. He has had several short stories published in the past, four of which appear in other, Living Dead Press anthologies. David is currently enjoying life and working on his next novel. He invites you to join his reader network at www.authornation.com/MCRIDER.

Michael W. Garza lives and works in southern California with his wife and two children. He has had work published or accepted by the Absent Willow Review, Residential Aliens, Morpheus Tales, The Horror Zine, Sounds of the Night, Blood Moon Rising, Living Dead Press, Midwest Literary Magazine, Dark Gothic Resurrection Magazine and Deadman's Tome. He has published three novels. For more information see www.mwgarza.com.

Anthony Giangregorio is the author and editor of more than 40 novels, almost all of them about zombies. His work has appeared in Dead Science by Coscomentertainment, Dead Worlds: Undead Stories Volumes 1-6, and Wolves of War by Library of the Living Dead Press. He also has stories in End of Days Vol. 1 -3, the Book of the Dead series Vol. 1-4 by LDP, and two anthologies with Pill Hill Press. He is also the creator of the popular action/zombie series titled Deadwater. Check out his website at www.undeadpress.com.

Dane T. Hatchell grew up in Baton Rouge Louisiana and has lived there all his life. In his youth he was a fan of old school horror movies, and a collector of magazines such as Creepy and Eerie. Now in his early fifty's, he is devoting his free time to writing to satisfy a lifelong passion. You can contact Dane on Facebook at Enadious@gmail.com or Enadious B. Neuman on Facebook.

Mark M. Johnson is a dedicated horror and sci/fi fanatic known on-line as, The Black Empty. His short fiction has appeared in: Bits of the Dead from Coscom Entertainment, Zombology 1, the upcoming anthology Letters From The Dead From Library of the Living Dead Press, and the upcoming Horrorology from Library of Horror Press. His work also appears in: Dead Worlds volumes 2 & 3, Book of the Dead vols 2, 3, and 4, Love is Dead, Dead history, and the Book of Cannibals, from Living Dead Press. Born and raised in Detroit , he currently resides in Warren MI with his wife Cindy, one graduated daughter, one high school son, one crazy dog, three cats and a python.

Keith Luethke lives in Knoxville, Tennessee and is the author of Dead House: A Zombie Ghost story and is a co-author of Human Harvest: Alien Abduction with Anthony Giangregorio. He enjoys talking to fans and can be reached through Facebook or at luethke@yahoo.com.

David Perlmutter is a freelance writer and university graduate student living in Winnipeg, Manitoba, Canada, where he has lived his whole life. His passions are American television animation (the subject of his forthcoming MA thesis and a projected historical monograph), literature (especially science fiction and fantasy) and music (rhythm& blues, soul, funk and jazz.) This explains why much of his writing is as nonconventional and defiant as it is. He is challenged with Asperger's Syndrome, but considers it an asset more than a disability.

C.H. Potter was born and raised in the hills of Western New York, where lonely dirt roads are always just a short drive away. His work has also been published in The Copperfield Review and The Monsters Next Door, as well as several anthologies from Living Dead Press, including Dead Worlds: Undead Stories Volume 1, and The Book of the Dead Volumes 1 and 2.

Jessy Marie Roberts lives in a "haunted" house in Western Nebraska with her husband and two dogs. She grew up in Morgan Hill, California. She has been published in various small press venues, including many appearances in anthologies by Living Dead Press, and is the Editor-in-Chief of Pill Hill Press (www.pillhillpress.com).

KM Rockwood enjoys most types of fiction and has a special fondness for subtly terrifying stories. Several stories have been published in both print and e-zine format.

Tommy Ryan VII is a graduate of the University of Michigan (Ann Arbor) with a degree in English. He lives in Farmington Hills, MI--a Detroit suburb. **Mark Rivett** is a Graduate of the Art Institute of Pittsburgh, and resides in Pittsburgh, PA. Tommy and Mark have been hunting werewolves together since their youth, and they collaborate via e-mail.

Spencer Wendleton has published two novels under his penname, "Alan Spencer." One is entitled, "The Body Cartel," the other, "Inside the Perimeter: Scavengers of the Dead." His work has appeared in numerous Living Dead Press anthologies and a variety of horror magazines and electronic media. The author welcomes e-mails at: alanspencer26@hotmail.com.

DEAD RAGE
by Anthony Giangregorio
Book 2 in the Rage virus series!

An unknown virus spreads across the globe, turning ordinary people into bloodthirsty, ravenous killers.

Only a small percentage of the population is immune and soon become prey to the infected.

Amongst the infected comes a man, stricken by the virus, yet still retaining his grasp on reality. His need to destroy the *normals* becomes an obsession and he raises an army of killers to seek out and kill all who aren't *changed* like himself. A few survivors gather together on the outskirts of Chicago and find themselves running for their lives as the specter of death looms over all.

The Dead Rage virus will find you, no matter where you hide.

CHRISTMAS IS DEAD: A ZOMBIE ANTHOLOGY
Edited by Anthony Giangregorio

Twas the night before Christmas and all through the house, not a creature was stirring, not even a. . . zombie?

That's right; this anthology explores what would happen at Christmas time if there was a full blown zombie outbreak. Reanimated turkeys, zombie Santas, and demon reindeers that turn people into flesh-eating ghouls are just some of the tales you will find in this merry undead book. So curl up under the Christmas tree with a cup of hot chocolate, and as the fireplace crackles with warmth, get ready to have your heart filled with holiday cheer. But of course, then it will be ripped from your heaving chest and fed upon by blood-thirsty elves with a craving for human flesh! For you see, Christmas is Dead!

And you will never look at the holiday season the same way again.

BLOOD RAGE
(The Prequel to DEAD RAGE)
by Anthony Giangregorio

The madness descended before anyone knew what was happening. Perfectly normal people suddenly became rage-fueled killers, tearing and slicing their way across the city. Within hours, Chicago was a battlefield, the dead strewn in the streets like trash.

Stacy, Chad and a few others are just a few of the immune, unaffected by the virus but not to the violence surrounding them. The *changed* are ravenous, sweeping across Chicago and perhaps the world, destroying any *normals* they come across. Fire, slaughter, and blood rule the land, and the few survivors are now an endangered species.

This is the story of the first days of the Dead Rage virus and the brave souls who struggle to live just one more day.

When the smoke clears, and the *changed* have maimed and killed all who stand in their way, only the strong will remain.

The rest will be left to rot in the sun.

THE BOOK OF CANNIBALS
Edited by Anthony Giangregorio

Human meat . . . the ultimate taboo.

Deep down, in the dark recesses of your mind, can you honestly say you never wondered how it might taste?

Honestly, never wondered if a chunk of thigh tasted like chicken or pork?

Or if a hunk of an arm was similar to steak? And what kind of wine would be served with it, red or white?

Would a human liver be no different than one from a cow, or a pig?

For all we know, human flesh is as tender as veal, better than the finest tenderloin. And that is what the stories in this book are about, eating each other. But be warned, after reading these tales of mastication, you may just become a vegetarian, or at the very least, think twice before taking your first bite of that juicy steak at your local restaurant.

DEADFREEZE
by Anthony Giangregorio
THIS IS WHAT HELL WOULD BE LIKE IF IT FROZE OVER!

When an experimental serum for hypothermia goes horribly wrong, a small research station in the middle of Antarctica becomes overrun with an army of the frozen dead.

Now a small group of survivors must battle the arctic weather and a horde of frozen zombies as they make their way across the frozen plains of Antarctica to a neighboring research station.

What they don't realize is that they are being hunted by an entity whose sole reason for existing is vengeance; and it will find them wherever they run.

VISIONS OF THE DEAD
A ZOMBIE STORY
by Anthony & Joseph Giangregorio

Jake Roberts felt like he was the luckiest man alive.

He had a great family, a beautiful girlfriend, who was soon to be his wife, and a job, that might not have been the best, but it paid the bills.

At least until the dead began to walk.

Now Jake is fighting to survive in a dead world while searching for his lost love, Melissa, knowing she's out there somewhere.

But the past isn't dead, and as he struggles for an uncertain future, the past threatens to consume him. With the present a constant battle between the living and the dead, Jake finds himself slipping in and out of the past, the visions of how it all happened haunting him. But Jake knows Melissa is out there somewhere and he'll find her or die trying.

In a world of the living dead, you can never escape your past.

DEAD MOURNING: A ZOMBIE HORROR STORY
by Anthony Giangregorio

Carl Jenkins was having a run of bad luck. Fresh out of jail, his probation tenuous, he'd lost every job he'd taken since being released. So now was his last chance, only one more job to prevent him from going back to prison. Assigned to work in a funeral home, he accidentally loses a shipment of embalming fluid. With nothing to lose, he substitutes it with a batch of chemicals from a nearby factory.

The results don't go as planned, though. While his screw-up goes unnoticed, his machinations revive the cadavers in the funeral home, unleashing an evil on the world that it has not seen before. Not wanting to become a snack for the rampaging dead, he flees the city, joining up with other survivors. An old, dilapidated zoo becomes their haven, while the dead wait outside the walls, hungry and patient.

But Carl is optimistic, after all, he's still alive, right? Perhaps his luck has changed and help will arrive to save them all?

Unfortunately, unknown to him and the other survivors, a serial killer has fallen into their group, trapped inside the zoo with them.

With the undead army clamoring outside the walls and a murderer within, it'll be a miracle if any of them live to see the next sunrise.

On second thought, maybe Carl would've been better off if he'd just gone back to jail.

ROAD KILL: A ZOMBIE TALE
by Anthony Giangregorio
ORDER UP!

In the summer of 2008, a rogue comet entered earth's orbit for 72 hours. During this time, a strange amber glow suffused the sky.

But something else happened; something in the comet's tail had an adverse affect on dead tissue and the result was the reanimation of every dead animal carcass on the planet.

A handful of survivors hole up in a diner in the backwoods of New Hampshire while the undead creatures of the night hunt for human prey.

There's a new blue plate special at DJ's Diner and Truck Stop, and it's you!

DEAD THINGS
by Anthony Giangregorio

Beneath the veil of reality we all know as truth, there is another world, one where creatures only seen in nightmares exist.

But what if these creatures do actually exist, and it is us that are only fleeting images, mere visions conjured up by some unknown being.

Werewolves, zombies, vampires, and other lost things that go bump in the night, inhabit the world of imagination and myth, but all will be found in this collection of tales.   But in this world, fiction becomes fact, and what lurks in the shadows is real. Beware the next time you sense you are being watched or catch movement in the corner of your eye, for though it may be nothing, it might just be your doom.

INCLUDES THE EXCLUSIVE DEADWATER STORY: DEAD GRAVE

THE DARK

by Anthony Giangregorio

DARKNESS FALLS

The darkness came without warning.

First New York, then the rest of United States, and then the world became enveloped in a perpetual night without end.

With no sunlight, eventually the planet will wither and die, bringing on a new Ice Age. But that isn't problem for the human race, for humanity will be dead long before that happens.

There is something in the dark, creatures only seen in nightmares, and they are on the prowl. Evolution has changed and man is no longer the dominant species. When we are children, we're told not to fear the dark, that what we believe to exist in the shadows is false.

Unfortunately, that is no longer true.

SOULEATER

by Anthony Giangregorio

Twenty years ago, Jason Lawson witnessed the brutal death of his father by something only seen in nightmares, something so horrible he'd blocked it from his mind.

Now twenty years later the creature is back, this time for his son.

Jason won't let that happen.

He'll travel to the demon's world, struggling every second to rescue his son from its clutches.

But what he doesn't know is that the portal will only be open for a finite time and if he doesn't return with his son before it closes, then he'll be trapped in the demon's dimension forever.

SEE HOW IT ALL BEGAN IN THE NEW DOUBLE-SIZED 460 PAGE SPECIAL EDITION!

DEADWATER: EXPANDED EDITION

by Anthony Giangregorio

Through a series of tragic mishaps, a small town's water supply is contaminated with a deadly bacterium that transforms the town's population into flesh eating ghouls.

Without warning, Henry Watson finds himself thrown into a living hell where the living dead walk and want nothing more than to feed on the living.

Now Henry's trying to escape the undead town before he becomes the next victim.

With the military on one side, shooting civilians on sight, and a horde of bloodthirsty zombies on the other, Henry must try to battle his way to freedom.

With a small group of survivors, including a beautiful secretary and a wise-cracking janitor to aid him, the ragtag group will do their best to stay alive and escape the city codenamed: **Deadwater**.

DEAD END: A ZOMBIE NOVEL
by Anthony Giangregorio
THE DEAD WALK!

Newspapers everywhere proclaim the dead have returned to feast on the living!

A small group of survivors hole up in a cellar, afraid to brave the masses of animated corpses, but when food runs out, they have no choice but to venture out into a world gone mad.

What they will discover, however, is that the fall of civilization has brought out the worst in their fellow man.

Cannibals, psychotic preachers and rapists are just some of the atrocities they must face.

In a world turned upside down, it is life that has hit a Dead End.

BOOK OF THE DEAD 2: NOT DEAD YET
A ZOMBIE ANTHOLOGY
Edited by Anthony Giangregorio

Out of the ashes of death and decay, comes the second volume filled with the walking dead.

In this tomb, there are only slow, shambling monstrosities that were once human.

No one knows why the dead walk; only that they do, and that they are hungry for human flesh.

But these aren't your neighbors, your co-workers, or your family.
Now they are the living dead, and they will tear your throat out at a moment's notice.

So be warned as you delve into the pages of this book; the dead will find you, no matter where you hide.

ANOTHER EXCITING ADVENTURE IN THE DEADWATER SERIES!
DEAD SALVATION
BOOK 9
by Anthony Giangregorio
HANGMAN'S NOOSE!

After one of the group is hurt, the need for transportation is solved by a roving cannie convoy. Attacking the camp, the companions save a man who invites them back to his home.

Cement City it's called and at first the group is welcomed with thanks for saving one of their own. But when a bar fight goes wrong, the companions find themselves awaiting the hangman's noose.

Their only salvation is a suicide mission into a raider camp to save captured townspeople.

Though the odds are long, it's a chance, and Henry knows in the land of the walking dead, sometimes a chance is all you can hope for.

In the world of the dead, life is a struggle, where the only victor is death.

INSIDE THE PERIMETER: SCAVENGERS OF THE DEAD
by Alan Spencer

In the middle of nowhere, the vestiges of an abandoned town are surrounded by inescapably high concrete barriers, permitting no trespass or escape. The town is dormant of human life, but rampant with the living dead, who choose not to eat flesh, but to instead continue their survival by cruder means.

Boyd Broman, a detective arrested and falsely imprisoned, has been transferred into the secret town. He is given an ultimatum: recapture Hayden Grubaugh, the cannibal serial killer, who has been banished to the town, in exchange for his freedom.

During Boyd's search, he discovers why the psychotic cannibal must really be captured and the sinister secrets the dead town holds.

With no chance of escape, Broman finds himself trapped among the ravenous, violent dead.

With the cannibal feeding on the animated cadavers and the undead searching for Boyd, he must fulfill his end of the deal before the rotting corpses turn him into an unwilling organ donor.

But Boyd wasn't told that no one gets out alive, that the town is a death sentence.

For there is no escape from *Inside the Perimeter*.

DEADFALL
by Anthony Giangregorio

It's Halloween in the small suburban town of Wakefield, Mass.

While parents take their children trick or treating and others throw costume parties, a swarm of meteorites enter the earth's atmosphere and crash to earth.

Inside are small parasitic worms, no larger than maggots.

The worms quickly infect the corpses at a local cemetery and so begins the rise of the undead.

The walking dead soon get the upper hand, with no one believing the truth. That the dead now walk.

Will a small group of survivors live through the zombie apocalypse?

Or will they, too, succumb to the Deadfall.

LOVE IS DEAD: A ZOMBIE ANTHOLOGY
Edited by Anthony Giangregorio
THE DEATH OF LOVE

Valentine's Day is a day when young love is fulfilled.

Where hopeful young men bring candy and flowers to their sweethearts, in hopes of a kiss...or perhaps more. But not in this anthology.

For you see, LOVE IS DEAD, and in this tome, the dead walk, wanting to feed on those same hearts that once pumped in chests, bursting with love.

So toss aside that heart-shaped box of candy and throw away those red roses, you won't need them any longer. Instead, strap on a handgun, or pick up a shotgun and defend yourself from the ravenous undead.

Because in a world where the dead walk, even love isn't safe.

ETERNAL NIGHT: A VAMPIRE ANTHOLOGY

Edited by Anthony Giangregorio

Blood, fangs, darkness and terror...these are the calling cards of the vampire mythos.

Inside this tome are stories that embrace vampire history but seek to introduce a new literary spin on this longstanding fictional monster. Follow a dark journey through cigarette-smoking creatures hunted by rogue angels, vampires that feed off of thoughts instead of blood, immortals presenting the fantastic in a local rock band, to a legendary monster on the far reaches of town.

Forget what you know about vampires; this anthology will destroy historical mythos and embrace incredible new twists on this celebrated, fictional character.

Welcome to a world of the undead, welcome to the world of Eternal Night.

BOOK OF THE DEAD
A ZOMBIE ANTHOLOGY VOL 1
ISBN 978-1-935458-25-8

Edited by Anthony Giangregorio

This is the most faithful, truest zombie anthology ever written, and we invite you along for the ride. Every single story in this book is filled with slack-jawed, eyes glazed, slow moving, shambling zombies set in a world where the dead have risen and only want to eat the flesh of the living. In these pages, the rules are sacrosanct. There is no deviation from what a zombie should be or how they came about. The Dead Walk.

There is no reason, though rumors and suppositions fill the radio and television stations. But the only thing that is fact is that the walking dead are here and they will not go away. So prepare yourself for the ultimate homage to the master of zombie legend. And remember... Aim for the head!

REVOLUTION OF THE DEAD
by Anthony Giangregorio
THE DEAD SHALL RISE AGAIN!

Five years ago, a deadly plague wiped out 97% of the world's population, America suffering tragically. Bodies were everywhere, far too many to bury or burn. But then, through a miracle of medical science, a way is found to reanimate the dead.

With the manpower of the United States depleted, and the remaining survivors not wanting to give up their internet and fast food restaurants, the undead are conscripted as slave labor.

Now they cut the grass, pick up the trash, and walk the dogs of the surviving humans.

But whether alive or dead, no race wants to be controlled, and sooner or later the dead will fight back, wanting the freedom they enjoyed in life.

The revolution has begun!

And when it's over, the dead will rule the land, and the remaining humans will become the slaves...or worse.

KINGDOM OF THE DEAD
by Anthony Giangregorio
THE DEAD HAVE RISEN!

In the dead city of Pittsburgh, two small enclaves struggle to survive, eking out an existence of hand to mouth.

But instead of working together, both groups battle for the last remaining fuel and supplies of a city filled with the living dead.

Six months after the initial outbreak, a lone helicopter arrives bearing two more survivors and a newborn baby. One enclave welcomes them, while the other schemes to steal their helicopter and escape the decaying city.

With no police, fire, or social services existing, the two will battle for dominance in the steel city of the walking dead. But when the dust settles, the question is: will the remaining humans be the winners, or the losers?

When the dead walk, the line between Heaven and Hell is so twisted and bent there is no line at all.

RISE OF THE DEAD
by Anthony Giangregorio
DEATH IS ONLY THE BEGINNING!

In less than forty-eight hours, more than half the globe was infected.
In another forty-eight, the rest would be enveloped.
The reason?
A science experiment gone horribly wrong which enabled the dead to walk, their flesh rotting on their bones even as they seek human prey.

Jeremy was an ordinary nineteen year old slacker. He partied too much and had done poorly in high school. After a night of drinking and drugs, he awoke to find the world a very different place from the one he'd left the night before.

The dead were walking and feeding on the living, and as Jeremy stepped out into a world gone mad, the dead spotting him alone and unarmed in the middle of the street, he had to wonder if he would live long enough to see his twentieth birthday.

THE CHRONICLES OF JACK PRIMUS
BOOK ONE
by Michael D. Griffiths

Beneath the world of normalcy we all live in lies another world, one where supernatural beings exist.

These creatures of the night hunt us; want to feed on our very souls, though only a few know of their existence.

One such man is Jack Primus, who accidentally pierces the veil between this world and the next. With no other choice if he wants to live, he finds himself on the run, hunted by beings called the Xemmoni, an ancient race that sees humans as nothing but cattle.   They want his soul, to feed on his very essence, and they will kill all who stand in their way.   But if they thought Jack would just lie down and accept his fate, they were sorely mistaken.

He didn't ask for this battle, but he knew he would fight them with everything at his disposal, for to lose is a fate worse than death.

He would win this war, and he would take down anyone who got in his way.

THE WAR AGAINST THEM: A ZOMBIE NOVEL
by Jose Alfredo Vazquez

Mankind wasn't prepared for the onslaught.

An ancient organism is reanimating the dead bodies of its victims, creating worldwide chaos and panic as the disease spreads to every corner of the globe. As governments struggle to contain the disease, courageous individuals across the planet learn what it truly means to make choices as they struggle to survive.

Geopolitics meet technology in a race to save mankind from the worst threat it has ever faced. Doctors, military and soldiers from all walks of life battle to find a cure. For the dead walk, and if not stopped, they will wipe out all life on Earth. Humanity is fighting a war they cannot win, for who can overcome Death itself? Man versus the walking dead with the winner ruling the planet. Welcome to *The War Against Them.*

DEADTOWN: A DEADWATER STORY
BOOK 8
by Anthony Giangregorio

The world is a very different place now. The dead walk the land and humans hide in small towns with walls of stone and debris for protection, constantly keeping the living dead at bay.

Social law is gone and right and wrong is defined by the size of your gun.

UNWELCOME VISITORS

Henry Watson and his band of warrior survivalists become guests in a fortified town in Michigan. But when the kidnapping of one of the companions goes bad and men die, the group finds themselves on the wrong side of the law, and a town out for blood.

Trapped in a hotel, surrounded on all sides, it will be up to Henry to save the day with a gamble that may not only take his life, but that of his friends as well.

In a dead world, when justice is not enough, there is always vengeance.

END OF DAYS: AN APOCALYPTIC ANTHOLOGY
VOLUMES 1 & 2
Edited by Anthony Giangregorio

Our world is a fragile place.

Meteors, famine, floods, nuclear war, solar flares, and hundreds of other calamities can plunge our small blue planet into turmoil in an instant.

What would you do if tomorrow the sun went super nova or the world was swallowed by water, submerging the world into the cold darkness of the ocean? This anthology explores some of those scenarios and plunges you into total annihilation.

But remember, it's only a book, and tomorrow will come as it always does. Or will it?

Eternal Night
A Vampire Anthology

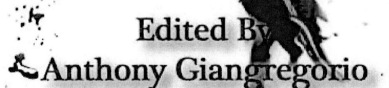

Edited By
Anthony Giangregorio

THE PLACE TO GO FOR ZOMBIE AND APOCALYPTIC FICTION

LIVING DEAD PRESS

WHERE THE DEAD WALK
www.livingdeadpress.com

THE BOOK OF CANNIBALS

ISBN 13: 978-1-935458-52-4   ISBN 10: 1-935458-52-3

ARE YOU HUNGRY YET?

THE BOOK
OF
CANNIBALS

KISS
THE
COOK

EDITED BY
ANTHONY
GIANGREGORIO

LaVergne, TN USA
15 August 2010
193412LV00004B/56/P